# A REGRETTABLE REUNION

Book Two in the
18 Karat Cold Mystery Series

*Book One: An Engaging End*

# A REGRETTABLE REUNION

AN 18 KARAT COLD MYSTERY

Mabry Hall

*A Regrettable Reunion*



*This is a work of fiction. Characters, places, events, and names are the work of the author's imagination or are used fictitiously. Any resemblance to actual events, locales, companies, organizations, or people, living or dead, is completely coincidental and non-intentional.*



*Cover design by Andrew Brown, Design for Writers*

*Endless thanks to*
*Rachel and Pat*

# Chapter One

"You want this. Stop pretending you don't care."

I didn't bother to deny it. Turning to leave, I stopped in spite of myself when he continued to speak. His low voice sent irresistible chills up the back of my neck.

"I know you too well, sweetheart. You get that tiny little crinkle at the corner of your smile when you want to give in to temptation. Come back here and give me your hand. Don't look. I'm about to make you very happy."

With a whimper of unwilling assent, I reached for him blindly with closed eyes. As he took my hand in his, I felt the warm touch of gold slide over my finger.

"Annalee! Honey, that ring was made for you! Finn, come in here and tell our Miss Wyatt that she better buy this thing even if it means Louisiana red beans and rice for the rest of her life. Food and shelter don't matter if you're wearing this, sweet girl."

I am not obsessed with personal adornment.

Yes, my friends might claim otherwise; they might say I can't leave the house without jewelry, or that I have an unseemly interest in it when worn by others to the point of swiveling my head like an owl when something particularly nice goes by. I have even on occasion heard myself referred to as an overly decorated Christmas tree. I refuse to take offense. My motto is: Put on all the pieces you want to wear; look in the mirror, and add one more thing. Maybe two. And don't forget the lipstick before you go out the door.

I'm lucky enough to have a job that allows me to indulge my interests. I buy it; I sell it, and I wear it myself in between. Wyatt's Pretties, Jewelry from the Past. I'm principal investor, owner, and sole employee. And right now I'm winding up a business trip with a detour through New Orleans.

"ANDY, IT'S BEAUTIFUL, but how can I justify spending the money on something like this for myself?" I asked, turning my hand back and forth to catch the late-afternoon rays of sun coming through the window of the Royal Street antique shop. The brilliant green of a demantoid garnet refracts light like no other stone, including the finest diamond. I was mesmerized by the sparkle and seized with the desire to acquire.

My long-time friend threw his hands up in exasperation. "How many years have you been drooling over my demantoid garnets? Finn, how many years?"

Andy's partner shrugged. "I haven't been counting, but it was way before she left Houston for the sticks."

I bristled. "Berryville is not the sticks. It's a small town in northwest Louisiana. Thirty minutes from Shreveport. Three hours from Dallas."

"Yes, sweet child, and you don't even live there. You live on a farm. With goats."

"They're not my goats," I said with a twinge of guilt. I'd grown quite fond of both the goats and their owner in the short time I'd been there.

"Whatever," he said dismissively, as he pulled out a bottle of Windex and began to clean the glass display counter. "All I can tell you is that it looks fabulous on you, and I'm making you a deal I wouldn't offer to anyone else. As in my cost, no mark-up, no profit."

My heart, and unfortunately my head, softened. "You don't have to do that, Andy. I know you got this at a bargain price and could sell it for five times as much. There weren't many demantoids mined of this size and quality."

He stopped his work and gazed at me with affection. "I know that. But you don't know how much your friendship means to me."

Finn came from behind and gave me a hug. "We'd give it to you if we could afford to, Annalee. You're the reason Andy's dad came to grips with the fact that his son was dating Finn and not Francine. We even went fishing together last week."

I wiped the sudden dampness from my eyes and laughed. "You're giving me way too much credit, but you've talked me into it. I'll use my fallback excuse—I can always turn around and sell it if I have to."

LIKE HELL I would. The three of us went for dinner at a trendy little spot in the Bywater neighborhood, and I spent as much time staring at my right hand as I did eating.

"I guess I'd be a bad salesman if I hadn't talked myself into spending the money. I pride myself on how I can close a deal with a customer who's teetering on the brink of handing me her credit card." I leaned back in contentment as our handsome waiter removed my dinner plate.

"I'm going to talk you both into ordering dessert," warned Finn. "There are too many things I want to taste on this menu to settle on just one."

There's something about a lemon dessert that makes me feel like I'm not overindulging, so I chose a Shaker Meyer lemon pie, while Andy went with a blueberry meringue with hyssop syrup and anise. Finn selected grapefruit gelato, and any hint of calorie restriction that grapefruit implies was vanquished with the first taste of its creamy perfection.

We sat in satisfied silence and nibbled freely from each other's plates till our espressos arrived, and we returned to the subject of jewelry.

"No one can be satisfied with one demantoid piece," Andy said. "Once you're hooked, you're forever on the prowl."

"Yeah," agreed Finn. "You'll be back for another. Next time maybe you'll pick one of the salamander pins. We sold one last week to somebody who didn't know what the heck she was buying. She argued with me that it was an alligator."

"Eww, I could do an alligator, but those salamanders give me the creeps. I don't do lizard jewelry. Now, one of those enameled insect brooches, maybe a butterfly, would make me happy. Not for a year or so, though. I need to let my bank account recover from the hole this put in it."

During the night a fall chill made its way from the north to bayou country. The air lost that breathe-and-you'll-drown humidity that's characteristic of New Orleans. I hoped to find the same agreeable conditions in north Louisiana after my five-hour drive home. I left my friends' Garden District cottage and began the slow drive down St. Charles Avenue under moss-draped oaks that spread from one side of the street to the other. I passed a clanging street car and my alma mater, Tulane, along the way. That's where I'd gotten the art history degree that left me stymied on the job front. Those hours spent walking up and down Royal Street when I should have been studying, trying on antique jewelry just like I could afford to buy it, turned out not to be a waste of time when I took a position in a ritzy Houston antique and estate jewelry store. I'd learned as much there as I had in four years of college.

Two hours later I was on the stretch of state highway that runs between Baton Rouge and Opelousas, trying to pay attention to the road instead of looking at the sugar cane harvest going on in the fields as I passed. A traffic jam stopped my progress just in front of a roadside stand selling boiled peanuts (don't make a face, they're good), and the proprietor and I discussed the reason for the delay.

"I hope this is due to a fender-bender, and not a bad wreck," I said, as I watched a sheriff's car go by on the shoulder of the road.

"Naw, ain't no wreck at all," the elderly man answered. "My nephew called me a few minutes ago. He said he'd gone out to check his duck blind in the swamp and found a dead body. I reckon every deputy in the parish is at the turn-off, and it don't take much to back up traffic on this road."

The man was so calm and matter-of-fact that it took me a minute to process what he'd said. "A dead body? Was it someone he knew? That's creepy."

"He said the animals had gotten to her; leastways he thinks it's a her. She was wearin' a dress."

I couldn't think of a single reply to that. Adding a soda to my purchase, I opened it and took a few deep swigs, willing my stomach to return to the calm I'd felt before stopping.

I got in my car and eased back into the slow-moving traffic. The murder mystery audiobook I'd been listening to had lost its charm, and I switched to a blues station on my satellite radio. I had at least three hours to go and a bagful of biodegradable peanut shells to be tossed out the window one by one as I emptied them.

Pulling off the road onto my dusty gravel driveway always makes me smile. That smile would be broader if Uncle Raine and Aunt Josie were still here to welcome me, but I'm always grateful I was the one in this generation chosen to inherit Goat Hill Farm. I drove slowly up the gravel drive, watching the dust settle on the crape myrtles behind me in my rearview mirror.

We've been in this little corner of northwest Louisiana since 1840. The house isn't nearly that old; it only dates to 1885. I don't live in some Gone with the Wind Southern plantation with big white columns and restored quarters out behind. My home is a two story white farmhouse with screened porches across the front and back and a tin roof that almost jingles when the rain comes down hard. You reach it by following a drive encircling four acres of old pecan trees that provide a little bit of a cash crop each fall.

Pudge waddled out to meet me when I parked the car under a pecan tree. "Hi, sweet dog, where'd you get that big bone?" He gave a muffled basset hound yodel, unwilling to drop his prize so as to give me the full benefit of his bass to tenor range. I skritched him between the ears and went inside to see if Montrose would give me a welcome as pleasant.

"Hiya, cat, did you miss me?" She left her seat by the window and padded into the wide entry hall to wind herself around my ankles, leaving the customary wreath of orange fur in her wake. A quick rub beneath her chin, and she was happy to go back to her nap.

A scratchy voice came out of a sunlight-filled corner. "Hey, you sexy thang. Can I buy you a drink?"

Lafitte, my newly acquired African Grey parrot, spent his formative years in a bar in Baton Rouge and has the pick-up lines to prove it.

"No, Lafitte, it's broad daylight. I'll take you up on that later this evening." He's only been a member of my little family for a few weeks, and I still have to remind myself that he isn't really carrying on a conversation when he speaks to me.

It was nice to come home to warm greetings, though. I wondered what it would be like to come home to a warm guy. I was sort of dating my neighbor. I know, probably not a good idea, especially since I was also his landlord. Ralph Bright has the farm next door and has leased the Goat Hill pastures for several years. Now that his son Caleb has moved back home, they've added a herd of goats to their Beefmaster and Charolais cattle.

Caleb is kind of cute, if you like six-foot-four hunks of lean muscle. I find his appearance inordinately pleasing, especially when he's wearing a pair of jeans and cowboy boots. Oh, heck, combine the physique, the brown eyes, the blonde hair, and the personality, and I don't have a thing to complain about. Did I say he's smart? He's smart. You really ought to see his rear end in that pair of jeans, but I guess I should pretend I'm more impressed with his brain.

All of these attributes combined had caused a serious loss of judgement just recently. I'd committed myself to attending Caleb's high school reunion dance Saturday night. If you'd told me four months ago that my move from Houston to Berryville would involve me in such an occasion, I'd have rudely laughed in your face. I heard footsteps on the porch.

"Sugar, you back home? Need me to help you bring anything inside?"

This generous offer came from Clotille, my neighbor. I could refer to her as a tenant, but she was born and raised in the cottage she occupies at Goat Hill. In my mind she's family and belongs here even more than I do. She watches the animals when I go out of town, since her house lies just across the yard and down the driveway a bit. She's in her late seventies, but that wouldn't stop her bringing in my suitcase or jewelry display cases.

I gave her a task to do inside. "I picked up a few groceries at Bubba's. Can you put the milk in the fridge for me?"

She wandered off to the kitchen, and I went back out to the car. A short time later I moved Lafitte's perch to the screened front porch, and we were all, including Pudge and Montrose, enjoying the beautiful day.

"How was the antique show? Did you sell much jewelry?" Clotille asked.

"Mobile is almost as pretty in the fall as it is in the spring, so even if I hadn't sold enough to have the house painted, it would have been a nice trip," I answered.

She demonstrated her delight and surprise by bringing her hands together and clapping with gusto. Her enthusiasm brought her rocking chair down on Pudge's tail, and he gave her the accusing look he usually reserves for my misdeeds. "You thought it would be next year before you could afford that. Does this mean you'll be able to redo the bathroom soon?"

"Let's not get carried away," I cautioned, as I lifted the big basset up onto the porch swing beside me. "Something is bound to break in the meantime. This place is too old to be carefree."

"That's the way it goes. Even though my little house is newer, there's always something that needs to be fixed, and of course, you pay for that too. I've had a new bathroom for ten years, and the one in the big house hasn't been redone in about fifty."

"Does it bother you that you grew up in that house but don't own it?" I asked.

"Well, let me think about that. You pay the upkeep; you pay the taxes, and I've never been charged a penny to live there. I'd have to say I'm happy with our arrangement."

"Good, because I don't know what I'd do if you left. I'd give the house to you if I could—"

"But you don't set the Goat Hill rules," she finished for me. "You're just the latest in the family line to live here." She reached over to squeeze my hand and gasped. "You have a ring the color of Carey's eyes," she said, her voice soft. Her eyes filled with quick tears.

I remembered then the bright, unusual green of her late husband's gaze. "You're right. No wonder I loved it so much."

"Is it an emerald?"

"No, let me tell you about it."

# Chapter Two

Tuesday was my day at the Magnolia Blossom antique mall in Berryville, about five miles from home. My drive to work took me by a small wood-framed church on the edge of town whose current sign read:

NOTHING RUINS THE TRUTH LIKE
STRETCHING IT.

I was reminded of my New Orleans conversation about my adopted home town. In spite of my quick rebuttal to Finn's judgement of my living arrangements, it's true that it isn't much of a metropolis. The original name of the town was *Berreville,* supposedly after some long lost Frenchman who wandered through in the 1700s, but it has long since been corrupted both in spelling and pronunciation. Say *Berravull* and folks will think you grew up here. Ok, don't get your hopes up; they won't really think that because everyone knows everybody else. You'll be pegged as an outsider the minute you drive past the city limits sign. You're an out-of-towner no matter how you say Berryville, but at least it will make you feel like you belong.

Anyway. We're in northwest Louisiana, in the Piney Woods, not in bayou country. Not too many folks make their living on their farms or in Berryville itself any more. Most of them work in Shreveport and Bossier City, which sit on opposite sides of the Red River thirty or so miles north.

Some people have made beaucoup money lately from natural gas. There's thousands of acres that seem to be on top of something called the Haynesville Shale. Not my land. Goat Hill and the farms near me are drilling rig free, which means I'm gas royalty free, too. That's okay; I have my jewelry business, and I lease my land to my neighbor for his livestock. I do just fine, and I don't have to worry about the energy business tearing up my pastures.

I do get a secondary benefit. There are lots of women in the parish who can treat themselves to a nice piece of jewelry now and then. I sell vintage costume jewelry as well as the real stuff, and I've been surprised at what a brisk business I do in town. There are also husbands and boyfriends who like the convenience of walking from the barber shop or Katie's Kitchen at the very last minute to buy a gift they know will be appreciated. I still travel the South doing antique shows, but I'm not as dependent on them for all my income.

The drive into town went quickly, and soon I parked by the side of the building and took a heavy canvas satchel from the passenger seat. Pete looked up from rearranging his model trains and greeted me as I pushed open the tall front door, its heavy brass hinges announcing my presence. My first week working, Pete caught me with a can of WD-40 and snatched it away before I spoiled the unofficial door chime.

"Don't tell me you're bringing back all the jewelry you took to Mobile last week," he said.

"Nope, I sold over half of it. Combined with my trip to Little Rock the week before that, I've sold two thirds of my inventory," I bragged. "These are new things I bought online."

"Congratulations. You deserved a good weekend after what you went through a while back. Walk by this Lionel set I'm working on and let some of your luck rub off. I thought I had it sold this weekend till the man's wife convinced him a new washing machine was more important."

"Where are her priorities?" I scoffed. "That's the type of person who thinks she's dressed with one piece of jewelry."

WE HAD A good morning even though I didn't sell any of my own inventory. One of our occasional Dallas customers stopped by on her way to Lake Charles and bought the eight foot tall Eastlake burled walnut secretary I'd been eying for the last three months. That was okay; I couldn't wear it on my wrist or hang it on a chain around my neck. Heaven knows there isn't room for another piece of furniture at Goat Hill. One hundred and thirty years of habitation by the same family leads to a serious accumulation of collectibles. I haven't been in the attic since I was a teenager; for all I know I already own an Eastlake secretary. I mentally added a look through the attic to my things-to-do list.

When Pete and I work together, one of us usually goes across the street to Katie's Kitchen and brings back the daily plate lunch. Nancy Crosby, the Magnolia Blossom owner, was in the store today, so I walked over to Katie's and met my best friend, who seldom gets a lunch break at all. The delicious aroma of freshly baked rolls wafted toward me, and Katie herself greeted me as I walked through the door.

"The doc is in the back corner booth," she said. "Iced tea?"

"That would be perfect." I navigated carefully between the tables on my way to the rear, trying not to knock anyone in the head with my purse. At least half the diners were friends and acquaintances, and I exchanged greetings as I passed.

Frankie sat on the bench facing the wall, doubtless hoping not to be spotted by any of her patients. I gave her low blond ponytail a pull before settling into the opposite side of the booth.

"Ouch," she said. "I wish I'd ordered the liver and onions for you instead of chicken and dumplings."

"You're not that mean. Usually. Have you been listening to symptoms outside of the exam room again?" As one of Sebastian Parish's three general practitioners, she's often hit up for free medical consults when we are together. It is amazing what people will ask in public, and with me standing right there listening. Do they think I can't hear them? It seems to me that the health privacy law isn't needed in Berryville when the local population is more than willing to discuss anything from bowel habits to sexual problems in front of a jewelry saleswoman.

"As always. A very reserved, well-mannered woman whose name I will not divulge just gave me a graphic description of a rash, and I only barely managed to stop her from lifting her shirt up to her neck in front of me and everybody in the restaurant. I asked her to call the clinic and tell Barbie to work her into this afternoon's schedule. I don't know if I'll be seeing a heat rash or something rare and interesting, but I sure as heck didn't want to look at it right before I ate my lunch."

I shuddered. "Thank goodness I wasn't here yet. I get so grossed out by the dermatology problems."

Katie dropped my tea off at the table and promised to return soon with our food. Frankie took advantage of the delay to check out my jewelry.

"What are you decked out in today?" She leaned across the table and moved my hair behind my ears with her hand. "Those earrings are new and look like they cost more than I make in a year. I've never seen you in diamond studs before."

"They're not real. Cubic zirconia."

"You're kidding. They don't look fake."

"I promise. There's no way I'd wear four carats of real diamonds. I would for sure lose one. The setting is white gold, though, so that helps to fool the eye." I lifted my right hand and fiddled with the earring. I wasn't going to point out my new purchase, but I didn't mind trying to catch her attention.

"And how many bangles are you wearing? Thank goodness there's too much noise in here for me to hear them clanking together. I'd rather hear a waitress drop a tray of silverware on the floor."

"Only three. They all belonged to Aunt Josie, so you've been seeing them on her wrist or mine for as long as you've been alive."

"Take them off and let me look at them. That ugly old ring you're waving around in front of my face is distracting me."

I met her eyes and saw she was fighting back laughter. "When did you notice it?"

"The minute you sat down. That's the most unbelievably bright emerald I've ever seen. How could I miss it?" She grabbed my hand and tugged it across the table so she could get a close-up. "It's gorgeous!"

"It's not an emerald. It's a demantoid garnet."

"I've never heard of them. Are they something new, like tanzanite? I remember your lesson on those; weren't they discovered in Africa not too long ago?"

"You do listen to me. I've often wondered if you just tune me out when I drone on about my job."

"Of course I listen. I haven't given up hope that you'll say something important."

"Your insults don't bother me, Dr. Lacasse. I'm always happy to increase your store of knowledge outside of medicine. Tanzanites were discovered in Africa in the late 1960s, and demantoids were discovered in the Ural Mountains in Russia about a hundred years earlier. The mines pretty much played out in the 1920s, so most of what you find is in antique pieces, many of which are Russian. I'll show you the Russian hallmark inside the band the next time you come out to the house. You can see the detail with magnification.

"And they're nearly all small stones. This one is unusually large. You remember Finn and Andy down in New Orleans, don't you? Their store has a tradition of carrying these when they can find them, because they're—"

"Stop right there. I haven't heard you this excited about a piece of jewelry since the day we made macaroni necklaces in Vacation Bible School, but it's too much information all at one time. Lunch is here. Let's eat, and you can finish the lesson later."

ALTHOUGH WE AGREED that dessert was out of the question after such a heavy lunch, we ordered coffee and decided to split one of Katie's peanut butter cookies. In my opinion, cookies classify as snack food, and a little snack never hurt anyone. Plus, peanut butter? Protein.

"Have you seen Caleb since you got home?" Frankie asked around a mouthful of cookie.

"I was only away for a week, and I just got home yesterday afternoon."

"And? Your mouth is moving, but you haven't answered my question."

"Why are you so nosy?"

"Why are you so evasive? It's been a long time since you had a fella, and the pheromones you two emit when you're together are about a 17 on a scale of 10. If there's going to be a mating dance, I want a ringside seat with popcorn and a Diet Coke. Boots does too, for that matter. He says he sees enough of the sordid side of life as parish sheriff. He's ready for a love story."

And this was one of the reasons Caleb and I were taking things very slowly. It doesn't take much to get everybody all up in your business in a small town. If we do decide to get serious, there will be lots of folks watching and commenting upon our every move. Since we'll be living next door to each other for the rest of our lives, a failed romance could be permanently problematic.

I decided to throw her a crumb. "He came by for a few minutes last night. We sat on the porch swing and talked about raising goats. They're a lot more interesting than you'd think. Do you want to hear what I learned? They're almost as fascinating as demantoid garnets."

"Stop threatening me. I'll back off. No goat tutorial, please. Are you still going to Caleb's tenth high school reunion this weekend?"

"Unless I have an attack of good sense before then," I said. "I didn't even go to my own reunion; I don't know why I agreed to go to his. I tend to lose my good judgement around that man."

"Good, because my good judgement says he's perfect for you. And I read something one time that says it's easier to go to someone else's reunion than your own. Something about the stakes being higher for you if you're facing your own past."

"I'm expecting a boring evening, since I won't know anyone except Caleb. I met a lot of your classmates when I visited through the years, but since he's two years younger than we are, I'm not expecting any familiar faces."

"You'll be surprised at how many people you'll recognize. I'll bet you come home with some juicy gossip about someone getting drunk and doing something embarrassing. I hope you won't be as closed mouth about that as you are about Caleb."

"Sorry." I reached across the table and patted her hand. "It's just sort of touchy right now till we figure out if we're going to risk changing our relationship. You'll be the first to know, I promise. In the meantime, I won't keep any gossip from you unless it involves me."

# Chapter Three

I DROVE HOME to Goat Hill and spent the afternoon cleaning the house. A dirt and gravel driveway produces lots of dust, which inevitably finds its way inside. A house built in the 1880s wouldn't have been airtight the day it was finished, and a hundred plus years of settling and shifting hadn't helped. As if that weren't bad enough, I'd added Lafitte to my menagerie, which meant the addition of gray feathers to the cat and dog hair that already threatened to take over. My many dust bunnies were beginning to look like a genetic experiment gone crazy.

I'd just finished mopping the upstairs when I glanced at the grandfather clock on the landing and saw it was almost time for my appointment with the house painter. Slipping my jewelry off, I put it in the top drawer of my dresser. It was part of my job to wear fancy fripperies (I love that word), but I'd learned the hard way it was best not to be too well decorated when I was getting a bid for work. It played heck with haggling for a lower price.

The bell rang. As I went to open the door, Lafitte called out "Hey, baby, come on in! The beer is cold, and you're hot!"

Geez, another new one. And as usual, his diction was perfectly clear. He's easier to understand than I am. Hoping the painter had a sense of humor, I pulled the door back and saw a laughing face.

"Hi, I'm Gideon. You have the Sessions' parrot, because I'd know that voice anywhere."

I liked him immediately. "You know Lafitte?"

"Like a bad relation. As a matter of fact, this isn't the first time he's put the moves on me. We painted his house a couple of years ago, and he was a lot more pleasant than the owner, although I shouldn't be saying that to you. One time he called me Sweet Cheeks and asked me to take him home. I felt guilty that I couldn't."

"It's okay. I know her too, and I have to agree with you. Let me slip on my shoes, and we'll walk around the outside of the house."

TWENTY MINUTES LATER he had all the information he needed to work up his bid. He seemed to know his field; he told me he could tell the house had been scraped the last time it was painted. When he saw my blank look, he explained it meant his job would be easier and my cost would be less. I understood that with no problem.

"I'll email you tonight with an estimate. Right now I have a team full of eight-year-old soccer players waiting for me to lead practice. I'm surprised my daughter isn't texting me already to find out where I am."

As he opened the door to his panel van, he paused and handed me his business card. "I almost forgot; I was so surprised by the parrot."

I slipped it into my pocket without looking at it and went back inside to finish cleaning.

THREE HOURS LATER my house was clean, and I was too. I slipped on my jammies, poured a glass of wine, and sat down in the living room with a murder mystery. I had marked my place with Gideon's business card when I brought the book downstairs, and I looked at it for the first time.

***A Perfect Finish: Painting by Gideon and Silas Nelson***

Nelson? I was involved in an unfortunate Berryville event with a Nelson when I was a senior in high school and visiting Frankie, but there had to be more than one family of Nelsons in town. Gideon didn't look a darn thing like Valonda. He was almost a foot taller and had dark hair. Of course I had no idea what color of hair Valonda really had. It was a different variation of blonde every time I saw her. He didn't have her little turned-up nose or blue eyes, either. I have to admit, the girl's eyes are exceptionally pretty.

The first names also didn't seem to belong in the same family. Silas and Gideon were both Biblical and old style. Valonda? I'm not sure where that came from, but it didn't seem likely to be attached to the same family tree as theirs. I'd have to ask Tennie Martin at lunch the next day since she'd referred them to me. And also since she knows everything about everybody in town and is willing to spill it.

I SPENT THE rest of the evening bumping into walls and tripping over the cat. It's hard to read and walk at the same time, but my book was too absorbing to waste time looking where I was going. Dinner was a peanut butter and plum jam sandwich held in one hand while the other held the paperback. We recently had a murder in Berryville, so the book felt awfully real, except maybe for the haunted house and the sexy vampires.

My farm is haunted, by the way, but for better or worse, I lack sexy vampires. Goat Hill has a ghost goat named Repentance. I'm fine with that; he stays outside and hangs out with the goats my neighbors are raising on my property. No trotting through the house and squeaking the floorboards. He's been here for over a hundred years, and he'll be here long after I'm dust in the wind. He's part of the Southern-fried ambiance, but since he's a goat, he isn't a bit scary. The ghost in the mystery was menacing and creepy, the kind of creepy that made me wish I lived in a brand new apartment equipped with halogen light bulbs.

I'd managed to get my teeth brushed, the alarm armed, all the lights off except my bedside lamp, and had crawled into bed while still reading. I can be pretty coordinated when I need to be. The protagonist was about to be attacked by either the ghost or the vampire. One of them was a good guy, but I hadn't figured out which yet. Very good plotting.

My phone rang, and I slung the book upward so it hit the ceiling fan and careened off toward the hall door. Thank goodness I wasn't reading on a tablet. Montrose leaped down and ran under the bed after I screamed in her ear, right before I hit the floor and ducked like I was under attack. Pudge began to howl, and from below I could hear Lafitte offering his

X-rated commentary on the disruption of his beauty sleep.

By the time I got my heartrate back to normal and crawled across the floor to retrieve my book, the phone had rolled over to voicemail. Maybe I need to switch to nonfiction. Maybe a riveting biography of Eleanor Roosevelt. At the very least, I should read scary stories downstairs with all the lights on, but then I'd have the problem of ascending my creaky staircase to my empty bedroom afterward.

I listened to my message.

"Hey, Annalee, I just wanted to make sure we're still on for the reunion this weekend. I'm so busy with work that I won't get the chance to see you before Saturday."

It was Caleb. He does something called database managing systems, in addition to raising cattle and goats with his dad. He tried to explain it to me once, but my eyes must have glazed over pretty quickly. He'd dumped the MIT grad school words and pared it down to computers, work from home, and lucrative enough that he could spend his free time learning to make goat cheese. Speak to me in simple terms, and I'm right there with you.

I sank into my pillows and returned his call. "What's wrong; you didn't believe me when I said I'd go with you?"

"You said yes, but your expression said something completely different. I thought it wise to double check."

"I'll admit it wouldn't be my first choice for a Saturday night, but I won't stand you up, especially since your dad is going to the football game with you Friday instead of me."

I heard him laugh.

"He wouldn't miss it. He was there every time we played a game in high school, and traveled to most of the out of town ones. Mom was always nervous I'd get hurt, but I don't think he gave that a thought. That year we didn't make it to State because the quarterback was drunk before the regional championship game nearly killed him."

That brought Valonda to mind. "I regret my part in that. What a weekend for me to be visiting Frankie from Houston."

"Your part? What did you have to do with it? I'm pretty sure I never heard your name mentioned."

"I can't believe you don't know. I thought everyone did. Valonda has sure as heck never forgotten," I answered. "Frankie and I were going past the athletic building that Saturday morning on our way to walk the track. I'm the one who saw Valonda's feet sticking out from under the shrubbery. *And* I'm the one who started screaming that she was dead. Heck, she looked dead. Both of them did, although in retrospect I should have clued into the fact that they were almost naked and surrounded by empty booze bottles. I'm telling you, I was traumatized for life. It was almost as bad as the time you threw me in the pond with the imaginary alligators when I was eight."

As always, he pretended he hadn't heard the reminder of his own involvement in a traumatic incident in my past.

"I had no idea you were at the scene. I heard Valonda and Ryan Dawson were so drunk they'd spent the whole night under those azaleas. Coach threatened all of us with the same suspension he gave Ryan if we talked about it, and the gossip died before it even started. Now there would be pictures all over the Internet."

"That was before everyone had a smart phone with them at all times. I just had a little flip phone with a pitiful camera, but even if I'd had today's technology, I wouldn't have taken a picture of the star quarterback in his underwear. What was he, six foot two and 220 pounds or so?"

"Yeah, he was a big guy, but totally easy-going. Outsized ego, though. If you'd taken a picture he would have assumed it was because you couldn't resist the opportunity to blow it up and put it on your wall. He's happily married now, and his wife was in my class. If they show up Saturday, you can get a socially respectable look at him. I think you'll like them both."

I decided to change the subject. "Here's the eternal female question. What should I wear?"

"I see you in yoga pants most often, but you might want to up the ante a bit. My vote is for something short and shiny that won't seriously outclass my sports-coat and tie."

"Duly noted. I'll do my best."

We ended the call, and I gave a brief thought to my wardrobe. I have a closet full of cute things from my former life in Houston, and nobody here has seen them. Between that and my myriad jewelry choices, I might not have to buy anything new for years. I could even pull something off the rack that was short and shiny.

I had never seen Ryan Dawson in anything but tightie whities. I hoped he would follow Caleb's plan and show up fully dressed. And I also hoped he was as forgetful of my involvement in his downfall as my date was.

# Chapter Four

WHEN YOU SPEND as much time on the road as I do, your car takes a beating. I drive a used BMW SUV that has over a hundred thousand miles on it. I have some special cases to display the jewelry I sell at antique shows, and they nestle snugly into the back. There's a compartment in the floor of the hatchback area that has a lift-up flap, so the jewelry itself is hidden under the weight of the display cases. But maybe most important, the GPS system keeps me navigating in the right direction. Most of the time. As long as I'm not too deeply into an audiobook.

Anyway, it's a sturdy, reliable car, and even though it looks rather stodgy, it's a lot more comfortable than Uncle Raine's old GMC pickup that I drive around town. It even gets better gas mileage.

Unfortunately it likes high dollar tires, and that's why I was sitting in the local Goodyear store Wednesday morning waiting for them to install the two new ones they ordered for me. I try never to be caught without something to read, but my tablet's battery ran down during the second chapter of my latest Janet Evanovich book. Maybe the woman sitting next to me had done some sort of voodoo on it when I cackled out loud and startled her out of her nap.

I poured myself a cup of overcooked coffee from the complimentary caffeine dispenser and looked idly out the window at the heavy equipment dealer next door. New and used large scale machinery covered an acre of asphalt and beckoned to me in temptation. What the heck, even though I'll never get to operate a bulldozer, I could walk over there and sit in the driver's seat of one. I'd take a selfie and sent it to Charlie, my baby brother. Wednesday morning was his physics class; he would welcome a diversion.

I dumped the paper cup of oily brown liquid into the trash can and walked out into the cool November morning. Ahead of me sat a panoply of construction equipment under strings of fluttering, multicolored pennants. I was looking at a real life version of Charlie's bedroom bookcase with its rows of Tonka toys. There was no one on the lot, so I didn't have to explain my visit. I could just wander freely and indulge my curiosity.

There were commercial strength tractors, bulldozers, one of those cherry picker trucks that lifts you up high in the air, a great big backhoe, and lots of farm equipment. I wasn't sure how to navigate climbing up on bulldozer treads, so I headed for a big yellow front-end loader with tires almost as tall as I am. That's pretty darn big for a tire, because I stopped growing two inches short of six feet. The loader was thoughtfully equipped with narrow metal steps ascending to the enclosed cab.

I looked around furtively. I really didn't want anyone to come by and force me to justify my avid interest in such an unusual subject. The lot was still vacant, and the guys at the tire dealership were paying attention to their jobs, not a crazy female about to clamber up to a place where she definitely didn't belong. I tossed my hair over my shoulders and went for it, glad I had put on slacks and flats that morning.

Fantastic. They were careless enough to leave the cab unlocked. Very considerate of them. I sat on the padded black vinyl bucket seat and looked around curiously. No steering wheel? There was a gear shift; why wasn't there a way to drive the thing? How do you make it go where you want it to?

I looked at the gear shift more closely and determined it wasn't. A shift, that is. It seemed to be much more involved and had various little yellow buttons and green trigger type thingies on it. I decided it provided the means to run the whole show, kind of like a video game joystick. Too bad I hadn't spent more time playing games with Charlie.

Below the front window were five dials, most of which seemed to measure things that weren't on my car dashboard. To the upper right was a video screen for a view of what was behind. That would be a necessity; if I backed into something with one of these, my Liberty Mutual guy would go ballistic. I saw a top-name radio and two cup holders that were a definite improvement on the ones in my car.

I looked out of the expansive windshield. I could see everywhere except directly behind me, which would be taken care of by the aforementioned camera. My car was up on the rack in the Goodyear garage, where I saw a guy removing the first of the two bad tires. I decided to see if any of the other vehicles were open for me to climb into. A dump truck might be interesting.

As I swung my feet out of the cab onto the top step, I heard the sharp voice of someone who wasn't pleased.

"Hey! Excuse me! May I help you? We don't allow our customers to climb on the machinery without a salesman. It's against our insurance policy regulations."

There was a bit of familiarity to that voice. I was almost positive it belonged to someone I knew, and the sound of it kicked in an automatic sense of dread. I turned my head slowly, and unfortunately had my gut feeling vindicated.

"Why, what in the heck are you doing on that front end loader, Annalee Wyatt? I don't for a minute believe you're going to buy one."

Valonda Nelson. What I wouldn't give to fire the sucker up and front-end-load her into the next parish.

But I decided I'd be nice if it gave me a hernia. "Hello, Valonda, what are you doing here?"

"I asked first. That's a very expensive piece of machinery, not playground equipment."

Nice. I would be nice. "Yes, you're right. I've always wanted to see what one was like from the control center, and since I'm waiting on my car to be ready next door, it seemed like the perfect time. I didn't intend to do anything but look inside, but when I found the cab unlocked I couldn't resist. Do you work here?"

She grabbed the bottom of her tight red sweater and pulled it back down over the waistband of her skirt with a practiced gesture. I'd never seen her in anything that didn't threaten an unwanted peek at features most women left covered in public.

"My Uncle Allen is the manager, and I'm filling in for the receptionist, although if Dinah doesn't show up, or at least call, I'll be taking over the job permanently.

It's ridiculous that girl thinks she can just disappear and expect to come back to work whenever she's in the mood.

"Anyway, all the guys are in a sales meeting, and I'm supposed to be looking after things till they're finished. I was shocked to see someone inside the cab of this thing."

"You're doing a great job of guarding the merchandise. You caught me fair and square."

She looked somewhat mollified by my compliment. "I guess there's no harm, but you need to be careful climbing down."

I agreed and slowly descended, keeping my hands tightly around the safety railing till I felt my feet touch ground. When I turned to face her, she was staring at my new ring.

"That's really pretty. It's so different. I've never seen a stone like that. Is it old?"

I'll admit I was surprised and impressed that she didn't think it was an emerald or a peridot, the second likely guess for most people. I gave her an edited version of the special garnet and let her try on the ring. Her face brightened and took on that look of desire I love to see on my customers.

"You wear such pretty things, Annalee. Sometimes I go into the Magnolia Blossom just to look at what you have to sell. Someday if I'm lucky maybe I won't just look."

She sounded sincere, and I believed her. I noticed she was wearing a tasteful pair of gold hoops. "I would be happy to help you find something you love, Valonda. Come in any time and try on everything in the case if you want. I have all price ranges, but it doesn't matter if you can't buy anything yet."

She smiled at me for the first time ever and waved good-bye as she walked back inside to her desk.

As I drove away later on my new tires, I saw her near the front loader again. This time she wasn't fending off unauthorized climbers, as a matter of fact, she wasn't doing any fending off at all. Some guy had her backed up against one of the gigantic tires giving her a kiss that came close to being X-rated. As for Valonda, her hands were plunged down the back of his khakis, and I don't think she was checking his wallet. Good grief. Maybe that was why she had gone onto the lot in the first place. Maybe my presence interfered with a secret assignation.

Oh, well, none of my business. I wished I could unsee the two of them, but for all I knew they'd been dating for months and had no reason but lust to meet amid the heavy equipment in the middle of a workday.

I pulled out of the parking lot toward home. The church had updated its sign appropriately for the day:

IT WASN'T THE APPLE—IT WAS THE PAIR

# Chapter Five

If there's one thing I've learned in the jewelry business, it's that disorganization will do you in. For example, if you make your living selling bulldozers, it's not that hard to keep up with your inventory. You should be able to count your supply from the office window. It's not so easy for me to keep track of rings and bracelets and necklaces and all the other things I buy and sell.

I've trained myself to be careful and repetitive with my pretties. I don't leave anything out loose on my work surface; whether I'm appraising or repairing, I always place items in one of the little bowls I keep on my desk. I never ever leave the room with something in my hand. If I take a ring to another part of the house, for example, I slip it on my finger even if it only fits my pinkie. Some of the things I sell could be lost in the spaces between the boards of the floor. The cypress logs were milled 140 years ago, and there's been shrinkage in the meantime.

In spite of my careful practices, I'd spent the better part of the morning crawling around in the study with a flashlight in my hand. I was missing a matte gold and cabochon ruby tuxedo shirt stud. The art deco set consisted of two cuff links and four studs, and the loss of one of them lowered the value of the set by almost half.

Montrose reached down from her favorite chair and tapped my head as I made another circle of the room on my knees. I stopped and gave her a suspicious look. "Do you know anything about this?" She yawned and closed her golden eyes, then placed a paw over them as if it were all too much to bear.

On a hunch, I moved my search up a couple of feet. Maybe the big orange cat really was the culprit. If she was involved, she might have swiped the item off the top of my desk with her paw, and it could be almost anywhere in the room. She loved to see things fly through the air. She could have batted the darn thing out the door and down the hall if she was in the mood to play. I hoped she hadn't been so energetic.

I saw a flash of gold from the windowsill and detected the smooth red surface of the domed ruby. The trajectory from the desk to the window was easy to visualize; a smooth arc precipitated by a fast swat.

No wonder I hadn't noticed it. The piece of flaking paint it hid behind was large enough to obscure a pair of chandelier earrings. I hoped the Nelson brothers would offer me as good a price on touching up problems inside the house as the one Gideon emailed me for the exterior.

My lunch date with Tennie was set late enough that we could feel free to sit and talk with no worry we were keeping someone waiting for our spot. I hate to feel hungry eyes on me while I'm eating. I walked through the door at Katie's Kitchen at 1:30 and saw her near the front of the room at one of the scarred wooden tables, rather than the back booth that Frankie and I occupied earlier in the week.

Katie Johnson's figure shows little evidence she owns a cafe that's been written up in national magazines as a don't-miss spot. I met her look of surprise with a guilty blush before she said a word.

"You're here twice in a week?" she asked. "I thought your dietary restrictions didn't allow it."

Tennie looked interested. "I've never known you to turn down a good meal. Are you on some sort of exotic diet?"

I sighed and confessed my weakness. "Nothing exotic; I've just gained five very solid pounds since I moved to Louisiana, and it has to stop. I know there are reasonable items on the menu that don't contain my entire calorie count for the day, but those aren't the ones that appeal to me. I walk through the door and see the daily special on the chalkboard, and I don't even look at the healthier choices."

My dining companion narrowed her eyes and squinted as she looked over my shoulder to the sun-filled window. It was so bright that the painted tin ceiling reflected a bilious green glow on the room.

"That one hasn't let a few pounds stop her fun," she said.

Katie and I followed her gaze into the parking lot across the street. All I could see at first was Tennie's metallic blue 1979 Pontiac GTO. Then I realized everyone in the restaurant was being treated to a view of Valonda Nelson wrapped around a man like a snake on a tree limb. "That's the second guy I've seen her with in two days," I said. "And it's almost the same pose. She's pretty limber." I probably sounded impressed, because in a way, I was. I've been practicing yoga for fifteen years, and I'm not sure I could get myself into such a creative position.

"I think they need to get a room," said Tennie. "If they get any closer together their clothes may melt off from the heat, or even worse, they may melt the paint off my car. It might be 65 degrees, but they're doing their part to increase global warming right there on Main Street. Where else did you see her?"

"In the parking lot at the heavy equipment dealer."

"What the heck was she doing there?"

"According to her, Dinah, the receptionist disappeared, and she's taking her place. Maybe the job description includes filling in for Dinah with the guy, too."

Katie shook her head in disapproval. "That Dinah Morrison had better grow up and stop leaving town on the spur of the moment. She's been taking off for weeks at a time since middle school without a by-your-leave. It's a wonder she graduated, but she has a child now. Her mama can't step in and take over just because that girl wants to go catting around. The last time she disappeared, she came back three months afterward and three months pregnant.

"As for Valonda, thank goodness it isn't an hour later. The kids walking home from school would get the sex education that the legislature won't let the teachers give them. Y'all give me your orders, and I'll deliver your meals and eat with you if you don't mind. We'll catch up on the Berryville news."

GREAT-AUNT JOSIE AND Tennie Martin were friends for years, and I had it on good authority (Clotille's) that

Great-uncle Raine shuddered in worried anticipation whenever the two of them were in each other's company without supervision. I guess it isn't surprising that we've become good friends in spite of our age difference. She misses my aunt and uncle, and I've proved myself willing to follow along on some schemes that were less than sensible. While we don't exactly hang out, we do seem to fall into a seamless rhythm when we're together. Maybe I channel Aunt Josie's spirit.

"What are you wearing Saturday night? Something short and sassy?" she asked, as we waited for our lunch.

I stopped squeezing the lemon wedge into my tea and stared at her. "I shouldn't be surprised, but how do you know I'm going somewhere?"

"I saw Caleb's mother at my water aerobics class yesterday, and Sarah is over the moon that you two are seeing each other. She said Valonda was cozying up to her at the grocery store last month, and she was afraid Caleb was in her sights."

I laughed as I scooted my chair to make room for Katie. "As if she has time to add another guy to her schedule, even if Caleb was susceptible to her charms."

Katie put down her plate of the day's vegetables and pointed across the street, where the display of affection had lost a few degrees of heat but looked like it could flame up again at any moment. "I don't know who you saw her with yesterday, but I'm pretty sure she'd dump that guy she's with now in a hurry for someone like Caleb. Mr. Right-right-now is her ex. He married her after the deal with Nancy's Jerry, but it didn't last. Now I think they're friends with benefits, although I don't think he's the only one."

"Wait a minute," I said. "That's who Nancy Crosby's ex-husband had the affair with? Wasn't that at least ten years ago? How old would Valonda have been, eighteen?"

"That sounds right," answered Tennie. "He was forty. He hired her right out of high school to be the secretary at his land surveying business."

Katie continued. "Nancy caught him measuring some elevations and contours that had nothing to do with Sebastian Parish topography. She had him out of their house so fast that Doppler radar reported a tornado in the vicinity."

Tennie and I both burst into laughter at Katie's vivid imagery.

"Oh my, that was a fun day except for the pain he caused Nancy," said Tennie, wiping her eyes. "I remember their front yard was covered with all his clothes. I'd never seen so many pastel golf shirts. She gave his clubs to the university down at Natchitoches for their golf team and changed the locks on the doors and all the passwords on their accounts until she could get her lawyer involved."

"But she never said a bad work about him to their kids," Katie said. "I admired her for that. She's still close to his mom, too. As a matter of fact, Jerry's mom completely sided with her. Nancy told him he should move himself out of town, because she wasn't going back to Texas. He lives in Baton Rouge now. Last I heard he was married to another woman who's too good for him."

"I wonder if Valonda will be at the homecoming party Saturday night," I mused. "And if she'll have a date. One of those two guys, or maybe bachelor number three."

"Maybe you shouldn't count on the bachelor bit, given her history, but we definitely want a full report," Tennie said. "Be sure to notice if the quarterback is there with his wife, too. A reunion of those two ought to be good for some excitement. There's plenty of folks here in town who remember that year. Football's darn near a religion in Louisiana, and Berryville was the top team in the state till that little incident."

"I hate to disappoint you, but I'm hoping for a non-event. Surely he's been forgiven by now."

Tennie looked doubtful. "I don't know about forgiveness, but I'll bet most of the men in town can still describe every play of the game that went on without him. I know my husband can. If that boy hadn't made the football team at LSU, he still wouldn't be able to show his face in town."

# Chapter Six

I STOPPED AT the drugstore for mascara, and I'll be darned, I ran into Valonda again. I know I live in a small town, but I might as well be tailing her like a private detective. I wished there was someone I could bill for my time. We exchanged hellos, and I ducked around the corner to the cosmetic aisle.

Barbie Andre, the wife of one of Frankie's partners as well as the office manager of the practice, was perusing the nail polish. "Hey, Annalee, I'm thinking about this Wedgewood blue. Do I get it with the silver sparkles or not?"

"Toes and fingernails both?"

"It would be nice to have the option."

"I'd leave off the iridescence if you're going to wear it on your fingernails at the office. Just my personal thoughts, but sparkling nails on my health care professional seem a bit flippant," I said. "I want to feel like my aches and pains are taken very seriously."

She dropped the small bottle into the plastic basket that hung on her arm. "I didn't realize that. When you come in for your flu shot, I'll scream and clutch my chest."

"You'll look more impressive when you do that if you're wearing an aquamarine on your finger that matches the polish. That's the kind of sparkle I can get behind, and it just so happens I have a nice one over at the Magnolia Blossom."

As I listened to her decide what occasion such a purchase could celebrate, I saw an end aisle display of jumbo pack toilet tissue go bouncing to the floor. Barbie stopped in the middle of "Halloween's over, and besides, it isn't orange or black . . ."

She looked over her shoulder, and we both flattened ourselves against the L'Oréal display as Valonda stormed past us and out the door. In her wake, a petite woman dressed in what looked like a Little House on the Prairie costume struggled with the packages of tissue, evidently determined to place them back in order.

I was the tallest of the three of us, so I walked over and helped finish the job. As she thanked me, I noticed she looked oddly like the woman who had just rushed past me. The bright blue eyes and facial features matched, but she seemed softened somehow. I could detect no trace of makeup, not even mascara. Her hair was a natural shade of brown, worn simply in a thick braid that trailed down her back, with no evidence of hairspray on the flyaway wisps around her face. She was the same height, and I caught a hint of curves like Valonda's beneath the shapeless dress she wore. She appeared to be in her early twenties, but that may have been due to the fact that she was dressed like my grandmother's great-grandmother.

"I'm Annalee Wyatt. Please excuse my nosiness, but are you related to Valonda? You look like you could be sisters."

"Yes," she said, and hesitated. "She's my older sister. I'm Dorcas." She gave me a sweet smile, then left the store almost as quickly as her sister had.

"I wonder what that was about."

Barbie shrugged. "They don't get along. Valonda is the family hellion, and Dorcas toes the line. Their dad is a minister, so the line is extremely well-defined. I think Valonda pole-vaulted over it in middle school and never looked back."

FRIDAY AND SATURDAY went by in a blur of yard work and jewelry repair, leaving me in a rush to get ready for the homecoming event. I'd just finished going over every square inch of my dress with a lint roller when the doorbell rang. A good-lookin' hunk of man stood on my porch.

"Wow, you look fantastic," said Caleb.

He circled me slowly as I stood in the foyer. The appraisal was a bit unnerving, but the judgement was gratifying. I'd been apprehensive that I'd eaten too many of Clotille's biscuits to fit into my favorite cocktail dress, but the zipper required only a slightly harder tug than usual to close. There was no danger I would burst out of the lacy number on the dance floor.

I tossed my hair over my shoulder and batted my false lashes at him. "Will I make the cut for the tenth reunion of the Berryville High Class of 2006?"

"The only change you need to make is your choice of footwear. As in, you need to wear some shoes."

"I figured you for someone with impossible standards." I turned on the alarm, then slipped my feet into a pair of crazy-high Louboutins and followed Caleb out of the house.

"Those are some hot shoes, but you know this dance is in the gym. You'll probably have to take them off so you won't ruin the basketball court."

"That's why I didn't have them on in the house. They make little tiny indentations in my cypress floors, but I'll look fashionable for the drive over," I said, secretly pleased that he thought I looked hot. True, he was describing the shoes, but close enough.

I settled into his dad's plush pickup truck and ran my hand over the leather seat. "Your dad gave you his pride and joy for date night. I'm impressed."

"Tonight is nothing like my homecoming dance 12 years ago. I brought home a C in English that week, and they made me take Mom's old Pontiac. That was a weird day all over town. Everyone's parents were on edge after Ryan and Valonda were found drunk and passed out. If the perfect Ryan Dawson could screw up so badly, what were their own little sweethearts doing on the sly?"

I tried to suppress an unexpected twinge of jealousy. It was inexplicable, but nevertheless, I felt the pinch of the green-eyed monster. "Who was your date? Do you think she'll be there tonight?" *Please let me look better than she does* was my selfish thought.

"Jenny Sanders. According to the reunion website, she just had her third kid and won't be able to make the trip up from Hammond."

Poor woman. She was post-partum and probably exhausted, and I'd sent jealous thoughts her way. As we entered the parking lot, I sent her some mental good wishes.

THE BLACK-TOPPED LOT was already half full of cars and pickups when we arrived. As I slid from the high passenger seat, I took a deep breath of the crisp fall air. It may be environmentally unsound, but I love the smell of burning leaves, and someone's afternoon raking was still perfuming the breeze.

Pausing in the lobby for me to remove my shoes, I slipped them into the shelves that had been placed there for the purpose. We held hands as we walked into the darkened gymnasium, and I felt like I was a teenager again. Excitement and anticipation mixed with a little apprehension, and I clutched Caleb's fingers tightly. We stopped at the bar and picked up a beer for him and a glass of wine for me, and I surveyed the crowd as we stood on the sideline.

For the most part it was a fashionable group. Berryville may be a small town, but we're not isolated. The current styles make their way here as soon as they do to Houston. My bronze lace sheath fit in nicely, and I was relieved to see that mine weren't the only bare feet. I remembered my grandmother talking about something she called a "sock hop" in her high school days, where she danced in the gym, I guess in her socks. I felt like she would recognize the occasion if not the dress code. Would she have been shocked at the cut-outs and sheer fabric on display, or would she have been the most outré one there? Probably the latter.

The reunion committee opted for a DJ rather than a live band, and to my delight, Caleb dragged me onto the dance floor right away, squeezing us into an opening in the crowd. I didn't let dancing stop my people-watching.

I recognized Hal, the butcher at Bubba's Buy-It-Low, even without his white apron and gigantic cleaver. There was no mistaking that prematurely bald pate and rotund middle. His wife was shaped just like him, but had all her hair and was rocking some great rhinestone earrings. Christie Jenkins gyrated past with a guy I recognized from the local bank. He looked pretty straight-laced compared to her bright blue hair color and garishly tattooed calf. Christie had joined her mom at Tiny's Beauty Boutique and Gift Shoppe, where she offered an alternative to the tight curls and traditional coifs that her mom produced day after day for the older women in town. The asymmetrical cut she sported tonight was a perfect advertisement for her up-to-date scissor skills.

After five songs, we left the floor fanning ourselves and retrieved our drinks. I noticed a ripple of interest in the crowd. It slowly parted, and the two people who made their way through the center moved like royalty accepting fealty and homage from their subjects. A roar of appreciation erupted, complete with cheers and clapping. I turned to Caleb, bemused by the spectacle.

"It's Ryan and Stacey," he said. "I haven't seen them since college, but you'll love both of them. Come on—I'll introduce you."

# Chapter Seven

We waited our turn. One after another, the other attendees approached the star couple and did what passed for genuflection. The guys shook Ryan's hand and made some comment about his football career, while the women giggled and complimented Stacey on her looks.

She did look striking, if a bit too perfect for my taste. Long, silken blonde locks cascaded over her shoulders, falling on either side of a face that a teen magazine would declare to be heart-shaped. Her lips, just a little too pillowy, glistened with so much shimmering gloss that I could have used them as a mirror, and her eyes were the gray of a January sky, framed with unbelievably long black lashes. Heck, they might even have been real, although I was betting on more expensive fakes than I wore myself. I saw high-carat diamond hoops dangling from her ears. They may have been fake, too, but they were gorgeous.

I took advantage of our wait to assess the rest of her look, mainly the jewelry. I'm good at it. Give me a couple of minutes to mentally add and subtract, and I can usually come within a hundred bucks or so of a total wholesale price on what someone is wearing. Retail? I'm not quite as sharp on that. Mark-up in the business varies quite a bit unless it's a well-known designer.

Stacey wore a gold crochet knit jumpsuit, stretchy and form-fitting. Built like a Victoria's Secret model, her cleavage pushed the boundaries of the deep V neck, and I hoped there were sturdy pieces of double-sided dress tape holding it in place. The whole look could have come from a 1970s Soul Train rerun, or Cher's closet. Oodles of shiny gold jewelry blended with the gold outfit, and she had dusted every exposed inch of herself with glittering bronzer. Is it still called bronzer if it's gold? Anyway, she shimmered all over.

Jewelry designer David Yurman makes beautiful contemporary things in a wide price range, and I'd say she had at least $15,000 of his distinctive work on each arm. Hard to believe, but even I don't wear that many bangles. Eighteen karat twists with colored stones anchoring the ends marched up her forearms above her wrists. Multiple gold chains lay artfully entangled around her neck as well. Her left hand was adorned with a $20-to-$30,000 pear-shaped diamond that probably hit 3 carats, but her right was almost naked, sporting only a Yurman pave pinky ring. Nice to see she could exercise restraint in the middle of her conspicuous consumption.

While totally not my style, I have to admit that she put the flash in flashy. Unlike the other women at the party, she hadn't removed her gold stilettos, gym floor be damned.

As Caleb brought me forward for introductions, I noticed a tiny lizard brooch almost hidden on the shoulder strap of her jumpsuit. I shook her hand and immediately said "Demantoid?"

She was understandably nonplussed. "I beg your pardon?"

Caleb laughed and stepped into the awkward breech. "You'll have to excuse Annalee; she's a jewelry dealer."

With that helpful comment Stacey recovered quickly. "You mean the alligator? It's a piece of second-hand jewelry I picked up in New Orleans for the reunion. You know, the Berryville Gators. I forget what they told me about the stones, but I think they're off-color emeralds. I'm not sure the guy who sold it to me told me the truth, anyway."

Omigosh, she had to be Andy and Finn's "alligator" customer, but I vowed not to say a word. Here was a woman with a lovely piece of jewelry and she didn't even know what she'd bought. She thought good quality demantoids were poor quality emeralds, and there's no way the guys let her out of the store without a written description of her purchase. I'd excuse her for thinking a lizard was an alligator before I'd excuse her for gem ignorance. The obnoxious smacks against second-hand jewelry and my friends' trustworthiness were just lagniappe, even if she didn't know I knew the guys.

Stacey's beautiful gray eyes narrowed as she did her own inner financial appraisal of the collection of Victorian lockets on a gold chain that encircled my neck. She didn't miss the dangling Victorian gold tassel earrings, either. "That's an *unusual* look."

Could it be that I didn't meet her standards? I resisted the urge to wave my Napoleon III French bangle bracelet in front of her nose. "Yes, I like antique and estate jewelry. That's what I collect and sell."

Her collagen-plumped smile oozed condescension. "How interesting. I guess there's a market for that; not everyone can afford to purchase good things."

*And luckily for me, not everyone wants to look like she spent all her money at the same cash register,* I thought. But I said, "You might be surprised at the realities of the jewelry business. Come see me if you'd like some vintage Bulgari or Cartier. I also have a few Tiffany pieces right now. Be prepared for a shock, though, because some of them sell for a minimum of five to ten times what they originally cost." That got me a dirty look, but it was worth it. I didn't bother showing her my own ring. Don't cast your pearls before swine applies to demantoid garnets, too.

I turned to listen to Caleb's conversation with Ryan. The star quarterback hadn't held up quite as well as his wife. His brown hair was so perfect I could believe his stylist had cut it with manicure scissors. That is not a compliment. The white oxford-cloth shirt he wore looked well-made but ready to pop a button across the room, and his sports coat, while fashionable, fit about as well as the shirt. He could afford the nice clothes, but the salesman must not have told him he needed a larger size.

I expected to hear the guys rehashing old games. Instead I saw my date's jaw clenched in a strained smile. He stood rigidly still while Ryan paced back and forth dramatically as if he were in a courtroom.

"Like I told the jury, the wreck was an accident that could happen to anyone. My client made the mistake of not realizing he was intoxicated, but he was only seventeen. He didn't have the maturity to know that he shouldn't be driving. He felt terrible that people lost their lives, but honestly, it wasn't his fault. Those people shouldn't have built their house so close to the road. If it had been a reasonable distance away, his truck would have stopped before it reached the bedroom. It's the very definition of an accident."

"As fast as he was going, they'd have had to be a half mile away from the pavement. Did you really feel that probation was appropriate in light of the fact he was too drunk to know where he was? I remember the backlash went national on that case. I know darn well you and I knew that we shouldn't drive drunk at that age."

"Oh, lighten up. His dad didn't give a rat's ass about a few politically correct complaints. He thought my bill was well worth it," Ryan replied, accompanying his words with unrepentant laughter. "He sent me quite a few referrals, in addition to switching all of his company work to me. That alone paid for my house on the beach at Galveston. You oughta come visit—we'll go deep-sea fishing on my boat." He stopped talking and narrowed his eyes at me, suddenly a little too interested. "Have we met before?"

I took an involuntary step back and began to fumble an answer, but Caleb put his arm around my waist and pulled me close.

"She's new in town. Just moved here a few months ago."

Before Ryan could question that, we were joined by another reunion celebrant. Valonda eased her way into our conversational circle and slipped her arm around Stacey's waist. "Hi, y'all, it's so nice to see you," she squealed, her enthusiasm sounding a little forced.

Stacey quickly stepped free of the contact, her distaste quite obvious. "Hello, Valonda, I might have known

I'd see you here. Have you passed out under any azaleas lately?"

The petite woman smiled politely and handled the unkind remark with surprising grace. "I have not, and I doubt Ryan has either. That's old news. You look great, Stacey. I love your new hair color."

Stacey flushed an angry red and tossed her head, causing the golden mass to fly back over her shoulders. I noticed an extension coming loose. "It's the same natural color it's always been. I don't do a thing to it."

Like hell. Her "natural" color cost big bucks and took several hours in the salon chair. She really should find someone else to take care of it. There's no excuse for shedding your extensions.

Valonda picked up on her misstep and changed the subject. Turning to me, she said, "Is Stacey's lizard pin set with those stones like your new ring, Annalee? Didn't you say they were some sort of garnet?"

I smiled warmly and mentally awarded her a gold star. She'd gotten the animal and the gemstone correct. "Yes, you're right. That lizard, or salamander, is a classic piece set with demantoid garnets and diamonds, probably Edwardian, from the early 1900's."

Stacey sniffed unattractively. "I don't understand the interest. It's just something cheap I bought for the reunion. I don't normally wear used jewelry."

I felt my ears getting hot. That cheap pin probably set her back at least three thousand dollars. I pulled forth some of my salesperson charm. "Your other jewelry is just *lovely*. It certainly doesn't appear to be used." Just as I expected, she preened under my appreciative glance.

"Ryan is the most perfect hubby in the world. He never says no when I want something new." She pulled on his arm to demand his attention. "Aren't you, Ryan? The most perfect hubby ever?"

A flash of annoyance went across his face, and I realized he'd been staring at Valonda since she joined us. As he replied to Stacey, his gaze continued to travel up and down the newcomer. His expression said he approved of her strapless red dress and upswept hair.

"Yeah, I'm the best," he said. "Valonda, you're looking good. Gimme a kiss for old times." He swooped in before she could object.

I swear that creep stuck his tongue in her ear. It was quick, but it was there like a bullfrog after a dragonfly. Lord have mercy, had everything I'd heard about his sterling character been lies? I think everyone standing there except Ryan turned red, but Stacey's face indicated rage, rather than embarrassment.

Valonda's date chose that moment to wander over, and Stacey took the opportunity to drag her husband across the room to another group of his admirers. We weren't worthy of even a backward glance.

Caleb ignored their abrupt departure and went into Southern Gentleman mode. "Annalee, I'd like you to meet Ed Nelson."

I found myself smiling at a cute brown-eyed guy in his late twenties wearing a plaid shirt, starched Levis, and cowboy boots. Even though I couldn't see if his butt looked familiar, I was sure this was the front view of Valonda's partner in her recent Main Street public display of affection.

"Hi, I'm Valonda's ex-husband, date for the evening,

and 5th cousin," he said with a grin. "I hear you have a secret desire to be a heavy equipment operator."

There was nothing to do but laugh. After Caleb got a brief explanation, he joined in and made a promise to let me drive his dad's tractor next year when they baled hay.

"The last time I was at the dealership, Dinah was in charge of the desk. Did she do another runner?" Caleb asked.

I promised myself to find out more about this woman who had a hard time staying put.

Valonda answered his question. "That's what we all thought, but her mom is getting worried. Dinah has behaved herself since she had her son. She hasn't even gone to Shreveport overnight without clearing it with her mom. Mrs. Morrison talked to the sheriff's office, and they're treating her as a missing person as of yesterday."

# Chapter Eight

THE NEXT COUPLE of hours were pleasant. We danced some more, ate Natchitoches meat pies and barbecue, and chatted up a lot of Caleb's old friends. None were as unpleasant as the Golden Couple, as I'd come to think of them. There was the occasional remark about the season-ruining behavior of the former quarterback, but it was interesting to find that almost no mention was made of Valonda's part in the debacle. I didn't hear a word uttered about my own involvement. I suppose it had been much more significant to me than anyone else. I'd worried all week long for no reason.

As Caleb talked, I found myself observing Ryan and Stacey. He was having a good time. His white shirt was untucked and a few buttons were undone. The level of the beer in his glass changed often enough that I was sure he wasn't nursing the same one. His voice grew louder and his laughter more boisterous, and his dance moves required more and more space on the floor. All in all, I'd say he was enjoying himself a helluva lot more than his wife, and the more he drank, the more women he kissed. I caught several more attempts on Valonda, but she dodged his clutches with alacrity; one ear wash had been enough for her.

I didn't witness a single woman who welcomed his overt affection; no surprise when it seemed more sexual than friendly. There were dirty looks thrown his way by more than one husband, but he was unfazed and undeterred. He looked like a man accustomed to getting what he wanted.

Stacey's smile grew more strained as the evening went on, and I occasionally heard a shrill "Ryan!" above the music. If she intended to slow him down, she was several beers too late. Although I'd taken an immediate dislike to her, I couldn't help but sympathize. I wouldn't wish an experience like that on anyone. True, my conversation with her was unpleasant, but perhaps several years of marriage to Ryan had shaped her personality for the worse.

Caleb and I were talking to some of his old buddies from the tennis team when Merribeth Horton burst through our group and hid behind Parker Burns. "Don't let him see me," she hissed.

Ryan walked past, loudly calling her name. "Merribeth, you good-lookin' thang. C'mon back over here, and I'll get you a drink."

Caleb cocked his head at me. "Has he been hanging around Lafitte? I swear I've heard the parrot use that line."

"I hope he doesn't have any more success with it than Lafitte does," I said. "The parrot has a much better personality."

"That SOB better watch himself when he walks to his car tonight," said Parker. "There'll be a line-up of guys waiting to get him alone and punch his lights out, and he's too wasted to even see it coming. He's not the star quarterback anymore."

WHEN WE'D HAD all the fun we could stand, we returned to the front entry to retrieve my shoes. Quarreling voices from a nearby hallway reached us, and I instinctively lowered my own, not with the intention of listening, but rather from the desire not to invade someone's privacy.

There was no mistaking the speaker. Stacey Dawson was reaming someone out, and that someone could be no one but her husband. Caleb and I exchanged nervous glances. I don't know about him, but I wished we had turned around and gone back into the gym the moment we realized we were privy to a fight.

"This is why we live in Texas! We come back to Berryville, and you think you're still the whoop-de-do quarterback! Never mind that you blew it your senior year; everyone has forgiven you for that, because you're such a great guy." Her voice became more strident. "Well, I've had it. Is there a woman here you haven't kissed? I'm surprised one of the guys hasn't socked you in your big, red, drunk nose. If you'd looked at Jason's face when you grabbed his wife's boobs, you'd be afraid to walk to your car in the dark.

"In addition to that, watching you strut around all evening wasn't enough; you had to publicly humiliate me with Valonda Nelson. Don't think I'm stupid. I know about the two of you."

"Whatter ya goin' to do about it?" came Ryan's drunken reply. "Leave me? Who'll buy you all that jewelry you like so much?"

Her voice was low and vicious. "That jewelry you've bought to keep me quiet about your bad behavior? Yes, you self-satisfied ass, our marriage is over. When I get through with you, I'll have enough money to buy better things than you've ever given me."

"I'd like to see you try," was his unoriginal response, followed by a wall-rattling belch. "Aren't you supposed to be president of the Junior League next year? You won't have time to be the Queen Bee if you have to get a J-O-B."

"You're too drunk to even focus your eyes, Ryan. In case you're seeing two of me, we both hate your guts. Go back inside and decide who you're going home with tonight, because it won't be me. I'm walking the three blocks to my parents' house. Try not to wrap your damn Corvette around a tree when you leave."

I dashed out the door barefoot, my shoes in hand, with Caleb hot on my heels. We hid behind the azaleas, not easy at our height, afraid we would meet Stacey in the parking lot. We ducked amid the greenery until she stormed past us.

"That was more than I wanted to know," whispered Caleb.

"You and me both. I guess you never can tell what life is like behind the facade, and they have a shiny one. Two hours ago she told us he's the most perfect hubby ever in the whole wide world."

"And now she's walking home to her folks by herself after telling Mr. Perfect she's divorcing him. Let's get in the truck and make sure she gets home okay."

Stacey's home was close enough to the school that we were able to watch her without her realizing she was under observation. Not that Berryville is high crime, but it was eleven at night in a town that shuts down at nine, and I was relieved to see her go safely inside and close the front door behind her.

As we drove up my driveway we saw Pudge under the pecan trees, snuffling along after a fat possum. Every time he got too close, the possum turned around and hissed at him, showing his inch-long front teeth. Pudge would stop a moment; they would exchange glares; then they'd begin their trip across the yard again.

"I wonder if he's ever caught one of the ugly things?" Caleb asked.

"I don't know that he really tries," I answered. "I've never seen him move fast enough to catch anything, even in his younger years, although there have been times when I thought he would bark something to death."

We went inside, and I poured us a nightcap of single-malt Scotch. Caleb flipped on the TV, and we settled into the couch to watch Saturday Night Live from the beginning, thanks to the magic of my digital recorder. It wasn't until we made it to the musical guest that either of us brought up the subject of the Dawson debacle.

"I feel confused," said Caleb. "Like a big part of my high school years was spent with my head in the sand."

"What are you talking about?"

"I looked up to Ryan Dawson. He was a better athlete than I was; he was president of the class every year; he dated the prettiest girls, and he even made reasonably good grades. He was a nice guy. The guy who came to the reunion wasn't the Ryan I remember. Was I just dumb? Can someone change that much in ten years?"

"As a licensed psychologist, I—"

"You're a licensed psychologist?"

"Gotcha. Of course not. But I do have an opinion, based on years of reading advice columns. Your description of Ryan in high school makes him sound like a Golden Boy. I think that good athletes are cut a lot of slack, especially in a place as football crazy as Louisiana. Class president is pretty much a popularity contest, and I can't imagine a quarterback who couldn't get a date with whoever he wanted. How successful was he in college sports?"

"Not so much. He only got to start in a couple of games his junior year. It was like he lost his mojo when he graduated high school. He couldn't complete a pass if the receiver was standing wide open and waving his hands."

"That had to be hard on his ego. How did he react?"

"We hung out with different groups, so I don't have first-hand knowledge. He was doing a liberal arts degree, and I was in engineering. I don't think he was king of the world, like he was at Berryville High. We ran into each other occasionally, and he always managed to sound like his life was perfect."

"And Stacey? Did they date all through college?"

He grinned. "Supposedly, but remember, she and I were both two years behind him. She did a pretty good job of being true-blue those last two years of high school, but rumor had it that he wasn't quite as trustworthy. They should both have been dating other people. There aren't too many couples that start in high school and have a successful marriage."

"Wise words," I said. "My priorities certainly changed as I got older."

Caleb's expression grew amused as he drew me to him. "My current priorities no longer involve talking about Ryan and Stacey."

"How about we don't talk at all?"

I SLEPT IN the next morning, awakening to the sound of Pudge's heavy breathing. His paws rested on the edge of my mattress, and his damp nose was about an inch from mine.

"Geez, dog, I hope my breath isn't as toxic as yours." I dragged myself from my warm cocoon and stumbled downstairs to let him out the back door. Montrose was close behind him. The Bright's herd of cattle stood on the other side of the fence, looking with yearning at my hydrangea bushes. I glanced at the swinging gate to make sure the new latch was tightly fastened before turning my back on the always-hungry group.

After plugging in the coffee pot, I went back up to retrieve my cell phone and a warm robe. I'd felt the briskness of the morning air when I let the animals outside, and I wanted to be comfortable on the porch while I drank my coffee. I filled an insulated mug and went out to the swing. Someone on a neighboring farm was burning leaves; the drifting smell was faint and pleasant.

A text from Frankie awaited me, sent two hours before I woke.

*Walk today at 3 pm?*
*Meet you at track?*
*Bring gossip!*

I sent her a smiley face emoji, followed by a thumbs up. She had been in Ryan's class in high school and college. It was perfectly acceptable to let my busybody flag fly with Frankie; she wouldn't blab any tales I shared.

WE PARKED WHERE we always do, in the coach's lot back behind the football field. The day had warmed up, as fall days usually do in Louisiana, and we both were in shorts, old T's, and baseball caps. Starting slowly, we began our first lap around the track.

"How was the party?" Frankie asked.

"I mostly had a good time," I answered. "First, let me say that no one there mentioned my part in the Ryan/Valonda scene."

"I'm not surprised. I don't remember any discussion at the time of your involvement, or mine either, for that matter. I was with you, which you always seem to leave out when you worry about the story."

"Yeah, you were there, but I was the one screaming that the two of them were dead. I guess I can lay that whole thing to rest. Ten years of nagging worry, plus last week's hard core apprehension, for nothing."

"It's good that nobody talked about it. Maybe Ryan finally lived it down."

"Oh, I didn't say the occasion itself wasn't discussed. I heard several guys ragging him. He just laughed it off, but Stacey didn't look amused. Plus I think he was on the verge of recognizing me, but Caleb changed the subject. He may figure it out later, but I hope I don't ever have to see him again."

"At least till Caleb's fifteenth reunion," she said innocently.

I felt myself flushing, and, of course, Frankie noticed.

"Should I ask how the after party was? You're working on quite a blush."

I could tell I was getting pinker. "He came in for a drink, and we watched SNL. Nothing happened."

"Really."

"Sort of really." I gave up. "Okay, we had a great evening. He's a lot of fun. I like him. I think he likes me, too. Is that enough?"

Her laughter echoed across the empty stadium. "You poor thing. You're finally admitting what Boots and I have known all along. We'll be standing by for further developments."

We made it only once around the track before we stopped by the field house at the water fountain. Frankie brushed a few fallen leaves from the spigot and leaned forward to catch the arc of cold water. I took the time to put my heel against the cinder block wall and stretch my hamstrings.

A large charcoal and blue swallowtail butterfly bobbed its way past my nose, and I indulged my inner nature girl by following it to a nearby stand of cardinal flowers. "Look at this butterfly, Frankie."

She joined me and we continued to track its wobbling flight path around the building until it disappeared over the wood fence. "Ready to go back to work?" I asked. "Our pit-stop was early; we have eleven more trips for our usual three miles."

As we skirted a big mound of raked leaves, Frankie caught her foot on something and pitched forward directly into the dry brown pile. I squatted to check on her. She hadn't jumped to her feet as quickly as she should have.

"Are you okay? Did you hurt your knee or twist your ankle?"

She stayed unmoving on her hands and knees, her face drained of color, so white I thought she might faint. "I think . . . I think there's somebody under here," she whispered.

"What do you mean? Somebody under the leaves?" I asked. What was she talking about? We didn't have vagrants in Berryville. I knelt and swept a few of the leaves to the side.

We screamed, but we weren't loud enough to wake the dead.

# Chapter Nine

THERE WAS NO need to call 911. The sheriff's department headquarters was around the corner and across the street, and our cries roused everyone within two blocks. One of Boots' deputies arrived quickly, gun in hand, with a growing crowd of neighbors behind him.

"Dr. Lacasse! Are you hurt? What's going on?"

I was relieved when Deputy Hammett holstered his gun before kneeling next to us. He didn't look old enough to carry a BB gun, much less something that looked like it could put a hole through an anvil.

"Hi, Seth," said Frankie, with a slight tremor in her voice. "I'm okay, just shook up." She pointed to the body barely visible beneath a thick blanket of leaves.

"Holy crap, pardon me, ma'am," he said.

"That's okay. Holy crap is mild compared to what I'm feeling," she said. "Do you have back-up coming? Not that this guy is going anywhere, but there's quite a group behind you."

He turned his head and noticed his audience for the first time. "Alright, folks, I'm asking you to step back onto the other side of the drive. Or better yet, go on home and let us take care of this."

Like that was going to happen. The crowd made a perfunctory step backwards. I saw Mrs. Gautreaux, the secretary at Our Lady of the Cedars, texting away like mad on her cell. I hoped she was notifying the priest; I felt like I could use some pastoral care from any denomination willing to give it. Her husband had his own phone out and was taking pictures. One of the teenagers in attendance looked like she was shooting a video. Would we appear on YouTube or Facebook first? I wished I'd worn nicer clothes.

Within a few minutes, more law enforcement arrived and staked off a large perimeter with crime scene tape. As Frankie and I looked on, the remaining leaves were removed from the body. Ryan Dawson lay face up, arms by his side, eyes open to the trees above. Frankie and I grabbed each other for support.

"He's dead, right?" I squeaked. "I mean, he looks dead to me, but you're a doctor. Is he?"

"Yes. He is. Are you okay?"

I looked past her to the bright blue November sky. I could hear a flock of geese high above, honking as they made their way south. The view was a total disconnect from what lay in front of me on the ground. "I guess so. I'm feeling a little spooked. Two dead bodies in a month's time seems like more than my fair share."

"I know what you mean," she said, "and there's no chance this was natural, or even accidental."

We stepped back to let the coroner's office do their job.

"Did you notice the wound, Dr. Lacasse?" one of the guys asked.

"Yes, but I didn't do any sort of examination. I just saw the slit in his shirt and a little bit of blood."

I clutched her arm, and she turned back to me. "How can he be dead if he didn't bleed? Do you think someone hit him on the head?"

"No, it was probably a knife wound to his aorta. See how his abdomen looks so round? That's where the blood is."

"Excuse me." I went behind the field house and threw up, stopping by the water fountain on the way back to rinse my face. "I think I've had enough walking for the day. Can I go home?"

Frankie threw her arms around me and gave me a tight hug. "Poor Annalee. This is a long way from diamonds and pearls, isn't it? You and I have to stay here and give our statements, but I sent one of the lookie-loos to get us something to drink. You'll feel better after a Diet Coke."

Boots arrived a short time later, having been at his hunting lease in the next parish for the past two days. I could hear his dogs baying from the back of his SUV. By the time he showed up, we were sitting on a wooden bench in the shade of a live oak. He stopped for a brief moment to talk to the coroner's office employees, then joined us.

"You two could have been sitting on the porch drinking iced tea and complaining about the men in your lives, but no, you have to be over here getting yourselves in the thick of things."

Frankie glared at her husband. "Not funny, Boots Lacasse. We were having a perfectly nice afternoon when I tripped over Ryan's foot. I don't know about Annalee, but it took a year off my life."

"Two years off mine," I chimed in.

"I'm sorry, honey. Somebody besides me will be getting your official statements, but in the meantime, do we know if his wife has been told?"

I pointed across the practice field toward Stacey's parents' house. "Here she comes, but I don't know what she knows." She was in floral-print skinny jeans, a red Tee, and red Keds, and the sun reflected off her long blonde ponytail. She walked purposefully, but her face was relaxed. Boots met her halfway to the crime scene, and within seconds we saw her collapse into his arms. He turned and cast a pleading look toward his wife. She sighed and went to join them.

A couple of hours later, the two of us sat on my front porch. That's where all the important talk goes on at Goat Hill. The screens keep out the bugs; there are tables for your wine or tea or what-have-you, and it's easy to up the amperage on the rocking chairs or swing to match your mood. Frankie had her rocker near the tipping point.

"Where is that husband of mine? He'd better not make me wait till bedtime to find out what he knows."

"Do you need more wine or another bite of goat cheese? Will alcohol or fat push your calm-down button?" I asked. "If it's sugar you need, I have a secret stash of Pepperidge Farm cookies that I'll break into."

She looked embarrassed. "I am a little worked up. It's just that it was Ryan. We went steady in the fifth grade. He was the first boy I ever kissed, and I may be the only girl who dumped him. Tate Stevens wasn't as cute, but he had a Shetland pony."

"Your first kiss happened when you were ten? Kind of racy, weren't you?"

A laugh broke through her distress. "It was a

playground kiss, five years before. I was a kindergarten floozy. He'd been eating a red sucker, and he smooched a sticky mess on my cheek. Come to think of it, that was the whole reason behind the kiss; there wasn't even a hint of romance."

Now that I knew why she was taking this so personally, I could try to distract her from today's awful event. "So was he already playing football in fifth grade? In one of those kid leagues?"

"If he was, I don't remember it. Ryan was always a leader. Good at all sports, better than average in the classroom, and able to sweet-talk his way out of anything. His parents were strict and did their best to keep his ego in check, but he knew just what to say to other adults to make them forget all about anything he'd done that was wrong. By the time he finished explaining, they were looking around for the bad boys who must have led dear little Ryan into trouble."

"The other kids didn't resent getting blamed while he got off?"

"No, not that I could tell. I think everyone was in on the deception. He accepted the adulation as his right."

I gave her a pointed look. "You aren't making him sound very appealing to me. I'm picking up self-important jerk from way back."

"Well . . ." her voice trailed off.

"Be honest. If he truly was that perfect, why would someone murder him?" I saw a brief flash of dismay in her eyes and momentarily regretted my words. "I'm sorry. That was an insensitive thing to say." But it was true. Someone disliked the guy badly enough to stick a knife in him.

"I need another glass of wine. Then I'll try to be more objective."

I poured her another four ounces of sauvignon blanc and waited.

"Everything came easy for Ryan until it didn't. I guess the first thing he couldn't talk himself out of was the suspension Coach gave him for getting drunk before the game. Berryville was the favorite to win the state championship that year, and I'm sure he saw it as a foregone conclusion. It might as well have been ordained in the stars. He tried to act cool afterward, but I know it bothered him more than he let on. His folks totally backed up the coach's decision, which wasn't surprising.

"As for our classmates, we saw he had the proverbial feet of clay. Looking back on it now, I think that may have hurt him more than losing the state championship. There were a couple of other guys who had always been in his shadow who came to the forefront. It must have rattled his confidence for the first time in his life."

"How did he handle it?"

"It made a difference. He got a little wilder. I remember the drinking picked up quite a bit, or so I heard. He skipped school a few times, but honestly, that wasn't unusual for the senior class, especially after the acceptance letters from college came in. Stacey still treated him like he was king of the world."

I remembered Stacey's words from the night before. Did we merely overhear a marital spat? Perhaps they always solved their differences with loud and nasty arguments, and her threats were empty. Ryan didn't seem to take them seriously, as a matter of fact, his responses made it sound like she'd told him she was leaving before.

Whatever the truth, given the current circumstances I didn't feel comfortable telling Frankie what Caleb and I had been privy to.

I chose to be circumspect. "Last night she told us he was the best husband in the world, but I noticed her glaring at him as the evening went on. He spent a lot of time with the ladies."

Frankie scoffed. "If dirty looks count, I hope none of the neighbors were watching me and Boots try to assemble our new patio furniture last weekend. We needed a referee and time-outs before we finished, and we still wound up with a bolt left over. No matter what happened last night, it was plain to see that Stacey was devastated by the news today."

I decided to drop the subject. "Come into the study, and I'll show you a new estate lot I bought. It arrived Friday, and I've just begun to go through it."

She, Pudge, and Montrose followed me into Uncle Raine's old office, which I had appropriated for my jewelry work. The plaster walls are painted a buttery yellow, and the room has a tall window with a southern exposure next to the old partner's desk of cypress and tulip poplar. Made in the early 1800s by a member of my uncle's family, I'm the sixth generation to use it. The tooled leather top is marred by years of use, but it's the perfect surface for jewelry, soft and forgiving.

Frankie pulled a chair opposite mine and waited for me to unlock the six-foot-high steel gun safe that I use for storage. I placed a tray of assorted jewelry in front of her, and we tried to temporarily forget the disastrous consequences of our afternoon exercise.

# Chapter Ten

I WAS WALKING the fence line behind the house and watching the moon come up when Caleb arrived in his pickup. He carried our dinner from Dairy Kreme in a white paper bag, and I could smell the scent of onion rings in competition with rich smell of damp earth and grass. Henry, his Welsh corgi, was with him, but he darted off to chase a rabbit.

"When we made this plan last night I had no idea I'd be hungry enough for two burgers. I've been out helping Dad repair a fence since early afternoon. When we finished I went right to the computer and ordered a post hole digger that attaches to the tractor and has a power auger. I'll have to dress it up like a ghost and give it to him as a late Halloween present, otherwise he'll insist that I take it back. He's not much on modern conveniences."

I settled him into a lawn chair next to the old log cabin that still occupies a place of pride on the farm, then went inside and got him a beer. When I came back out, he gave me the side-eye.

"Is your goat out here with us?"

"What goat? Do you think I stole one of yours? Or are you talking about the one who lived here in 1890?"

He scowled. "What other goat would I be talking about? Is he going to watch us eat our burgers?"

"Probably not, but I make no promises. Repentance usually doesn't show until later in the evening, but the cabin is one of his favorite places. He likes to climb on the roof and survey the farm."

He turned cautiously and looked behind us. "Is he there?"

"Do you *see* him?"

"No."

"That's because he isn't there. We have more important things to talk about than ghosts. I'll bet you haven't heard the news."

"Whagd nuzh?" he said, around a mouthful of burger.

"Someone killed Ryan Dawson last night. Frankie and I found his body this afternoon." I jumped up to pound him on the back when he choked on his burger. "Sorry, I guess I should have done a more gentle lead-in. I sort of jumped right into it."

He gave me an accusing look as he wiped ketchup off his chin. "No kidding. Where was he? What happened?"

I told him what I knew, which didn't amount to much, finishing with, "Frankie thought she would hear from Boots, but when he called, he just asked her to meet him at home."

"So, no suspects?"

I could barely see him in the dusk, but I guess he could imagine the look I was giving him.

He took another drink of his beer and carefully set the bottle back down in the grass. "Do you think Stacey was that mad?"

Thank goodness. I wasn't alone in my suspicions. "I don't know. How can you tell from overhearing one conversation? I don't feel comfortable volunteering that information to law enforcement. It just seems sleazy, somehow, to tell something I wasn't meant to hear."

"Will you tell Frankie? I know you two tell each other almost everything," he said.

I reached for another onion ring, glad he'd doubled up on that order as well as his own two burgers. "I kinda sorta tried to—no specifics, mind you—and she almost got indignant. She chalked it up to typical marital squabbling."

I watched him dig around in the bag and grinned when he didn't find another onion ring. I'd been just in time. He wiped his hands on his already greasy napkin, then pointed his index finger at me.

"You're pushing it, Wyatt. Do I have to get three orders next time?" Finishing his beer, he spoke more seriously. "Let's agree that right now we won't bring up what we heard. We'll see how things progress. It was probably a robbery; he was wearing a chunk of a gold Rolex."

I shook my head. "It was on his wrist when we found him today. After my exposure to him last night, I'd guess the motive was personal."

I AWOKE MONDAY morning with a sense of disquiet. Something was wrong. I shimmied into a caftan, then scooped Montrose off the foot of the bed and threw her over my shoulder as I went downstairs. Lafitte broke the silence with, "Hey, honey, I got a rocket in my pocket!" and I remembered Sunday's events with a shudder. No wonder I felt out of sorts.

Clotille was in my kitchen getting out an iron skillet. "Hey, sugar, I heard about Ryan Dawson last night at church. I figured you might be out of sorts this morning; might need a little breakfast to get going."

"You're my guardian angel. I should wait till after I exercise to eat, but the thought of an egg and a piece of toast is too tempting." I poured myself a mug of the coffee waiting in the carafe, shoveled in some raw sugar, and added a little milk. "I can't believe I didn't hear you come in. I thought the aroma of coffee was wishful thinking."

"You've already stopped using your alarm system. I didn't even have to put in the code," she said, her tone disapproving. "It's barely been a month since you got it."

I settled in at the chrome and Formica dinette and took my first sip. I could feel my brain begin to work. Lafitte still carried on a conversation with an imaginary bar patron in the living room, and Pudge was scratching to get in at the screened door, finished with his morning business. It was hard to reconcile the normality of my morning with what had happened the day before.

The sudden appearance of a plate holding two fried eggs, a couple of pieces of bacon, and two of Clotille's heavenly biscuits put a stop to my mental processes and awakened the primitive part of my brain. "Clotille, I ate a cheeseburger and onion rings last night. This will finish up my calorie allotment for the week!"

She smiled with satisfaction. "But you're happy, right?"

"I'm happy. I do hope there aren't any leftovers, though."

"No, I knew you'd complain like always, so I baked the biscuits and fried the bacon at home. That's all I brought to you."

"In my heart I'm disappointed, but my head is glad. You know my will-power is nonexistent when it comes to your biscuits."

She took the wild plum preserves out of the refrigerator and sat across from me. "Time's up. Tell me about Ryan."

It's almost impossible for me to tell a linear story. I'm one of those people who goes around the world with a tale—I throw in so much background and nonessential information that by the time I finish, you may have forgotten what you asked me. So I started this one with the buildup Caleb gave me on Ryan and Stacey, contrasted it with my opinion of them, tossed in the overheard fight, and finished up with Sunday's gruesome discovery.

"Let me guess—you think Stacey was so mad that she killed him."

I wiggled uncomfortably in my chair. "Am I that easy to read?"

"To someone who's known you since you were a baby? Completely. For what it's worth, it isn't that unusual for a married couple to have an argument, but I imagine following through with murder doesn't happen very often. Want some more coffee?"

I got up to refill both of our cups and returned to the table to defend myself. "Don't forget I'm the daughter of Mariah Leighton Wyatt, etc., etc., etc. I've overheard plenty of marital disputes in my lifetime." I stopped and thought for a moment. "Yes, you're right. I have definitely heard my mom sound mad enough to do in one of her husbands. I never took her seriously, but I know Jack Clements did. He was packed and out of their condo so fast that I'm surprised he waited for the elevator. If they hadn't lived on the twenty-fourth floor, I think he'd have thrown his clothes over the balcony and jumped after them."

Clotille's laughter filled the kitchen. "Were you there? That sounds like an eye-witness account."

"I'd made the mistake of going back to the condo with them after our Thanksgiving meal at their country club. Charlie was still in high school and wanted his big sister there as a buffer. I spent the next couple of hours picking up broken dishes that Mom threw at the door when Jack left. My cowardly brother locked himself in his bedroom with a video game."

She nodded. "I remember Mariah was a thrower, even when she was little. It didn't matter what your grandmother did to punish her, either. I didn't figure she'd ever get married, but she proved me wrong. Four times."

"Four different men who were intrigued by her spirit and volatility until they shared a house with her. Maybe Stacey's personality is like my mom's. She may have told Ryan she was leaving him once a month, and we just overheard the November installment."

# Chapter Eleven

After Clotille left, I cleaned up the kitchen. I scoured the skillet with salt, then rinsed it and put it on a stove burner to dry. The cast iron utensil was a least a hundred years old and seasoned to a glossy finish. I love the sense of continuity I feel in taking care of my home. I heard the sound of tires on the gravel drive and went to the living room window. The sight of the painters' truck reminded me that caretaking had its downside.

Gideon knocked at the front door. "Good morning. We finished up our last job, and I thought we'd take advantage of the good weather to get started on your place. I should have called to warn you, but I figured you wouldn't care."

I stepped outside to greet him and meet his brother. "Hi, you must be Silas." I shook hands with the male version of Valonda, if she were six inches taller, had a full beard, and was too shy to meet my eyes. I decided to ask. "Are you two related to Valonda? Or maybe Ed? I met him this weekend."

Silas looked toward his brother and waited for him to answer my question.

"She's our big sister. We're related to Ed, too, but that tracks back several generations. We don't even go to the same family reunions since the two of them divorced."

"And Dorcas?"

"She's the last one. You won't meet any more of us unless you run into our wives or kids."

"There's Mama and Daddy," mumbled Silas.

"You're not likely to meet them unless you go to his church and subject yourself to a couple of hours of hellfire and brimstone," said Gideon.

That sounded interesting. For the first time, I looked at their truck and noticed there was an angel wearing a halo and holding a paintbrush above the name of the business. Gideon followed my gaze.

"We got in trouble for that angel. Dad thinks it's sacrilegious. He's the preacher at the First Church of the Devil's Destruction."

I stifled an inadvertent laugh. You wouldn't find a better name in a Monty Python movie. Turning my amusement into a cough, I confessed that I wasn't familiar with that house of worship.

Gideon grinned. "You drive by it every time you go into Berryville from here. I know you've read the nuggets of wisdom he posts on the sign out front. If the spirit moves him, he sometimes changes them two or three times a week. What did it say today, Silas?"

"STOP, DROP, AND ROLL WILL NOT PUT OUT THE FIRE IN HELL." answered his brother, with a shy smile.

"You said that with a soft voice, but I hear it in all caps. That's your dad? I always look at that sign for my daily life instructions," I said, then worried I'd offended them with my light-hearted tone of voice.

"He's a doom and destruction kind of guy," Gideon said. "We've been a disappointment to him. The only one of us who toes the line anymore is Dorcas, and we hope she'll grow out of it. It was a pretty restrictive way to grow up."

Silas made his first unprompted contribution to the conversation. "I go to the Baptist church now, and you'd think I was twerking with the devil. My wife sings in the choir, which is another sin. Daddy doesn't believe in music in church."

I rolled my eyes heavenward. "I hope I never hear what he thinks about Episcopalians."

"They're half a notch above Catholics," laughed Gideon. "We're gonna get to work. If the weather holds, we'll finish by the weekend."

I went back inside, changed into some jeans, and began to clean jewelry. It's a delicate process, and the many different materials that compose antique pieces require special care. Today I was working with gold and precious stones, so a diluted solution of ammonia and gentle dish soap was safe to use. I buy soft-bristled toothbrushes for cleaning around settings, and the ones they sell for babies and toddlers are perfect. And for gosh sakes, use a big bowl *and* plug up the sink drain! I once had to take a P-trap apart to retrieve a diamond ring, and it's not a skill set I want to use again. The experience did, however, provide me with blackmail material for Frankie that I've yet to use. Boots would be so upset to hear that story.

AFTER TWO HOURS of painstaking work, I needed an activity break. Between Clotille's and the painters' unexpected appearances, my morning exercise routine had fallen off the schedule. It's hard for me to focus on the tiny little details of jewelry without the tension relief of my usual yoga or Pilates.

I grabbed my mat from the hall closet and went to the open space of the living room floor, but was caught up short when I saw Silas through the front window. I didn't want to do my stretching in front of an audience, and he looked like he'd be busy on the porch for the rest of the afternoon. Montrose sat on top of the mahogany side table and swatted the pane of glass as he worked, as if she could reach through the pane and touch him. I made a mental note to encourage her to sleep downstairs. If she missed her usual all-day nap, she'd be so tired that she would snore and keep me awake.

The yoga mat went back into the closet, and I went up the stairs. I might as well put on some makeup and go to the grocery. Tonight's meal had to be healthier than the burger and onion rings I'd shared with Caleb.

Aunt Josie had used a skirted, very feminine dressing table to apply her "face" each day. As a child, I'd thought it glamorous, like something out of an old movie. The kidney-shaped top was covered in the same pale pink satin that repeated itself in a skirt that cascaded to the floor beneath three side-by-side drawers. A thick piece of glass protected the surface, and a large oval mirror hung above it. I tried to keep the top clear of anything that wasn't beautiful. My aunt's half-full bottle of Arpege stood beside a silver-framed portrait of my uncle, and I kept my daily jewelry in a Belleek china dish she brought home from a trip to Ireland.

For a few months after moving into Goat Hill, I'd tried to do my makeup in the bathroom. The vanity was too much a part of my aunt; I still felt like a little kid playing dress-up when I sat down at it. One day, as I was once again chasing my mascara tube around the bathroom floor after it fell off the edge of the sink, I decided maybe I was a big girl after all. I moved everything to the dressing table, and now I primp like a movie star getting ready for her close-up.

But today I was just going to Bubba's Buy-It-Low. No paparazzi anticipated. As I smoothed sunblock over my cheeks, I remembered Stacey's golden glow. I hoped it was a spray tan. I was pretty sure she was already hitting the Botox; there would be no point in adding wrinkles from the sun at the same time. Wrinkles would be the least of her worries now, though. I said a little prayer that she was holding up to the tragic event of the day before.

Before going to the grocery, I stopped in at the Magnolia Blossom. Nancy was behind the counter, swathing a pressed glass cake stand in bubble wrap for a customer. "I want you to take a picture of your famous coconut cake on this and send it to me, Irene. I'll put it on our Facebook page. I love it when somebody buys something old and actually uses it," she said.

"A picture would be nice, but I think you should ask for a piece of the cake, Nancy," I said, after the woman walked out the door.

Nancy shook her head in disagreement. "I've had her cake, and it's from a box mix and has canned frosting. She tints the coconut according to the holiday. Orange for Halloween, green and red for Christmas, yellow for

Easter. You get the idea. She even does black for April 15th, in honor of income tax. That's why you have to be careful when you brag on someone's cooking. I'll bet her family hasn't had anything but that cake for dessert since the first time she made it. What are you doing in here today? You aren't scheduled to work until Friday."

"I got your message about the jewelry that sold this weekend and thought I should come by and decide what to bring in later to restock the case," I answered.

"Will that take very long? I hate to impose on you, but I'd love to run home and take the dog out for a minute. She's in heat, and I'm driving her to Minden tomorrow to meet a nice French bulldog guy. Unfortunately, every mutt in Sebastian Parish seems to know Coco is in a friendly mood. My son has football practice this afternoon, and I don't know if she can hold her little knees together till 5:30."

"How can I say no to Coco? All that's on my schedule is a trip to the grocery. Take your time."

Nancy picked up her keys and dashed out the door with a wave of thanks. I went to my jewelry case and began to survey the merchandise. I was down three rings, two pair of earrings, and four gold-filled bracelets. Not bad at all for a weekend. Someone had also purchased the elaborate rhinestone tiara from the 1950s. Doesn't every little girl harbor thoughts of being a princess at least once? I'd had a hard time putting that up for sale, but first I wore it for an entire weekend, including a trip to my favorite pizza place in Shreveport.

Mondays are seldom busy, but we like to keep the store open every day. I used the quiet time to Windex the glass cases, which attract fingerprints every time someone walks past them. I had just finished cleaning the barrister's bookcases, which held some valuable pieces of Newcomb pottery, when the bell over the front door jingled. I turned and saw Valonda peer around inside, then furtively enter the shop.

# Chapter Twelve

"Hi, Valonda," I said, stepping forward. She must have realized I noticed her odd entrance, because she offered an explanation.

"I try not to come in when Nancy's here," she said. "I mean, I guess you know what happened. It's awkward, and it's my fault."

She was obviously referring to her affair with Nancy's ex-husband, but I pretended she hadn't said anything. I saw no reason to increase her embarrassment. "I'm happy you're here. Do you want to look at some jewelry?"

We moved to the display and I pulled out the tray of rings that she indicated. She slipped several on and off before she mentioned the happenings of the weekend.

"I heard about you and Frankie finding Ryan," she said. "I just can't believe he's dead. Who would think you could get robbed and killed in a little town like this?"

So she thought the motive was robbery. Interesting. Was that just an assumption? I wondered if Boots and his department had turned up something I hadn't heard about. Maybe Ryan's wallet was taken, and the killer just didn't see his gold watch. In that case, the robber was incompetent as well as deadly. I commiserated with her distress, but didn't add my first-hand observations to the town rumor mill.

"Have you heard anything about Stacey? I wonder how she's holding up. Didn't Ryan's folks move to Georgia?"

"Yes," she answered. "They weren't originally from here. His dad came to work at the papermill when Ryan was in kindergarten, and he was promoted and transferred when Ryan was in college. I saw a car with Georgia plates at the Oak Glen Bed and Breakfast this morning that must be theirs. They probably drove all night, poor things."

Valonda's interest in jewelry on such a day was a surprise. Maybe she had just seen me through the glass storefront and wanted to talk about Ryan, because she wasn't focusing her attention on the things I showed her. "Did you stay till the end of the party on Saturday? It's a good thing you were with Ed, since we know there were criminals in the area."

"Ed left shortly after you and Caleb. He had to work a Sunday morning shift at the mill. I stayed for another hour, but I parked underneath one of the streetlights next to the gym door, so I guess I was pretty safe. I didn't see anything unusual."

She paused and looked up, and I had the feeling we were about to get to the real reason for her visit.

"Annalee, I know it doesn't sound right to be envious of Stacey right now, but I loved that pin she was wearing; the lizard with the garnets. How much money would I have to save to buy one of those? She said it was cheap."

Uh oh, she had the jewelry bug for sure. Time for a friendly reality check. "I've learned through the years that people have different thresholds for cheap. She most likely paid anywhere from $3000 to $5000 for that little fellow."

I smiled sympathetically at her gasp and continued. "That might be cheap to the Stacey Dawsons of the world, but it's a fair-sized chunk of change to most of us."

"No kidding! I guess I'll never have one. Why are they so expensive?"

"The size of the stones, the workmanship, the quality of the diamonds that are often a part of the design—I've seen them for almost $20,000 before. I'll admit I've seen a couple for less than $2000, but the demantoids weren't the bright yellow-green that Stacey's were."

We heard the tinkling bell and the squeak of the heavy wood door as Nancy breezed into the store, spouting apologies for the amount of time she'd been gone. She stopped mid-sentence when she recognized my customer, and Valonda quickly left the building with a muttered farewell.

"Was it something I said?" Nancy asked, with a wry smile.

"I think she's understandably self-conscious around you, given her history."

"You mean the history of my husband and his wandering eye? And his other wandering part?"

I laughed, glad she had a sense of humor about the situation. Of course it had probably taken several years for her to get to that point. "She said it was her fault, and she tries to come into the store when you aren't here."

"The more she buys, the more forgiving I'll feel. And if I'm honest, it wasn't her fault. Jerry has a history of taking off his pants in the wrong bedroom. That's why we moved here from Dallas in the first place. He had an affair when I was pregnant with our first child." She shook her head. "I was dumb enough to think he would behave himself if he lived in the same town as his mother. He's lucky Valonda didn't sue him for sexual harassment. She was an eighteen-year-old kid, for heaven's sake."

"Do I have your permission to tell her you don't hate her as much as she thinks you do? There's something about her that's sort of sad, in spite of her active love life."

"Sure, go ahead. I don't think we'll ever be friends, but I've forgiven her for her role in my marriage break-up. If not her, there would have been someone else. Hell, there probably *was* someone else, knowing Jerry. It's amazing a woman as sweet as my mother-in-law turned out a rat like that."

I left shortly after Nancy's return, but before I could get into the grocery store I got an all-caps text from Barbie at Frankie's office.

*FLU SHOT!*
*HOW ABOUT RIGHT NOW?*

Darn it, she must have seen Uncle Raine's pickup through the office window. Its pattern of rust was as distinctive as the spots on a leopard. I hoisted my purse over my shoulder and walked down the block from the grocery store parking lot to the town doctors' office.

When I walked through the front door, Barbie immediately buzzed me into the back. I shamelessly draw upon my friendship with Frankie and refuse to sit in the waiting room with anyone openly harboring germs. I usually park myself in her office, surrounded by medical journals festooned with gross pictures. As you can tell, I was never tempted to go into any of the healthcare professions.

Barbie placed her hands on the countertop. "Like my nail polish? I've just about talked myself into that matching aquamarine ring you mentioned to me last week."

"Gone."

"What?"

"Sold, this weekend. Ya snooze; ya lose."

"Unbelievable. I hadn't even gotten over to the shop to look at it. I guess it wasn't meant to be."

"That's how I console myself when something slips by. I didn't have sales duty at the Blossom this weekend, but several items of mine sold. I think maybe it was the reunion crowd."

Barbie's voice dropped to a softer volume. "I can't believe what happened to Ryan Dawson, or that you and Frankie were unlucky enough to find the body."

I used a quieter tone as well, mindful of the nearby waiting room. "Have you heard any news? I expected a phone call last night from Frankie, but it never came. It would be nice to know if everyone in the area should be worried, or if the sheriff's department thinks this was personal."

She held her finger up to silence me and turned to the front window. "No, Mr. Miller, I'm not sneaking patients in ahead of you. I know your appointment was five minutes ago. This lady is here on business." The elderly gentleman shot me a disgruntled look and returned to his seat.

"White lies make the world go 'round and the pushy patients sit down," she whispered.

As she checked a patient out, I saw Nita, the nurse practitioner, beckon me into the lab room. She held a small metal tray topped with a syringe, an alcohol wipe, and a rubber stoppered glass bottle. Pointing to a chair, she began to prepare the injection. "What's this story I hear about you and Frankie going for an afternoon stroll yesterday?"

"Oh, you know, just another peaceful day in small-town Louisiana," I answered, gritting my teeth in preparation for the huge, sharp, vicious needle she was about to jam into my arm. I closed my eyes. "Hurry up. I'm a gigantic chicken. Even the alcohol prep hurt."

Nita snapped her fingers in front of my nose. "Open up those eyes, wuss. The needle went in immediately after the alcohol. You're done."

"Oh. I feel a little silly."

"You are a little silly. What happened yesterday when you found the body? Did you close your eyes then?"

"No, but I did throw up. And although she may tell you otherwise, Frankie freaked out, too."

"It sounds like a freaky experience. I need to go by the Sawyer's house and visit with Stacey, but it may be too soon. Plus I'm not sure what the etiquette books say about offering condolences to someone whose husband was murdered. It seems like this should require something more than the usual 'I'm sorry.'"

"Are you friends? I didn't see you at the reunion Saturday night."

"We grew up next door to each other, but I'm a year younger."

I couldn't pass up the opportunity to find out more about the widow. "What is she like? I don't remember anything about her from my visits, but she looked like a million bucks Saturday night. She's so very blonde and tan, with a crazy-good figure, and she was decked out in buckets of gold jewelry. You know that comment means something when I make it. I understand they didn't have children." See how circumspect I can be? I didn't mention the overly plumped lips or shedding extensions.

Nita finished washing her hands and turned back to face me. "I think she could have done a lot more with her life than she has. By the time we hit high school, I didn't have much in common with her. She's a math whiz, but once she started dating Ryan, she had no goal in life except to marry him. She set her sights on him when she was fourteen, and she never gave up. He was her obsession. I don't think she's ever even kissed another guy. This is going to just kill her."

"And Ryan? Was he as crazy about her?" Watching my words again, I left out a description of his energetic attempts to openly seduce most of the women at the party.

She rolled her eyes heavenward in disgust. "He's a card-carrying horn dog. I wonder if that's what got him in trouble. I always thought he was lucky he hadn't been beaten up by a boyfriend or husband. Maybe his luck ran out."

I thought for a minute. "I think I read something recently about methods of murder. You know, like women are more likely to kill somebody with poison. I wonder who is more likely to stab someone?"

"I don't know the answer to that, but if he'd been done in with a shotgun, I'd suspect Stacey herself. She was the state champion trap shooter when she was a senior, and I remember how mad she was when she found out Ryan was cheating on her in college. Her dad confiscated her gun and hid all of the shotgun shells. Even though they had horrible fights, every time she caught him, she followed up with total forgiveness." She gave me a sly look as she paused at the open door." Frankie said for you to go on into her office and catch up with the latest medical news. I think the special subject for this month's pediatric journal is head lice." She was still laughing as she disappeared around the corner.

# Chapter Thirteen

"YOU'VE TOLD EVERYONE in the office that I can't even sit in the same room with your journals?" I asked Frankie.

"I told them you'd barfed behind the field house yesterday, and it sort of led into the medical picture thing. Did you find the one on lice?"

"You are *disgusting*. Didn't they teach you the importance of empathy in medical school?"

She cackled with unrestrained glee. "I needed a laugh today. Everything's been pretty crappy since yesterday afternoon."

"Glad I could be of some use. Does Boots know who did it yet?"

She sobered up immediately. "Not a clue, as far as I know, but I haven't talked to him today. He left before I got up. Why don't you come to dinner tonight? We'll see what we can get out of him."

Bubba's Buy-It-Low is a cornerstone of life in Berryville. The town is lucky to have a successful locally owned grocery store that is responsive to the needs of the community. It's a small store, but it has a real butcher, even if Hal doesn't stock the Fredericksburg, Texas lamb that I love to buy at Whole Foods in Shreveport. I can get freshly ground hamburger and the locally raised chicken that I marinate for fajitas, and they are never out of my favorite cereal. Everybody knows me, too, and I know all the employees and a lot of the customers. I love small town living.

Restocking the basics that afternoon didn't take long. Milk from our local dairy, cheese from Vermont, crackers from the little elves at Keebler, plus a bag of fall apples, and I was good to go. I cranked my head around like an oscillating fan as I drove past Stacey's parents' street. I didn't want to be so obvious as to drive past the house, but I was morbidly curious. I guess this is why people rubberneck at wrecks.

There were several cars in front of the house, including Ryan's Corvette. As I looked, a sheriff's car pulled up across the street, and Boots emerged. He glanced my way and tipped his hat. I waved and kept on going, right past the little church that I'd learned was pastored by Valonda's father.

The sign had been changed again, and I felt like this one was selected with me in mind.

## SPREAD THE GOSPEL—NOT THE GOSSIP

And here I was all excited that I would be at Frankie's for dinner and hoping Boots would fill me in on what he knew. But it wasn't really gossip if I'd been there when the murder victim was discovered. I considered it a fact-finding mission, I mean, free dinner.

My cell phone rang. "Hey, do you want to bring Caleb with you this evening?" asked Frankie.

"No, he's spending the evening working."

"What's he doing in the dark? Rocking the goats to sleep?"

"I see you're still looking for laughs. He's doing the work that pays the bills. He has online conferences set up with his computer clients in Chengdu."

"I thought he worked with businesses in China. Where's Chengdu?"

"It's a big city in central China. The pandas live nearby, and the food is great. Or so Caleb tells me. But he'll be up most of the night and probably useless tomorrow."

"Boots will just have to question him later. You'll be on his menu by yourself tonight."

"What? Is that why you're feeding me? Your husband has interrogation plans?"

"Mild ones. No torture planned, and I already told him you'll spill the beans for a good sauvignon blanc."

"It doesn't even have to be very good."

I waved to Clotille as I left the house. She spent as much time on her front porch as I did on my own, and this evening I could see her wrapped up in her favorite afghan, staying cozy as she watched the sun go down. I flipped on my brights when I turned out into the dark two-lane highway. It was the perfect time of the evening for raccoons to head out on their nightly raids. Sure enough, before I'd gone a quarter of a mile there was a family of four. I slowed for them to pass, then had to hit the brakes hard as a fifth one, smaller than the others, scampered out from the woods and belatedly followed them.

The way to Frankie's went back through Berryville to the other side of town. I swear, sometimes I think my car doesn't even need to be steered. It just knows where

I want to go within the Sebastian Parish limits. The light was on over Frankie's side door, and I heard her calling Boots' hunting dogs as I opened the car. The pack of them ignored her and continued their frantic dash to greet me.

I could see Mr. Jenkins through the front window of the house across the street. He was retired and not in the best of health, but I knew from Frankie that he got a lot of joy watching her try to outrun those darn dogs. They're sweet, very well trained, and make an overwhelming welcome party.

I walked in the door and caught myself on the kitchen counter as I tripped over a speckled puppy. "The eight outside aren't enough? Are you cloning them now?"

She sighed. "That's Miranda, after his favorite singer. She's the youngest, and she wasn't feeling well last week. I brought her inside, and now she won't leave."

The puppy rubbed her velvet nose against my hand. "She's awfully pretty. I'll bet when she gets a little older she can pitch her voice just as high and loud as Miranda Lambert, too."

"She passed that goal a couple of days ago. She already hits notes Mariah Carey can only dream of. Go on in and have a seat on the couch. Boots is waiting for you."

I walked through the kitchen with Miranda right on my heels. She scrambled into my lap as soon as I sat down, and I got her settled before taking my wine glass from Boots.

He sat in his own recliner, which was only a shade more stylish than the one in the window across the street. I still couldn't believe Frankie had agreed to put it in her beautifully decorated home, although they do say that a successful marriage involves compromise. I'd have thought the herd of dogs enough.

Boots drew my attention away from the décor.

"This is only a conversation between two friends," he said. "Nothing official, I'd just like your take, as a friend, on the party Saturday night."

"Have you found anything useful?" I asked.

"I'll tell you what I can afterward, but I don't want to put any ideas in your head before I get your view of the evening." He paused and looked toward the kitchen. "Frankie, sweet woman, is there anything I can promise to get you to bring me another beer? I'm sooo comfortable in this chair."

She gave him another bottle and said, "You owe me coffee in bed tomorrow."

"Will do. Now, tell me all about the reunion," he said, turning back to me.

I looked toward Frankie. "We didn't have time to talk about the dance when we were walking Sunday, so this will be new for her. I don't think she wants to hear what I have to say. She has fond memories that may be challenged."

She scowled. "I'm a grown-up. Go ahead and say whatever you want. I know people change."

I continued, still wary of her reaction. "I'd heard all sorts of flattering things about Ryan and Stacey both. I'd been worried that he would comment on my involvement with the drunk-in-the-bushes incident from high school, but he didn't put the pieces together." Boots nodded; he was aware of our history.

"The two of them came in like royalty. There are several people in their class who have done interesting things.

For example, Cathy Eggleston is finishing a pediatric heart surgery fellowship, and Sam Kennedy is working with one of the top designers in New York, and no one was impressed with that. But a faded high school jock? Whoop de doop de doodle do."

Boots laughed and reached for a tortilla chip. "You definitely are not a member of the American Church of the Holy Pigskin."

"Nope. Even if I was, I'd have been turned off by Ryan's tales of the criminals he's gotten off already during his few years of law practice. It didn't take him long to establish himself on the dark side. I know everyone is innocent unless a jury finds them guilty, but that doesn't make me happy about those few guilty ones who walk free, especially if I'm treated to the responsible attorney bragging about it. Did you know that he was the attorney who got that teenager off after he ran over all those folks in their house?"

Boots frowned. "No, I didn't realize. I remember the case. As a sheriff, I understand your disapproval. It's an occasional consequence of our system of checks and balances, but you can imagine how much it bothers those of us in law enforcement."

"So now that I've established I didn't like his professional behavior, let's move on to his social graces. There were none."

"Oh, come on, Annalee. Really? You're telling me that he had none of the charm left?" asked Frankie, with an uncharacteristic dose of sarcasm.

"I knew you couldn't handle it," I said, crossly. "Boots asked me what I thought. That comment bothers you, yet you didn't say anything about the caliber of clients he was willing to represent."

She glared at me. "Okay, I'll be quiet," she said, in a tone as annoyed as the one I had used.

Her husband gave her a look that said he expected her to follow through with her promise. "Go on, Annalee. This is helpful, because the line I've gotten paints that old, high-school picture. You're seeing this from an outsider's point of view."

"I found his behavior toward the women at the party disgusting." That really got Frankie's attention. She started to speak, and Boots held up his hand.

"You know, honey, a woman's place may not be in the kitchen, but right now I need you out of the room. You're too close to this, and if you're going to react to everything Annalee says, I'll have to take her down to the department and make this formal."

She left the family room in what could only be described as a huff. Miranda readjusted herself in my lap and put her head on my arm before falling back asleep.

"Sorry," said Boots.

"I do find it odd, considering the fact that she gave me a pretty complete rundown of his bad behavior herself the afternoon that we found him."

"I think it's like the situation where you can say bad things about your own kids, but nobody else is allowed to."

"That makes sense, I guess. I saw Ryan blatantly grab women by the boobs and on the fanny. He practiced full-frontal tight hugs complete with wiggling, if you get my drift, and kissed half of the women there. Not friendly pecks on the cheek, either. I got a close-up and personal view of him getting gross with Valonda's ear, and she did not welcome the attention."

His eyes narrowed. "I didn't hear any of this from the others I've interviewed. Was he drunk?"

"Not when he did the ear-washing maneuver. As the evening continued, he got plastered. Shortly before Caleb and I left, Merribeth Horton hid behind our group to get away from him."

"How about the husbands and boyfriends? Did you notice any reaction from them?"

"I saw a few who were obviously po'd, but I didn't catch any sort of confrontation with anyone. A lot of beer was consumed."

"I know that for a fact. My deputies got four attendees on drunk driving charges afterward."

"There's one other thing," I said. "Caleb and I overheard Ryan and Stacey having a fight, and it wasn't an ordinary tiff. Things were said that I wish I hadn't heard." There. It was out in the open. We had agreed not to say anything unless asked, and Boots had asked.

"Yeah, I know about that. Stacey told us. She's all torn up about it, because it was the last time they spoke."

Well, heck. Our big secret turned out not to be so big, or even a secret.

"FRANKIE, THIS MEAL is perfect. I feel like I'm eating in a trendy restaurant."

She gave me a grudging smile. "One of our favorite places in Shreveport used to have this on the menu. The grilled salmon on top of the salad with pistachios and grapes is healthy, and the dressing doesn't have many calories."

"She's trying to counteract the high-cal food I fix when it's my turn to cook," said Boots. "More wine?"

I held my hand over the top of my glass. "Not for me. I don't want to be a name on the Sebastian Parish DWI arrest record." I refilled my water glass from the pitcher on the table. "It's my turn to ask questions. Can you answer any?"

His face became serious. "I can, but you can't repeat anything. Frankie's told me in the past that no one keeps a secret like you do, so this is some of what we know. His body hadn't been moved, so he was stabbed there in the grove of oak trees. The knife wound was to the aorta, and it would have been quick. The coroner doesn't think he would have lived long enough to load onto an ambulance if one had been waiting in the parking lot."

"So he didn't suffer."

"He would have lost consciousness very quickly," said Frankie, quietly.

I reached across the table and took her hand. "I'm truly sorry. I know this is awful for you."

She squeezed my hand in return. "I'm sorry, too. I'll try not to be so cranky."

Boots cleared his throat. "All this emotional honesty is interfering with my testosterone level. I'm going back to a discussion of the crime."

"Yes, sweetie," said his wife.

"The coroner puts the time of death around midnight. Stacey left at 10:30 and walked home to her parents' house, according to her. The folks were already in bed, so there's no proof that she's telling the truth."

I held up my hand. "I'm a witness. Caleb and I watched her walk across the field, and then we drove around the corner to a spot where we could see her go in the door.

We had an uneasy feeling about her walking alone, and I guess there's something to be said for intuition."

"Good, that's very helpful," said Boots. "Ryan was one of the last guests to leave, at 11:30. The caterers were clearing away their equipment, and one of them saw him walk out the door by himself."

"I hope he didn't drive anywhere," I said. "He was weaving on his feet when we left."

"No, the Corvette was where he and Stacey parked it when they arrived. The key was in his pocket, along with his wallet."

"And we know he was still wearing his gold Rolex," said Frankie.

I felt a weight on my foot and looked under the table. Miranda had fallen asleep with my toes as a pillow. I'd finished my meal, so I pushed my chair back and picked her up. She snuggled into my lap without opening her eyes and continued to snooze. "It feels good to have a sleeping puppy in my lap. It's a nice counterpoint to the conversation."

"You can take her home—"

"You can't have her—"

"Don't get into an argument on my account. She isn't going home with me; I have more pets than I can handle. Let's get back on track. Robbery wasn't the motive unless someone panicked and ran before they had a chance to take anything. I didn't see anyone at the party who obviously wanted to kill him. Do you know who else stayed as long as he did?"

"The caterers came in from Natchitoches, so they weren't very useful on that score. I got a good description today of a woman who might be Valonda. Did you notice what she was wearing?"

"A short red strapless dress," I said.

"That's what the guy described. He said she was the last female there, and she left alone ten or fifteen minutes before Ryan and the other stragglers."

"She was there with Ed, her ex-husband, but he left before her because he had to be at work early the next morning. Every time I saw her she was trying to avoid Ryan, though. I'm surprised she stayed so late if most of the other people were gone."

"I'm going to talk to her tomorrow. I'm hoping she can give me the names of the guys who were still with him. I don't have much to go on so far."

Frankie rose from the table and came back with a pint of almond brittle ice cream and three tiny bowls.

"Look at that, she's rationing my ice cream, too. Have you ever seen such a small bowl?" he complained.

"It's one of those fancy saki cups your cousin gave us for a wedding present. It holds two ounces, and I'm giving you a demitasse spoon. We will take tiny, mindful bites and savor each molecule," she said.

"Boots," I whispered, "I'm going to Houston tomorrow. I'll go by my favorite bakery and pick up some French pastries for you, and I'll drop them by your office in a sealed box. But in the meantime, pick up your little silver spoon and smile for the camera. I'm posting this picture online."

# Chapter Fourteen

I LOVE HOUSTON, don't get me wrong, but I have even less tolerance for the traffic since I don't have to deal with it every day. I hit my favorite boutiques on Westheimer as soon as I got to town and picked up a few things on sale for my work wardrobe. I keep it simple, neutrals that allow the jewelry to take center stage.

I met my mom and her newest husband, still in honeymoon mode, for drinks. This is the third time I've observed this stage of one of her marriages, not having been present for the honeymoon that preceded my entrance into the world.

Lawrence is a handsome guy. They always are. And as long as their marriage lasts at least three years, I'll make some cash. My baby brother bet on two, but I've noticed Mom is not quite as flighty as she was when I was younger. Her attention span is longer.

We slid into a booth at Lawrence's favorite steakhouse, and he ordered a round of martinis after asking me what I'd like. Soon we were deep into a discussion of a death that occurred in Berryville just a month before.

"I'll never understand why you wanted to move to that farm," said my mom. "I don't care if it is a family tradition. And it's dangerous!"

"And Houston is so safe?"

"It's not that bad. Most of the shootings here supposedly are done by people who know the victim, not just some random criminal. I don't know a single person who's murdered someone."

"It's obviously better to have been properly introduced to your murderer," Lawrence said, with a sly wink.

"It's the same in Berryville," I said. "Frankie's husband is sure that the latest one was acquainted with the victim." *Now, why in the heck did I say that?*

"What do you mean, the latest one?" shrieked my mother.

"Mom, people are looking at you. Let's use our inside voices. A guy was killed Saturday night, but they think the victim knew the perpetrator." I knew the crime vocabulary, and that sounded a lot less scary than knife-wielding assassin.

"Did you know him?"

"I'd met him earlier that night, but he lived in Nacogdoches. He was an attorney there."

"East Texas? I'm familiar with a lot of the lawyers in that area through the state bar association," said Lawrence. I'd forgotten he was an attorney; it isn't easy keeping track of the different boyfriends and husbands my mother has collected through the years.

"Ryan Dawson. He was my age, but already had a successful practice, if you measure that by money made."

"Hmm, Dawson, Dawson. That sounds familiar." Lawrence finished his drink and ordered another, along with an appetizer of calamari for the table to share.

"I'm not sure he had many scruples. At the high school reunion, he was talking about a kid he got off for a drunk driving accident. He ran into a house," I said.

Lawrence slammed his fist down on the table with such force that a waiter dropped a tray.

"Now, honey," said Mother. "You won't be able to play golf tomorrow if you bruise your hand."

He ignored her. "I knew there was something unpleasant about that name. His behavior during and after the trial was scandalous. It's certainly not unusual to represent a client whose culpability may be in question, but it's very unethical to speak of the victims as he did in that case. He practically put them on trial for their living conditions. There was a lot of negative talk about him among the legal community."

This was interesting news. "So there's gossip among attorneys about things like that?"

"Of course. The national press coverage was horrendous. I have friends on the governing board of the state bar who wanted to bring him up on ethics charges. His partner went to bat for him, and that's all that saved him. The older guy has served on the board in the past, and he called in some favors to get it dropped."

I wanted to hear more, but Mom changed the subject to a discussion of their recent wedding in France, which I had missed. The rest of the evening was given over to food, wine, and the behavior of the various friends and family members who made the trip to Europe for the occasion.

When we parted, I went to my friend's apartment near downtown and crashed in the guest bedroom, happy that she was in California for the week. Not that I didn't want to see Cici, but I wasn't in the mood to justify my choice of rural Louisiana to another person.

WEDNESDAY MORNING WAS busy, as I went about the reason for my trip. The estate lot that I'd purchased online looked even better in person, plus I paid a fair price for it. After lunch with a friend from my old job, I was ready to return to the quiet peace of Goat Hill Farm. Cici's place had turned out to be on the city ambulances' main drag to the county hospital, and double-glazed windows had not protected my ears from the wail of sirens. I made quick work of my remaining jewelry-related business, stopped by the bakery for the promised pastries, and ascended the Highway 59 on-ramp for the drive back home.

Two hours of driving north put me on the outskirts of Nacogdoches. On a whim, I skipped the usual loop around the town and drove straight into the business district. I knew there had to be a jewelry store downtown; there always is. I could check out the inventory and maybe do a little nosing around about the Dawsons.

Red brick streets led to a pretty square, where a sign told me I was in the oldest town in Texas. I parked in front of a charming statue of a pioneer family, complete with dog, and got out of the car.

It wasn't hard to locate the store. I walked across the way to a nineteenth century building labeled Smith & Sons Jewelers and opened the heavy glass door in the middle of the red brick facade. As I glanced at the display cases, it was obvious that Stacey had not purchased her Yurman pieces there. The jewelry on view was attractive, but geared to a more modest budget.

A neatly dressed woman in her middle years rose from a desk in the back and approached me curiously.

"May I help you?"

I introduced myself and gave her my business card. "I drive through this area fairly often and realized I'd never stopped in," I said, as if it were an odd thing to have missed. "Do you carry any estate pieces?"

She introduced herself as Janice Smith and showed me to a case near her desk. She unlocked the back of it. "What would you like to see?"

There was nothing that stood out and screamed "Buy Me," but there were a few things I could resell, and perusing them would give me the opportunity to talk.

"Could I see the tray of rings?" She took it out and put it on top of the counter, and I removed my magnifying glass from my purse and began to examine anything that looked promising. I picked up a small, unusually shaped opal, and held it to my eye. "This is interesting. How about I put aside a few things, and we can talk price afterward?" I saw her eyes light up when she realized I might be good for a few purchases, even if I negotiated a volume discount.

As I planned my opening gambit, Janice looked at my card.

"Berryville, Louisiana." That got a look of recognition. "I think that might be where someone local got killed last weekend."

"Would that be Ryan Dawson?"

"Yes, that's him. He and his wife have lived here a few years." Her face was expressionless, which was odd, given the subject.

"It was a terrible thing," I said, with what I hoped

was the right touch of sympathy, although I must say, she didn't seem to be grieving. "I met him and his wife at a high school reunion party the evening before it happened. She wore some lovely jewelry. Did you sell any of it to her?"

That got a reaction.

"Oh, no, not a bit of it. She isn't too much on supporting the local merchants unless she wants a donation to a charity auction."

"That's a shame. I believe small businesses are the backbone of the country." That's true. Why else would I purchase most of my groceries at Bubba's? "And her husband? I remember he wore an expensive watch."

She wrinkled her nose in disdain. "The only reason a man needs a gold Rolex is to show off. Seiko and Bulova are good enough for our customers."

I'd come up against reverse snobbery before, and knew there was no advantage in arguing the exquisite workmanship that went into a Rolex, or that it was possible to get one with a simple leather strap. I was all too familiar with the kind of guy she mentioned, and I thought they were obnoxious, too.

"I understand he was a prominent attorney here. Was he in a group or in solo practice?" This was the right question. She took a deep breath and her eyes brightened with pleasure as she prepared to confide in me.

"He joined the practice with Everett Crockett after Eldon retired. Everett wanted someone young, a go-getter who would expand the firm and keep Crockett and Smith going for years to come, and neither of his own children went into law. I think he got more than he bargained for."

"Smith? One of your relatives, maybe?"

"Eldon is my husband's uncle. A lovely man, but getting a little too forgetful to practice law."

I'd stumbled into a fountain of information. I selected a dainty gold ring set with a faceted amethyst for my keeper stack, asked for the tray of necklaces and continued looking.

Picking up a small gold and garnet cross on a chain, I paused and looked conspiratorially at the saleswoman. "Janice, I hope I'm not out of line, but it seems to me that you have some reservations about the Dawsons. Like I said, I only met them Saturday night, but he seemed to be a little, um, a little . . ."

"Full of himself," she finished for me.

"I have heard that description used for him," I confided, keeping my tone as conspiratorial as I could manage.

"And his *wife*. They've only been here three years and already she's going to be president of the League. *That* required more than good deeds and volunteer hours. I wonder if Bonnie Crockett wishes she hadn't been so welcoming when they moved to town. That job was supposed to go to her daughter this year."

"Did she do something illegal to get chosen?" I was genuinely curious. I'd never thought of the Junior League as a criminal organization.

"I'm not saying that. But I can tell you that if the Crocketts spent as much time promoting their own kids as they have those two, their daughter would be president of the school board instead of teaching first grade, and their son would be running the bank, not working as a junior loan officer. And then there's the bad publicity Ryan brought to the town with that awful wreck. I'm not glad he's dead, but there aren't too many folks around here who'll miss him. My goodness, that doesn't sound very nice, but it's true."

I finished shopping, and we agreed on a price. As I wrote my check, another question occurred to me. "Do you think Stacey will move out of town now that she's widowed?"

"Lord have mercy, I hope so, or she'll be moving into the house with Everett and Bonnie. They'll insist on it.'"

# Chapter Fifteen

I REACHED GOAT Hill as Silas and Gideon were shutting down for the day. They were subdued and exchanged none of the cheerful banter I'd gotten used to. I'd planned to tease them about their dad's latest church sign:

THE FIRST THOUGHT IS TEMPTATION.
THE SECOND IS SIN

That totally fit my relationship with doughnuts. I congratulated myself on having left the unopened box of pastry with Boots' secretary.

I greeted my waiting menagerie and walked through the unlit hall past solemn portraits of my ancestors. I saw Aunt Josie's eyes in one, my mother's jawline in another, even Charlie's nose on someone who died a hundred years ago. My own face looked back at me from a 1912 photo of a great-great-grandmother. It gave me an oddly cozy feeling of permanence.

I checked the refrigerator. Clotille had called and said she'd brought over half a pork roast and some sweet potatoes before going to visit her sister Florette, and there they were. Life was good.

*

It gets dark pretty early in November, so I made sure I finished my outside chores while I could still see. I watered the flowerpots of mums, even though they were beginning to drop their bronze and yellow blooms. Maybe Saturday I'd plant them in the back flowerbed along with the others from bygone years, and their flowers would reappear next fall. The porch was in need of sweeping, but on the chance that the fresh paint was still damp, I deferred that chore. Floating dust would not make an attractive top coat.

I took a walk among the pecan trees and accumulated a burlap bag full of newly fallen nuts. It felt good to get some exercise after four hours of traveling. A gray squirrel and I exchanged nasty comments, in spite of the fact there would still be plenty of pecans for him and his fellow furry thieves when I ran out of the energy to pick them up.

I returned to the house before full nightfall and went to my cheerful kitchen. It's totally 1960's: turquoise Formica, black and white linoleum tiles on the floor, and ancient copper colored appliances, but the white enameled cabinets are shiny and bright. The place holds so many great memories of people and food that I'm almost hesitant to redo it when I get some extra money. Maybe I'd entertain the idea after I was taking my showers in a new bathroom.

I made myself a cup of hot jasmine tea and went to the living room, where I settled into the worn chintz sofa and flipped on the TV. Lafitte danced from side to side on the perch in his cage and flirted. "Hey, baby, lookin' good," he called.

"Really?" I asked. 'You're not very discriminating tonight. My hair's a mess, and I need a shower."

"Gimme a little kiss," he said, with a loud smoochy noise. He did a good job of reproducing the sound, considering he didn't have lips.

"You have birdseed breath, Lafitte, and I'm saving my kisses for Caleb."

He began singing "Don't mess with my toot toot," loudly and off-key. Montrose jumped onto the table next to him and stared. I couldn't tell if the cat was a music lover or wanted to shut down the performance.

My cell phone rang and I saw Caleb's name. It was nice to be dating someone who made real phone calls. I'd been going out with text-only guys for years.

"Hi, Lafitte's over here singing a Rockin' Sidney song. Do you want to come listen? I have pork roast and sweet potatoes, but I have to warn you that I look less than attractive."

"I hate to pass up such a high-class evening, but I have more work to do than I can handle right now with the folks in Chengdu. How was your trip?"

"Productive. I picked up the estate I purchased. It looks very promising; there are even a couple of Georgian items in it. Plus I heard things about the Dawsons from two different sources."

"That's strange. What're the chances of that in a city of over two million people?"

I helped Pudge onto the sofa and sank back into the cushions again. "My mom's new husband is an attorney, so he was aware of Ryan because of that awful case he bragged about to you. As for the other source, I stopped at a jewelry store in Nacogdoches. The woman working there was more than willing to let me know how much she disliked both of them."

"Stacey too?"

"Evidently she's stepped on a few toes in her rise to the top of the social heap, which is easy to do as a newcomer in a small town. I oughta know," I said. "Any news about who killed Ryan? I haven't heard from Frankie since I left."

"Nothing specific. I ran into Seth Hammett this afternoon when I was at the post office, and he said they had a 'person of interest.'"

"I suppose we'll have to wait like everyone else. I can't call Frankie and ask about something that's essentially none of my business, much as I'd like to. You go on and do your work, and I'll eat Clotille's dinner."

"Clotille? You didn't tell me it was her cooking. I might have tossed those Chinese tycoons by the side of the road to share that."

"Just for that, see if I ever cook for you again, Mr. Bright."

AFTER DINNER I spent an hour with my new jewelry. Valonda Nelson and I had an unpleasant history together, but my interactions with her over the last week had improved my opinion. I found myself looking at pieces with her budget in mind. I knew she couldn't afford to spend much, but sometimes I get things that aren't terribly valuable but are still striking and unusual.

I did a gentle polishing of a Victorian mixed-metal silver bangle bracelet, just enough to get a shine but not enough to remove the patina. The wide band of sterling was etched with daisies overlaid in yellow gold. Tiny silver balls marched along the edge of the bangle. It was too large for someone as tiny as Valonda, but I vowed to keep my eye out for something similar in a daintier size. She had the taste to appreciate it.

A modern 14K chain nestled in a pile in the bottom of the chest. It was heavy enough to blend nicely with the five or six necklaces Stacey had worn, but my guess was she wouldn't be in the market to purchase jewelry for quite a while. She would probably consider herself in desperate straits if she was faced with buying the "used" things that I sell.

I put the tray out of sight of the large side window and let Pudge out for his final circle of the house. I heard his "Scat, varmint," bark, and looked outside to see him facing off against the possum again. I never left him to sleep outside, lest he announce every night critter that prowled my hundred or so acres.

Twenty minutes later, dog inside and alarm on, I was ready to climb in bed and read myself to sleep. I picked up a nonfiction account of London and soon lost myself in a chapter describing the odors of the city. I fell asleep thankful for clean country air.

Gideon and Silas were no more talkative the next morning. My day went by quickly, filled with jewelry repair and paperwork. This year would be different—I planned to have all my tax information organized by the end of the year. No frantic scrambling about in April, no ma'am, December 31st would see a new me. My accountant might need to be resuscitated if I didn't have to file for an extension, but it was a risk I was willing to take.

Frankie texted mid-afternoon to ask for a ride to book club. Book club! Already? And what would I take for pot-luck? There wasn't nearly enough pork roast left to share. I exited the study and ran to the kitchen. Although there were at least ten pounds of unshelled pecans, I had no time to shell them, so no pie. A quick perusal of the fridge left me uninspired until I glimpsed a jar of tahini in the back corner. Hummus. Garlic, canned garbanzo beans, cumin, olive oil, a stout tablespoon of tahini, and lemon juice went into the food processor in quick succession. A bit of the drained liquid from the garbanzos thinned it out into the perfect consistency, and a heaping teaspoon of Aleppo pepper flakes added a slight punch and a pretty color. I even had an unopened box of crackers in the pantry. Disaster averted.

Now to read the book.

FRANKIE WALKED OUT of her office and locked the door behind her. She had changed from her work uniform of pastel scrubs into jeans and a blue and white striped Breton knit shirt. "You look like a French sailor," I said, as I leaned across and opened the door for her. She placed a covered cake plate on the floor of the car and climbed into the passenger seat.

"Better a sailor than Picasso," she answered. "Didn't he usually wear a shirt like this?"

"Him, too, I suppose. Did you read the book?"

"I always do. And you?"

"Nope. I wanted to, but I took a realistic look at the time and then didn't even look at the title. No last minute down-load today. I may try to sound noncommittal when it's my turn, so I won't have to own up to my failings. You always do, my fanny."

She grinned. "But I did today. That's what's going to count in the next hour or so."

# Chapter Sixteen

I PARKED BEHIND the community center underneath a bright street light. While I didn't feel unsafe, considering Saturday's killing perhaps I should be more careful than usual. Frankie and I entered through the back door and placed our food on the long side table. We had all copped to drinking more wine than we should have at the last meeting, so three women were designated to bring bottles rather than each one of us. I grabbed some bottled water to start with and joined the circle of women beginning to form in the middle of the room.

"Annalee didn't read the book," said Frankie.

"Nobody likes a tattletale. To be honest, I've been so disorganized I don't even know which book it is. I was going to look at the list this afternoon, but admitted to myself I'd waited too late."

"It's an oldie but a goodie," said Katie. "I picked it because I wanted an excuse to reread it. It's 'Rebecca', by Daphne DuMaurier."

"Hey, I have read it. When I was about fourteen. Does that count?"

"Depends on how much you remember," said Frankie. "You'll get a grade at the end of the discussion."

The plot came back to me as I listened to everyone's comments. The terrifying Mrs. Danvers, the handsome Maxim de Winter, and most of all, the heroine who was never given a name; all brought middle school memories that contrasted with the way the story felt to me now.

"I remember that it seemed so romantic when I was a teenager. I loved the way Max swept the young girl off her feet and insisted that they marry," I said. We had already agreed it was creepy that she wasn't named anywhere in the book.

"That's one of the reasons I wanted to read it again," said Katie. "Now I view him as a manipulative control freak."

"He's almost as scary as the housekeeper," added Cora.

"I'm not so sure about that," said her sister Maya. "She's the stuff of nightmares."

"I still think he'd sweep me off my feet," said Tennie. "You young girls are used to soft, agreeable men. My generation expected them to be forceful and commanding."

Eudora Jackson gave Tennie an indulgent look. "I'm older than you are, and I say you're remembering men like Clark Gable and Humphrey Bogart. The movies, in other words. Your husband Hoyt is rather mild-mannered."

"I won't admit to being that old, Eudora. Now if you want to reference Paul Newman, I'll go along with your theory."

"Very well, Paul it is. Robert Redford still makes my heart beat fast, too. This is the third time I've read 'Rebecca' myself, and I find that my own interpretation has changed. I believe that our little unnamed second wife has come into her own by the end of the book. She may not be living the life she envisioned for herself, but she now has power. Her husband must live with the knowledge that she knows the truth. I believe he will be watching his step for the rest of his life."

"That's a satisfactory conclusion," said Willow. "You never know what goes on behind closed doors in a marriage, but I'm vindictive enough that I'd want Rafe to walk in fear forever if he treated me the way Maxim treated Rebecca, wayward wife or not."

We admitted we shared her desire for vengeance and broke ranks for dinner. I watched Eudora eye my hummus with curiosity, then politely place a dab of it on her plate. I wondered if I should warn her about the garlic level, then decided that as a Louisiana native, she would be fine. I selected a couple of Tennie's pimiento cheese sandwich triangles and some of Willow's spiced pecans, then added Maya's corn casserole and her sister Cora's fresh collards sauteed with white wine and golden raisins. Nancy's chicken salad with grapes was always a winner, and Katie had provided cumin-dusted roasted carrots.

As we ate, the conversation turned to the murder. Frankie and I repeated our stories about finding Ryan's body and answered some questions that were more pointed than I would expect from a group of genteel women. No, there wasn't much blood. Yes, he was fully clothed, including tightly zipped slacks. That question was from Tennie. No, there was no lipstick on his cheeks, but we didn't notice his collar.

"I'm relieved you two are answering questions," said Maya. "Everyone wants to know about it since Seth was the first deputy who responded, and I've been keeping my mouth shut."

I looked at Maya in surprise. "I'd totally forgotten you're married to Deputy Hammett. He did a good job of taking charge of a difficult situation."

She beamed. "I'll pass along the compliment. It took him a long time to wind down when he got home that night."

"Has anyone talked to Stacey?" asked Ernestine Greener. "She's bound to be taking this hard. She fell for him her freshman year in high school, and nothing else mattered. I still remember the notebook she carried to my English class. There wasn't a square inch that didn't have Ryan's name doodled on it somewhere. I had her again junior year, and she was a sentimental fool when we studied 'Romeo and Juliet'. I swear she was disappointed that she and Ryan didn't have a star-crossed relationship. Worst case of puppy love I saw in thirty-five years of teaching."

"We've sent a few meals over to the house from the cafe," said Katie. "It's my understanding that she's not coping well at all. She does have a big support system. Ryan's law partner and his wife came up from Nacogdoches immediately and are staying at her parents' house, which to be honest, is a little bit odd. I mean, Ryan's own parents are at the Oak Glen B&B. Don't you think that's strange?"

I kept my mouth shut about what I'd learned in Nacogdoches. Let someone else agree it was odd; I didn't want my friends to think I'd been snooping around Texas like a stone-cold gossip.

As usual, Frankie's mother, Beth, arrived late. I don't know how Frankie wound up so punctual unless it was a reaction to growing up with a woman who never got anywhere on time. Tonight she had a good excuse. She prepared a plate of food for herself and settled in to talk.

"I ran into Stacey's mom at the grocery this afternoon, and let me tell you, that poor woman is on her last nerve. She's trying to take care of everyone around her while she grieves, too. Ryan's parents are at the house except for when they're asleep at the B&B, and those people from Nacogdoches! Lord in heaven! Celeste says she can't get rid of them. You know they just showed up Sunday night and moved right in!"

"Poor Celeste! Why are they here? I can see them coming up for the funeral, but they were business partners, not relatives," said Ernestine. "Are they at least being helpful?"

"From Celeste's description, I'd say she's taking care of them, in addition to everybody else. She said they're acting like Ryan was their own son. The poor woman is ready for this to be over. The coroner finally released the body, and the service is set for Saturday at the Methodist church."

I STOPPED BY Bubba's right before it closed to get the yogurt I'd forgotten to buy on Monday, and ran into Sarah Bright, Caleb's mother. She threw her arms around my neck and hugged me like I'd just returned from the French Foreign Legion.

"Annalee, it's so good to see you," she gushed, as she released me from her grasp. "You live right next door, and we just never get together. Maybe Caleb can bring you over for dinner soon. Ralph and I would like that."

I felt like an awkward little kid. On one hand, Mrs. Bright was a lovely woman, and I'd like to spend time with her. On the other hand, awkward. I was dating her son, but we weren't ready to take it seriously. Were we? I put that on my list of things to discuss with Himself, but in the meantime I smiled and agreed that I'd love to visit. She left with a promise to call me soon, and I got in line to check out.

While I can't claim to know everyone in town, I was pretty sure the older man ahead of me wasn't from Sebastian Parish. His starched blue jeans were too tight, hugging a butt that was almost nonexistent. I don't know why anyone would want to emphasize something that flat. The T-shirt was bright white and fit him too closely. Was he showing off an imaginary six-pack? Yes, he still had some muscle, but the overall effect was past its prime and stringy looking. Thinning white hair fell back in immaculate waves from his leathery forehead, and the overhead lights glinted off the shiny gold rims of his glasses. He moved with an arrogance that, coupled with his complaining voice, left me no doubt that this was a man who was accustomed to getting his way.

"I don't understand why your wine selection is so bad," he grumbled. He finished unloading his shopping basket as his voice rose into a whine. "And the cheese—all you have is cheddar and Monterrey Jack. And you don't have any Carr's Water Crackers."

"I'm sorry, sir, but most people buy their wine and fancy cheese in Shreveport. There isn't much call for anything exotic in Berryville." Bubba Jr. gave him a polite answer, but I had a pretty good idea of what he was thinking just by watching the way he swiped the items past the bar code scanner.

The man pulled an alligator wallet from his back pocket and removed a platinum American Express card. I noticed his bright white Converse Chuck Taylors worn without socks. Try-hard, much?

He continued his grousing. "It's no wonder Stacey and Ryan wanted to live in a more cosmopolitan city. We're going to keep her in Nacogdoches after this whole awful affair ends."

I choked off my impending laughter and turned it into a dainty cough. This could be none other than Everett Crockett, from the very cosmopolitan city of Nacogdoches, Texas, population in the neighborhood of 30,000, if I remembered the city limit sign correctly. He stomped out of the store, and I took my turn at the cash register.

"You can't satisfy all the customers," I said, as Bub ran my containers of yogurt over the scanner.

"Nope, and that's the second time today that guy hasn't been satisfied."

"You mean you let him down more than once? What else did he want? Caviar and truffles? Veuve Clicquot?"

"This morning it was free range eggs. Anybody around here who wants free range eggs is raising their own chickens in the back yard; I told him. The guy's from east Texas. He acts like he's from New York City. I bet he's a big shot in a little pond."

I looked at him curiously. "You mean a big fish?"

"Yeah. A big fish. More like a minnow who thinks he's a shark."

As I neared the edge of town, I was surprised to see the sign in front of the First Church of the Devil's Destruction had been changed again. The congregation should suggest to Brother Nelson that he spend his time sprucing up the aging building instead of rewriting slogans.

SIN MAY BE JUST A THREE LETTER WORD
BUT IF YOU CARRY IT AROUND LONG
ENOUGH IT CAN CAUSE DEATH

If I thought more than thirty seconds about it, it made no sense at all, but a quick read got the Rev's point across. I spent the drive home sifting through my conscience just in case.

# Chapter Seventeen

Gideon and Silas were on the second floor scaffolding by seven-thirty, arguing with each other as they opened paint cans. I could hear them loud and clear, because, dadgum it, they were outside my bedroom window, and I was still under the covers. I like to be up and dressed for the day by seven-thirty, but nightmares involving piles of fallen leaves had disturbed my sleep, and earlier I'd turned off my alarm and pulled the sheet over my head.

"I said I don't believe it," said Silas. "And if *you* do, I'm liable to knock you off this plank and see if you bounce when you hit the ground."

"There's no need for that," answered Gideon. "I didn't say I believe it; I just said it's worrisome. She hasn't always made good decisions, and you and I both know it."

I could hear the sound of paintbrushes sliding along the side of the house and wondered how I was going to get out of bed and to my closet without being seen. I don't sleep in the nude, but my 1974 Eagles T-shirt, pilfered from my dad, barely covered my fanny. It also had a few holes worn through it, quite possibly in embarrassing places. I peeked past the top of the sheet only to find Silas carefully painting the wood trim on the window.

It would be smarter to wait till they moved, but I desperately needed to go to the bathroom.

I scooched toward the side of the bed opposite the window. No sudden movements, still under the covers, just inch by inch till I got to the edge, all the while wondering who they were discussing.

"I don't understand why she called you instead of me," said Gideon, clearly annoyed. "I'm older than you are."

"What do you think this is about, who gets to ride shotgun? We aren't kids, and she knows I always had her back." This was followed by a long silence.

"You still blame me for that time Daddy locked her in the attic," Gideon said.

"Yeah, you stinking pile of chicken poop, I do. If you'd joined in with me, he wouldn't have dared to. It was a hundred degrees that day. She coulda died."

Another long silence. "I've always felt bad about that. You let her out and took a beating for it. You are a better brother, and it's time for me to step up."

I glimpsed them going in for a brotherly hug, and I edged a little too far and fell off the bed with a room-shaking thump.

"Hey, Miss Wyatt! Annalee! Everything okay in there?"

*Busted.* "I'm fine, but could you turn and face the pasture for a minute? I'm not dressed for an early morning visit."

"Sorry about that; I didn't think about anyone being in the room. We should have knocked on the door," said Gideon.

TWENTY MINUTES LATER I was dressed and out in the side yard with coffee and Pudge. He found an empty donut box at the base of the scaffolding and proceeded to push it around the yard with his nose, as if exercising it could make another hot dozen appear. I wished him luck in his endeavors and turned my attention to the painters.

"What's going on this morning, guys?" I called up to the second floor. I'm nosy, but I'm also polite. They took the bait, and I was surprised that quiet Silas was the one to enlighten me.

"Things aren't good, Miss Wyatt," he said. "Sheriff Lacasse took Valonda in for questioning yesterday about Ryan Dawson."

That knocked me for a loop. "You have to be kidding. Valonda? That sounds crazy. She's what, five feet tall?" I saw his chagrined look and realized that wasn't the right defense. "And of course she wouldn't do something so awful."

"Of course she wouldn't," echoed Gideon. "She's a spitfire, but she wouldn't hurt a flea."

The conversation I'd heard through my bedroom window made sense now. "I noticed you two were quieter than usual the last couple of days. Did you expect this?"

"We were afraid it was coming," said Silas, still looking down from his perch by the bedroom window. "Stacey Dawson has been calling everybody she knows, spreading rumors that Valonda and Ryan were seeing each other. She's always been a jealous person, even when there was no need."

"I'm bumfuzzled," I admitted, wondering why the gossip hadn't made its way to last night's book club. "This doesn't make a bit of sense. Do your parents know?"

Gideon gave a long sigh. "Yeah, they know. They aren't exactly rushing in to help. Dad even changed the sign in front of the church after he found out."

My mouth dropped open. "You mean the one about sin leading to death? I saw that last night when I left book club. That's cold."

"Dad's not a warm, fuzzy kind of guy. He's not happy with any of us except Dorcas, and he practically disowned Valonda after the thing with Mr. Crosby. She's family, but nobody treats her like she is except me and Silas."

"She's lucky to have you two. I hope it's all a misunderstanding."

I wandered back inside and shot a text to Frankie. *Why didn't you tell me Boots had questioned Valonda?* Too late I remembered I'd promised to stop texting her when she was at work. She would either ignore me or reply with a rude emoji.

Neither. I got a text back right away.

*You're my best friend but he's my best husband*

Well, pooh. I hadn't anticipated that reply at all.

SHOULD I DO my hair before my shift at the Magnolia Blossom or after? Caleb and I had a hot date for dinner in Shreveport, and there might not be time for the full-bore beauty routine when I got off at five-thirty. I stepped into the shower and began to scrub. Montrose occupied her usual spot on the back of the toilet, a poof of furry orange against the turquoise tiled walls. She batted the shower curtain and peeked around it to stare at me. I flicked water on her nose and was rewarded with the sound of a dainty sneeze. The cat was annoyed, but not stalk-out-of-the-room annoyed. She continued to stare.

I scrubbed, rinsed, toweled off, and thought about the latest news. It would take a surveillance video of the actual homicide to convince me Valonda Nelson killed Ryan Dawson, and even then I'd suspect special effects were used. It was just implausible.

What on earth could have led Boots to question her? Maybe her brothers were making too much of it. It would be understandably upsetting to have your family member called in to the sheriff's office, but surely she was just one of many people being interviewed. Why, if I hadn't been a family friend, Boots would have had me come into the office myself. Hadn't he threatened Frankie with that when she kept interrupting us at dinner Monday evening?

He had to be under a lot of pressure from the family. If Stacey was spreading her theory all over town, he didn't have a choice but to follow up. Boots is smart; there's no way he would think Valonda was the killer. I paused with my comb halfway through my wet hair.

Maybe I was asking the wrong questions. Why did Stacey think Valonda stabbed Ryan in the first place?

During the time Caleb and I were at the party, I'd witnessed nothing to indicate that the accused wanted anything at all to do with the victim. On the contrary, after his creepy attack on her ear, I'd watched her spend the rest of the evening running around the room to avoid him. I know what Valonda is like when she's receptive to an advance; I've seen her swapping spit with two different guys in full view of the whole parish.

If I didn't hear anything useful at the store, I was bound to at least pick up some rumors at lunch. I decided right then to work in a few hundred calories at Katie's. I'd say no to the cookie this time.

I PARKED UNDER a bare-limbed elm and admired the colors of the fallen yellow leaves on the red brick street. The Magnolia Blossom is down the block and across the way. We leave the parking spots free in front of the door for customers, and as I approached I was surprised to see a FedEx truck pulled up sideways across four spaces.

Pete greeted me as I opened the door. He was in the process of completing paperwork for the driver, who had two large boxes on a dolly.

"You're here early, Pete. I thought I was supposed to open up today," I said, walking behind the long wooden counter to put my purse in the file cabinet. "You must have been expecting a delivery."

"No ma'am, this isn't a delivery," he said with a self-satisfied smile. "I sold a mint prewar American Flyer set online last night. The buyer paid for overnight delivery, and I've been here for an hour already, packing train pieces."

"That sounds like a special one. I'm surprised you're willing to let it go. I always thought selling wasn't your main goal."

"You and my wife. She thinks it's just an excuse to buy more trains," he said, holding the door open for the delivery man to leave.

The morning sun came through the tall glass windows and illuminated every speck of dust. I used my time to wipe down the many pieces of antique furniture that filled the store. It was an endless job, and we all took turns when we weren't busy with customers. As I stood up from wiping the legs of a barley twist table, I noticed Pete looking into my jewelry case with more than his usual interest.

"Do you see something you like? I can help you spend all that money you just made on the train," I offered.

"My wife's birthday is tomorrow, and it might be fun to bring home a piece of jewelry for her. She always says she doesn't care about such things, but I sometimes notice her looking at the other ladies with more interest than she will admit. Plus the first thing she said after I sold the train was 'I'll bet you already have another one in mind to buy.' It would be fun to prove her wrong."

I perked up. I do love to help someone buy a gift. "Let's look. Do you have something in mind? A necklace? Earrings?"

"That cross you're wearing today is awfully pretty. I've heard you joke about selling what you have on. Any chance you'd part with that?"

My heart sank. I do hate to disappoint a customer, but the ornate gold and silver piece wasn't for sale. I could see why he wanted it, almost every time I wore it someone complimented me. Over two inches long, it was made of sterling, with eighteen karat gold leaves curving around five old rose-cut diamonds. I'd never seen another like it.

"Pete, you have heard me say that, and for the most part, I mean it. This cross was my great-great-grandmother's, though, and I never sell my few family pieces. I have at least three others on display, and there may be one on my shelf in the store safe."

It's a good thing we didn't have any customers, because we spent an hour going piece by piece through my selection. Pete examined rings, bracelets, brooches, and necklaces before deciding on the red garnet Victorian cross that I'd bought so recently in Nacogdoches. I placed the necklace in a pretty gift box and wrapped it in my signature paper that is covered in sprigs of lavender and violets. I tied it with a spring green bow that matched the leaves on the flowers.

"I'm sure she'll like it, Pete, but if she doesn't she can come in and select something different in exchange."

"I can't imagine why she'd want to do that, Annalee. Like you said, it's pretty, and it's simple enough for her to wear every day. I just hope I don't set a precedent with this. She might expect jewelry all the time now."

"Hey, that's how I run my business. Get 'em hooked and keep 'em coming," I said.

# Chapter Eighteen

PETE SAID HE would stay at the shop if I brought back the day's plate lunch from Katie's for him. I fetched my purse and turned left out the front door. I barely escaped being knocked flat by a short, round man who came barreling around the corner at the end of the block. He clutched my arm before I fell and muttered, "Sorry, ma'am," then looked at my neck and gave a flamboyant shake of his fist toward the sky. "Heathen! Blasphemer!" He jerked his other hand away from me and stomped on down the sidewalk without explanation or a backward glance. That's when I noticed a familiar young girl following him.

"Dorcas?" I asked, noting her nod of recognition. "Do you know that man? I don't understand what just happened."

"That's Daddy," she said, not meeting my eyes.

"He's a minister, isn't he? Why did he get so upset when he saw my necklace?"

"He doesn't approve of pretty crosses. He says they're a tool of the devil, and that true believers should only wear ones made out of nails." She stared at the ground for a moment, then ran down the sidewalk to catch up with her father.

I took a deep breath and continued to the cafe, thinking I just might need dessert after all.

"DID I SEE you holding hands with Reverend Nelson?" asked Katie.

"You saw him grab my arm after he nearly knocked me down, but it definitely wasn't a friendly exchange. What's the deal with that man? He took one look at my necklace and pronounced me a heathen."

She peered at the cross. "Strictly a guess, but I imagine he thinks it's frivolous."

"Frivolous? I was called a heathen and a blasphemer right there on the sidewalk."

"Could have been worse. He unplugged the amps for the band at the spring daffodil festival, because they played a Christian rock song. Then he used a portable microphone to lecture the crowd on sin."

"That's out of the ordinary, but I don't put it in the same rank as calling someone a heathen right to her face," I said.

"He's been known to carry bed sheets around with him to throw over women he considers inappropriately dressed," she continued.

"I'd like to see him try. No wonder Valonda doesn't get along with him." I eyed the room. "Is that Tennie by herself at the back booth?"

"Yes. Hoyt's out of town, and she came in for a well-balanced lunch, although I noticed she ordered chicken fried steak and mashed potatoes. She says she's having raisin bran for dinner, but I hope she has a salad on the side. Go sit with her, and I'll have Maxie come by to take your order."

Unlike Frankie, Tennie sat in her favorite spot with her back to the wall so she could keep an eye on everyone. She waved me toward her, and I slid onto the well-worn wooden bench.

"What's up, partner? I'm ready to solve some more crimes," she said.

Tennie and I have a history together, one that I've tried to forget. "I'm doing honest work today. I'm at the Blossom all day long. Pete is running things by himself while I eat lunch. He's treating me special, because I just sold him a piece of jewelry for his wife." I slapped my hand over my mouth. "That's a birthday secret. Don't say a word to anybody."

"Don't worry," she said, as she buttered a roll. "I wouldn't dream of spoiling Hildy's surprise. I'll bet she hasn't gotten jewelry from that man since he put that plain gold band on her finger."

I ordered tea and a vegetable plate, then told her about my run-in with Reverend Nelson.

She narrowed her eyes and inspected the offending necklace. "Beautiful. I remember your grandmother wearing it when I was a little girl. Terry definitely wouldn't approve."

"Terry? I would expect something more Biblical. Adam, or Ezekiel, or maybe Elisha."

"No, he's the first religion enthusiast in his family that I know of. Not that the Nelsons were heathens, by any means." She winked at me.

I ignored the provocation. "So what denomination is he? I can't fit him into the ones I'm familiar with."

"Why, the First Church of the Devil's Destruction, of course. Emphasis on *first.* I think he's making it up as he goes along."

"Does he make a living at that? It's an awfully tiny building."

"I think he's still a foreman on the parish road construction crew. Melinda, his wife, is an aide at the nursing home."

My food arrived, and I applied my fork first to the fried okra. I could get food almost as good as this in Houston, but it would be five times as expensive, served with unnecessary garnishes, and given some sort of heirloom name. The calorie count would no doubt be the same. "Do you happen to know why he doesn't get along with his kids?" I asked around a bite of corn muffin.

"It's only my theory, but he was a couple of years behind my children in school, and I remember what happened when Valonda was born. Melinda got pregnant while they were in high school, but they married before the baby came. Melinda was quiet and shy, and Terry was wild as a buck. They weren't even supposed to be dating; her parents had forbidden it. That spring it was the talk of the town.

"Anyway, Valonda was born about three months later, and she had a heart defect. Fixable, understand, they took care of it at Texas Children's Hospital in Houston, but Terry blamed himself. He said God punishes the wicked, and he was determined to be good from then on. He went overboard. You'll notice the next three kids have Biblical names."

I finished my cheese grits (hey, it's sort of a vegetable), and voiced my objection to the story. "God may or may not punish the wicked, but the baby was the one with the heart defect. Surely Mr. Nelson didn't believe that happened because of his bad behavior."

"People don't always require their beliefs to be rational," Tennie said. "Terry was crazy about that baby, but he's wound up pushing all of the kids away with his extreme rules and expectations. I think Valonda was the apple that fell right next to the tree trunk. She's not much different than her daddy was. Dorcas is the only one who still toes the line, and I wonder if that's just a matter of time. That girl needs to have some fun."

She leaned out of the booth, focused on something happening near the front of the cafe. "Looks like they're getting ready for a crowd. I wonder who the big group is? That's usually a weekend thing, when people have grandkids in town."

I turned to look and saw the wait staff moving tables together.

Tennie ducked back into her seat and answered her own question. "It's Stacey, her dad, a couple of aunts, and Ryan's parents. I hope her mom is home taking a nap. Poor Stacey's face is so swollen; it looks like she's been crying nonstop since Sunday. Oh, and there's another couple I don't know, early sixties maybe."

I'd be pretty conspicuous if I turned backwards to stare, but I was dying to know if it was the previous night's whining shopper. "Describe the guy to me," I said.

"Five-seven, maybe. Wearing blue jeans that are so stiff they look like they've been dipped in liquid starch. Who does that with jeans? And tight. The only man I know who wears jeans like that is the interior designer my sister uses in Birmingham, and he's at least thirty years younger. Old men lose their butts. It's a fact of life. He needs to look in a mirror if he won't listen to his wife. I bet she's told him, and he thinks she's jealous because he's thinner than she is."

I was hanging on to her every word and growing surer by the minute.

"Strange hair. It's an attractive shade of white, but why the heck is it so long on top? He doesn't have a comb over, but it's swooped back from his forehead like that television preacher; you know, the one that lives in a mansion down in Houston. I see tortoise shell glasses like we used to wear years ago. I guess they're in style again."

She put on her own glasses. She was getting into this. "The shoes are deck shoes that have never seen a boat, and he made the bad decision not to put socks on those scrawny white ankles, plus he rolled the jeans up into fussy little cuffs. Makes my eyes hurt. The shirt looks like the most expensive men's store in town was trying to get a little stylish. They sell clothes to make a regular old fart look like a ridiculous old fart."

I nearly spit my tea across the table. "You're so bad, Tennie. But you're right. I think you're looking at Everett Crockett, Ryan's former partner from Nacogdoches. He had on wire-rims and sneakers last night, but otherwise the description fits. Do you believe that's his wife with him?"

"Probably. She's extremely pretty; I can tell she has brown eyes even from this distance. They're warm and kind. Nicely done blonde hair, gorgeous skin. She's a tiny bit round, but it looks good on her. I can't stand those skin-stretched-over-bone women. The wife might be his age, but she looks a good ten years younger. And she's a helluva lot more appropriately dressed. I'll bet she's charming. I can tell she's working to keep a conversation going at the table, while her husband just sits there like a warty toad."

"Are you sure you didn't work for the FBI? They could put out an all-points bulletin based on your descriptions."

She grinned. "Did I not tell you I worked as a reporter in Dallas before Hoyt and I got married?"

"No! You're kidding! That's why you're so observant."

"And I'm naturally nosy," she responded. "To continue my report, Ryan's poor parents look like they're hanging on by a thread. I took dinner by the B&B last night so the two of them could eat in, and they're exhausted. They need to go home to Georgia and grieve. I'm glad the funeral will be tomorrow. The rest of the family is coming in this afternoon."

Maxie stopped by with Pete's lunch, and I reluctantly rose to return to work. Tennie, long since finished with her meal, ordered a cup of coffee.

"You're in no hurry to go home. Where is Hoyt, anyway?"

"Deep sea fishing with his brother. He won't be back until Sunday night, and I'm not going to do so much as fry an egg while he's gone. I can stay here and people-watch all afternoon if I want to."

I walked past Stacey's table and gave her what I hoped was a compassionate smile. As I exited, I saw a middle-aged woman walking down the sidewalk toward me with a blonde baby boy on her hip. His golden curls bounced with each step, and he waved his hand in my direction with a sunny grin. Charmed, I held the door for her as she entered the cafe. As I watched them walk in, I saw Ryan Dawson's mother leap to her feet, heard her scream, and watched her collapse into her husband's arms in a faint.

# Chapter Nineteen

Do you think I didn't want to stick around and find out what *that* was all about? There was no polite way for me to do it, plus Pete deserved to have his lunch delivered before it got cold. I left, but I walked looking back over my shoulder. It's a wonder I didn't crash into one of the genuine antique reproduction light posts. By the time I got to the door of the Blossom, the woman carrying the baby had exited Katie's and was on her way, walking very quickly, down the street. I could hear the little boy babbling happily.

Pete met me and took the container from my hand.

"Pete. Look down the block. Do you know who that woman with the baby is?"

"That's Lydia Morrison," he said, glancing that direction before he walked to the back of the store with his lunch. "That little cutie is her grandson, Danny. Her daughter is missing, or so I heard. All the talk in town has been about the murder that happened Saturday, but Dinah hasn't been seen in maybe three weeks. Albin and Lydia are just about frantic."

"I think I heard that. Did their daughter work at the heavy equipment dealership?"

"I believe so," he said. "She was a flighty girl. She dropped out of college and got a few small parts in some of the movies they film in New Orleans, but always had to waitress to make her bills. She would get discouraged and come home to save money and work for a little while, then head off again without much notice. Albin told me one time that she'd thought she could get by on pretty, but found out that the acting part was important too."

"I guess she came back here to be close to her parents after she had the baby," I ventured. "I think I heard it mentioned she was a single mom."

"That's true, and she has never breathed a word about who that baby's father is, as far as I know. Not even to her parents. Folks have wondered if maybe it was one of the actors she met in New Orleans. You know they film some big-time movies there, with big-time stars. Whoever it is, he helps take care of Danny. Lydia told my wife that a check goes into Dinah's account every month on the fifth. It's never late."

I WAS STILL turning the news around in my head when the door opened, and Tennie came barreling up the center aisle. She stopped directly in front of me and came close to knocking a Wedgwood vase off the counter when she threw her purse down. For a scary moment I thought she would launch herself across the glass display top and grab me by the collar.

"You're not going to believe this," she whispered dramatically. "It looks like that baby's daddy might be Ryan Dawson!"

"No!"

"Yes! That's why his mother fainted. Poor Lydia was so surprised that she whirled around and ran out the door before the Dawsons could talk to her."

CALEB AND I had spent enough time together over the past few weeks that I'd gotten a little more relaxed about dressing for our dates. Only two outfits went back on their hangers tonight before I settled on skinny black pants and an oversized jade green cotton sweater with a sort of plunging neckline. Not too low, mind you, just enough to catch his attention but not any breadcrumbs. I scattered five rhinestone brooches across my left shoulder and slipped a pair of gold hoops onto my ears before layering gold bracelets on my right wrist. Short booties completed the outfit, and I left my hair long and loose.

I descended the stairs to the piercing sound of a wolf whistle, followed by another one not quite as loud and a bit off-key.

"I'm embarrassed to be outdone by a parrot," Caleb grumbled.

"Lafitte's not your ordinary parrot. Not that you're just an ordinary guy, either," I said, patting his arm reassuringly.

"You're trying to keep my ego intact. I appreciate that. Every little bit helps."

I let Pudge in through the front door and set the alarm. "I didn't hear the truck drive up, and the dog didn't make a sound. I hope we aren't going to dinner in your electric utility vehicle."

"Not quite," he said, as I turned the key in the lock.

He held the screen door open for me, and I walked

down the steps and stopped in surprise beside a beautiful little brown metallic BMW coupe. "What the heck? Where's the pickup?"

"There are responsibilities that go along with having a hot girlfriend. When I saw you climb up into Dad's truck in your fancy dress last weekend, I knew it was time to buy a car. Not that I didn't appreciate the view, what with the high heels and short skirt."

"Girlfriend? That sounds both juvenile and interesting. I might like this new label."

He tucked me into the passenger seat like the gentleman he is and went around to the driver's side. His heart-stopping smile was warm and easy. "I took you to the big dance last weekend, didn't I? When a guy asks a girl to homecoming, it's serious."

"I don't know if I believe that. You didn't bring me one of those gigantic corsages. I'm also not wearing your football letter jacket, and I'm sure you have one. No, I think you're trifling with me." I thought that would get another laugh, but instead his face grew solemn.

"I heard Ryan's parents wanted to bury him with his high school jacket, but I think they settled for having it on display at the funeral. Stacey wanted to keep it."

We changed the subject and talked about the goats he and his dad were raising and how soon they would get their cheese-making project off and running. Maybe if Everett Crockett came back to Berryville he would find the grocery shopping improved.

We pulled into the parking lot and looked for a sweet spot to leave Caleb's new car. He found an empty space between an Infiniti and a new Lexus, still with the dealer tags. "This looks good," I said. "Both of these guys will be worried about their own cars and will make sure they don't ding your doors."

"If I was really concerned, I should have had you walk down to the road at your place and meet me. That gravel driveway at Goat Hill left me covered in dust," he said, running a finger across the hood of the car before we crossed the lot.

"Hot girlfriends don't do roadside delivery," I answered, as he held the heavy glass door open for me. There was a party going on in one of the back rooms that we could hear all the way out at the entry. I caught snippets of shouted toasts that called to mind a rehearsal dinner already heavily lubricated by alcohol.

We chose to eat at one of the tall tables in the expansive, dimly-lit bar. A jazz trio played in the corner. I didn't recognize any of the other patrons, but Caleb nodded and said hi to folks at a couple of different tables. He ordered a bottle of wine and the cheese plate to get the evening started.

I waited until we'd had a few sips of the excellent Rueda before telling him what happened at the cafe that afternoon. I'd expected him to be surprised, but I wasn't prepared for anger.

"Damn, was everything about Ryan a lie? How could he do that to Stacey?"

"And his parents," I added. "Imagine how his mom felt when she saw that baby. Mrs. Morrison might as well have brought a ghost into the room."

"And you know the kid is Ryan's?"

"No, no, I haven't heard anything except what Tennie told me, and she just reported what happened in the cafe. Pete, at the store, said he's not sure even Dinah's parents know who the father is. He did say that Dinah gets monetary support every month."

"And she's still missing," Caleb said.

"As far as I know."

He took another drink of wine and pointed his finger at me. "Maybe she killed him. Maybe he wouldn't leave Stacey, and they had a fight, and Dinah stabbed him."

I gave him a dubious look. "There's a gaping hole in your theory. She's missing. You're saying she snuck into town, met Ryan by the high school track and stabbed him, then snuck back out of town?"

"Hmm. Point made. That's probably the reason Boots doesn't call me for crime solving advice."

I saw a familiar face enter the room and waved. Nita Marren, the nurse practitioner from Frankie's office, walked over to our table and introduced her date.

"Hi, y'all, this is Ben. He was on call delivering babies all night long, so say hello now before he goes to sleep face-first in his salad."

Ben gave us both a good-natured hand-shake, accompanied by a big yawn, and they agreed to join us for a drink before going to their table.

"I've been telling Ben about all the craziness going on in Berryville lately," said Nita. "Have either of you heard anything about the murder? It's weird that nobody has been arrested, don't you think?"

"I'm completely out of the loop," I answered. "Frankie and I are best friends, but I haven't been able to shake anything out of her."

"Me either," she said. "Ryan's parents came in this afternoon and practically demanded to talk to her. The three of them went into her office and shut the door but didn't stay long. Mr. and Mrs. Dawson didn't look happy when they left, and neither did Frankie. I can't imagine what they were talking about, and I did everything to hear except press my stethoscope to the door."

Caleb and I exchanged glances, and I figured we were thinking the same thing. Had the Dawsons come in seeking information about little Danny Morrison? Frankie saw most of the children in town at the clinic. Maybe they thought she would tell them something that would confirm or negate their suspicions.

Nita looked over my shoulder toward the lobby and wrinkled her nose in distaste. "Look who's here."

I followed her gaze to the entrance. "I've been running into that guy everywhere." Everett and Bonnie Crockett stood next to the hostess desk. "And he always looks like nothing is measuring up to his expectations."

"I think that's default for him. You've heard of RBF?"

Caleb and Ben both looked confused as I laughed.

"Resting Bitch Face, guys. It refers to someone who normally looks sour even if they're in a good mood," I said.

"Keep up, boys," said Nita. "Mom said Stacey's mother had finally pushed them out of their guestroom and into a hotel here in Shreveport. Maybe they'll go back to Texas tomorrow after the funeral."

"I hope the food meets his lofty standards," I said, before recounting my experience in Bubba's the previous night. "I wonder how Mrs. Sawyer got them to leave. I can't believe the Crocketts stayed with them in the first place. I understand that they're close to Ryan and Stacey, but it's not like they're relatives. Nacogdoches is a little more than an hour away from Berryville. They could have been sleeping in their own bed."

The waiter arrived with their drinks, and our conversation paused for a moment. Then Nita lifted her martini glass in a salute to the three of us. "Here's to life getting back to normal."

We clinked our glasses together and watched Everett and Bonnie follow the hostess into the dining room behind us.

"His wife is really pretty," said Caleb. "He's a little overboard with the clothes and hair, don't you think?"

"His wife told my mom that Ryan was responsible for that. She said they were even better friends than they were partners, and that he'd encouraged Everett to dress a little younger. My mom said his wife found it amusing and that she and Stacey got a kick out of it, but they never dared let him know. I think he's known for a healthy ego," Nita said.

"I guess the friendship angle explains why they've been here all week," I said. "But I'll bet even Stacey will be happy to see them leave."

# Chapter Twenty

Caleb and his parents picked me up the next morning for the funeral. I hadn't known whether or not I should attend. My interactions with the deceased wouldn't classify me as a close friend, but there was nothing in the etiquette books about the obligations of the person who discovers the dead body of a murder victim. Would my presence be a distraction at the service?

Sarah Bright solved my dilemma when she called and matter-of-factly told me to be ready at 10:30. "I thought it would be nice if you rode with us," she said kindly.

I braided my hair and twisted it into a coil at the back of my neck, then slipped into a sedate navy dress. Pearls, both earrings and a long strand, completed the look. I started to slip on the stack of bracelets that lay in the Belleek dish, but knew I'd resort to jingling them without thinking. Inappropriate funeral behavior for sure, so the safest thing was to leave them at home, but boy, did I feel naked without them.

The Brights were in the fancy pickup. Caleb helped me into the back of the double cab, and we waved at Clotille as we went down the driveway. I took a good look at Caleb as we pulled onto the two-lane country highway. He wore a navy suit with a tiny pinstripe, a starched white shirt, and a blue and green striped tie.

"You look nice," I said.

"Hear that?" said Sarah. "Aren't you glad I wouldn't let you wear that sport coat?"

I watched a blush spread from just above his collar to the tops of his ears. "Alright, Mom," he muttered.

Ralph laughed. "It's nice to know we can still embarrass you, son."

I grinned at Caleb. "We're never too old."

He changed the subject to goats, always a safe topic. He and his dad just finished describing the new barn they were building when we went past the First Church of the Devil's Destruction.

GOD'S WOUNDS CURE, SIN'S KISSES KILL

"That seems a bit pointed," I said. "Do you suppose Reverend Nelson is referring to Ryan?"

"I don't know," said Sarah, "but it's an insensitive choice, in my opinion."

"The man hasn't been playing with a full deck for years," said Ralph. "Most everyone in town knows it, so maybe they won't pay much attention."

The venerable brick church was packed. We found a pew toward the back that had enough room for the four of us to squeeze in, but most of the people who arrived after us had to stand. Stacey and the Dawsons looked like they were hanging on by a thread. The loss of someone you love is always hard, then add murder to it, and, well, I just can't even imagine the pain.

After the service, the attendees were invited to a reception in the fellowship hall. Even though I felt more and more like a true member of the community with each day that passed, I wouldn't have attended by myself. My family has been in Sebastian Parish for 175 years, but I grew up in Houston. Sharing the occasion with the Brights was very comfortable.

We walked into a large room with a twenty-foot table draped in white linen, covered with food brought in by the ladies of the church. I couldn't draw my eyes away. It was Southern Living magazine come to life, and the dishes represented a span of three generations of home cooking. Caleb and I wandered away from his parents and cruised the buffet, just contemplating the largesse.

There was a huge platter of fried chicken that looked like it came from the Gas-n-Go. Before you turn up your nose at that, let me explain that Mrs. Blackwell has been frying up chicken there for at least twenty-five years, because I remember stopping by with my Uncle Raine when I was just a little girl. It's incredible, golden and crunchy and just the right amount of greasy. It anchored one end of the table, and a sliced ham was on the other.

A cut glass relish tray held pickles, olives, and dilled carrots, and there were three different plates, two made of cut glass and one of hand-painted porcelain, which held a dozen deviled eggs each. In this part of the South, your kitchen isn't complete without at least one egg plate, with its twelve oval indentations. As we walked by, a little boy ran up to the table, stretched his arm to the maximum, and nabbed one of the eggs. We watched him shove the whole thing in his mouth in one gigantic bite, just about the time his mother grabbed him by the shirt collar and threatened him with a pop on the fanny if he left her side again. As they walked away, he turned and opened his mouth wide, grinning at Caleb as he showed him a mouth full of his prize.

"I think you must have done that at some time in your life," I said. "He's looking at you like you're a co-conspirator."

Caleb kept his eye on the youngster and popped one of the eggs into his own mouth, then gave him a slow wink. The tot's eyes widened, and his grin was replaced with a look of admiration. Luckily his mother didn't turn around and see what was happening behind her back.

"You, sir, are a bad influence."

"I do my best," he said.

Tennie and Nancy wandered over and greeted us, followed closely by Ernestine Greener. I lifted my brows inquisitively at Tennie, but she shook her head. Evidently she hadn't heard anything else about little Danny Morrison's parentage.

Nancy tapped my shoulder and pointed toward the north end of the room. Another, smaller, table sat there, covered in a cloth in the high school colors and laden with desserts. "Guess what's on that table," she said.

I turned to Ernestine. "Caramel cake?" I asked hopefully.

"On the pressed glass cake stand. Right next to Eudora's coconut cake with lemon filling."

"Caleb, you go ahead and get yourself some ham. I'll start with dessert," I said.

Frankie came by a few minutes later with a plate of interesting things. She eyed my almost-gone pieces of cake. "You already hit dessert?"

"I started with it. I was afraid to wait till you got yours. What are those odd-looking things you're eating?"

"Chicken casserole made with cream of mushroom soup and lime Jell-O salad with crushed pineapple."

"What's the stuff on top of the casserole?"

"Corn flakes."

"Why? And what are those white blobs in the Jell-O?"

"I don't know why, but they're always there. The crunch is a vital part of the casserole experience. And I'm eating this salad in memory of Ryan. My mother served it at least once a week when we were little kids, and he hated it. He used to whisper gross things about the cottage cheese to me, while telling my mother how delicious it was. He always did have a way of working both sides of the fence."

"My grandmother made that at Easter every year, and my cousins and I had the same conversations," said Caleb. "I've seen Ryan put away two pimiento cheese sandwiches at lunch, so this is my memorial." He held a plate with several of the little triangles, plus a few made of curried chicken salad.

The guests included a fair number of people who had made the drive over from Texas, and we made a point of speaking to some of them. The atmosphere was slightly noisy and social, though not as much as it would have been for the death of someone who'd died of old age. Ryan's relative youth and the manner of his passing kept things more somber. Boots appeared at our side, accompanied by Seth and Maya Hammett.

"How often do you go to the funeral for a murder victim?" I asked Boots.

"We generally try to have someone from the department at every one," he answered. "There's always a possibility that the perpetrator will be there, since most victims are killed by someone they know."

"It's not like they'll feel guilty and jump up and confess in the middle of the eulogy, but their demeanor and actions may add up to something suspicious," said Seth. "But we're mainly here today because we knew the guy."

As we stood there watching the crowd, we saw Valonda approach Stacey. Though we were unable to hear what was said, there was no mistaking Stacey's dramatic pivot as she turned her back to the other woman.

"Wow," said Maya. "That was a total burn."

"I don't know what the woman expected, given the fact that the widow thinks she killed her husband," said a familiar voice. "And I think it's just a matter of time before the whole truth comes out."

We found ourselves joined by Everett and Bonnie Crockett. Introductions were made, but it was obvious that he and Boots were already acquainted.

"Sheriff Lacasse, it's good to talk to you again," he intoned. "Dare I hope you've made progress since we last spoke?" Crockett had chosen the tortoise shell glasses for today's event and wore a normal suit, but that annoying voice was unchanged.

Before Boots could reply, Bonnie interrupted. "Now, Everett, this is not the time for questions and demands. I'm sure the sheriff is doing his job."

I saw him stiffen at the rebuke, but her hand was on his arm with visible pressure, her knuckles white with force. He took a deep breath and said, "Yes, Bonnie, you're right. I apologize." I wondered if she often had to take such measures with him.

RALPH BECKONED FROM across the room, and Caleb and I said our goodbyes and left the building shortly after his parents. Before we reached the truck, I heard someone calling my name. I stopped, turned, and was surprised to see Everett and Bonnie close behind us. They introduced themselves to Ralph and Sarah as "Ryan and Stacey's other family."

A couple of minutes of chit chat was followed by an expression of sympathy for my ordeal in the discovery of the body.

"As an attorney, I deal with crime from a safe distance. It must have been very disturbing to come across something so brutal on your afternoon walk," Everett said.

"Yes, it was distressing," I agreed. "I'm glad there was so little outward evidence of his injury." Boots had coached me with this response, knowing there'd be people who wanted gruesome details.

"I still can't believe that law enforcement was unable to recover any worthwhile clues from the scene," Everett said. "We loved Ryan like a son, and I fear this case may come down to circumstantial evidence. Can you think of anything they might have overlooked? I'd be happy to pay for a private detective."

I admitted I was aware of nothing and hoped he would never find out I was doing my own snooping.

Bonnie shook her head. "We're so worried about

Stacey. We hoped she would come back home with us, but she isn't ready yet."

I watched the two of them as they walked to their Mercedes, and wondered if Stacey was as attached to them as they were to her.

# Chapter Twenty-One

Feeling at loose ends when I got home, I decided to do something to take my mind off the morning. I was right in the middle of a great yoga session on the front porch when my phone rang. Fighting the temptation to ignore it, I eased out of a headstand and answered.

"Hey, it's Frankie. I just wanted to let you know that Boots made an arrest this afternoon. It'll be in the news, but I feel just a tiny bit guilty for stonewalling you all week. A tiny bit."

This was a surprising report. "Well, don't keep me in suspense. Who is it?"

"Valonda Nelson."

I nearly fell off the porch swing. "What the heck? That's insane. There's no way she did it; I don't care what Stacey says."

"I admit it's unexpected, but he has enough evidence to charge her or he wouldn't have brought her in."

"So she's in jail?"

"Yes. She'll go before the judge Monday, and he will probably set bail."

"Wow. I'm not processing this. It makes no sense." I had a sudden remembrance of my conversation with her brothers. "Silas and Gideon are going to freak."

"How do you know them?"

"They're painting my house. They gave me a little background the other day on their dad. I don't think any of them had an easy childhood."

"Don't say that to Boots. Nothing flips his switch like a criminal blaming their parents."

"She's not convicted," I said a little sharply.

"You're right. Anyway, I just wanted to let you know. Talk to you later."

I HEARD THE sound of gravel crunching underfoot and looked up to see Clotille approaching.

"Hey, baby girl," she said, as she came up the steps. "Are you taking a nap on the swing?"

I moved Montrose off Clotille's favorite rocking chair and gave her a light blanket to put over her legs. "I'm pretending I didn't answer the phone when Frankie called. She gave me some very unwelcome news."

After listening to my story, Clotille agreed that the likelihood of Valonda Nelson having committed murder was as far-fetched as having killed Ryan herself. I then told her about the kerfluffle in the cafe the day before when Mrs. Morrison brought her grandson in.

"What a thing to have happen," she said. "I wonder if Mrs. Dawson was in such an emotional state that she imagined the baby looked like Ryan. Poor woman. And what a mess if it turns out to be true."

"Wouldn't it be a good thing?"

"Yes and no. I don't think they would have any legal rights, especially since Ryan and Dinah weren't married. Plus they'd have to face the fact that their son not only cheated on his wife, but he fathered a son and didn't claim him publicly. That's not showing a very high moral character in my opinion."

"You're right. I wonder if the baby has something to do with Ryan's murder. And I wonder if Boots even knows about it."

I DIDN'T HAVE to wonder very long. A surprising phone call from Boots with a polite request to stop by left me awash in curiosity until he knocked on the door ten minutes later.

He was wearing full sheriff regalia, all khaki except for the big black pistol strapped on his hip. With a polite smile, he asked if I would take a professional look at a piece of evidence.

"Me? Really? How could I possibly help you?" I was intrigued and excited. Was I a possible witness for the prosecution? Where were the television cameras?

"Frankie says you know as much or more about jewelry than anyone else in the parish."

"Oh, jewelry." So much for fame and notoriety. "Sure, if I don't know, I can direct you to the right resource. Come into the study where I have my tools and research books."

He followed me into Uncle Raine's old library, and I turned on the bright lights I use to examine the pieces I buy and repair. "Sit across from me at the partner's desk, and we'll have a look."

I placed a black velvet display board between us and waited for him to put the item in question on it. He unbuttoned his right shirt pocket and fished out something small wrapped in a paper towel. He set it on the velvet board and waited. Resting before me was a demantoid garnet salamander.

I gave one of those horror-movie style gasps and jerked back as if it were going to pounce on me. "Where did you get that?"

He eyed me with interest. "That's quite the reaction. It's not real, you know. It isn't going to crawl across the desk."

"I know that," I said defensively. "C'mon, Boots, where did you get it?"

He shook his head. "Not until you tell me everything you know about it. I don't want to prejudice your answer."

I picked it up and reached for a magnifying glass. "Okay. I'll give you a quick, nonbinding appraisal. Edwardian. 14K gold, demantoid garnets of good, but not excellent, quality. The color isn't quite as bright as the best grade. Faceted ruby eyes. Lines of small faceted rose cut diamonds on either side. These pins are referred to as salamanders or lizards, although the shape of the head is definitely salamander-like." I turned it over and checked the hallmarks in the gold. "Made in England, looks like it's been skillfully repaired at some point. Between three and four thousand retail. It could easily be double or triple that if the stones were better."

A look of surprise crossed his face. "That much for a little lizard pin? That's crazy."

I returned the brooch to the black velvet, where it sparkled in the bright light of my jeweler's lamp. "This piece hits several buttons for collectors. Demantoid garnet, Edwardian, and nature. There are people who love to collect different insects or frogs or lizards, or even things like grapes or leaves. I have one customer who likes brooches and earrings designed as clusters of grapes. She has them in jade, different colors of pearls, coral, amethysts—you name it, she'll buy it. I have her in mind every time I go shopping. Now. Tell me how this fellow wound up in your pocket."

"It was in Valonda Nelson's bedroom, tucked away in a tiny box under her pillow."

Oh, no. This was cataclysmically awful news. Why? Because the last time I saw it, Stacey Dawson had it fastened to her flashy gold jumpsuit. We eyed each other warily across the desk. He broke first.

"I know you have reservations about Valonda as a murder suspect, but I need you to be honest with me about this pin."

I took offense. Wouldn't you? I mean, really. "Have I given you reason to doubt my truthfulness, Boots?"

"Never," he answered quickly. "Forgive me. Chalk the comment up to the job, not our friendship."

"That's better. What else do you want to know?" I'd be darned if I were going to volunteer anything that might implicate Valonda. There's honesty, and there's over-sharing.

"Have you ever seen it before?"

"It's impossible to say. It's a common style. I've certainly never examined it before." I settled back in my chair and smiled.

He looked a bit annoyed. "Work with me, Annalee. Does this particular pin look familiar to you? Have you seen someone *recently* wearing one similar to it? Before you answer, remember that I've seen you describe and appraise a pair of earrings on someone stopped next to you at a red light."

I was wasting our time. "Yes, Boots, Stacey Dawson was wearing a pin that looked like this one at the dance last Saturday night. Are you happy now?"

"No, I'm not happy," he said. There was a sharp edge to his words. "I don't want Valonda to be guilty of murdering Stacey's husband. But if she did, it's my responsibility to provide the DA with the evidence."

I immediately felt guilty myself. The guy was just doing his job. "I'm sorry, Boots. You're right. I've had a change of opinion about Valonda over the last few weeks. It's surprised the heck out of me, but I sort of like her now, and I'd hate to find out she was the murderer."

"That's fine; maybe she isn't. You tell me what you know, and I promise I won't use it for anything other than finding out the truth. I will tell you I've met some extremely charming criminals in my line of work."

I reached out and picked up the brooch again. It felt warm and heavy in my hand, and I gave a brief thought to the life it must have lived before this. Surely it had never been implicated as evidence in a murder investigation before. Much as I disliked the idea, I had no choice but to help Boots discover the truth.

"I can't claim your offer isn't fair. However, you have to understand that these are only my observations. Stacey was decked out in thousands of dollars' worth of gold and diamonds, all contemporary. I recognized the designer, and I would say it had all been purchased within the last few years. That's why I was intrigued to see this little fellow clinging to her shoulder. When I singled it out for a comment it was obvious she didn't know anything about it. She thought she'd bought an alligator to wear in honor of the high school mascot."

"Was she pleased to find out it was something special?"

"Heck, no. She was dismissive of it, because it was 'used.' When Caleb told her I deal in antique jewelry, she looked at me as if I run garage sales for a living. She assumed I sell things to people who can't afford anything new."

Boots rubbed his forehead as if it hurt.

"Do you want some Excedrin?"

"Yes, please. That would be helpful."

I left the room and returned with a glass of iced tea, two pills, and a slice of pecan coffee cake made from this season's crop. He gave me an appreciative smile and downed the meds, then took a big bite of cake.

"I feel better already. You're a lifesaver. My next step is to figure out how that lizard came to be in Valonda's possession."

"Does she know you found it?"

"You bet, she was standing right there in her bedroom watching us. I had a search warrant when we went to her house this afternoon. I waited till after Ryan's funeral, because I didn't want to take the focus away from the service. You know a buzz would have gone through the church if I'd made my move before, and I don't consider her a flight risk."

I was still staggered by the news. How on earth had Stacey's jewelry turned up in Valonda's house? My confused brain couldn't come up with a plausible scenario. "Can I ask what she told you? Or is that something I'm not allowed to know?"

He waited till he'd finished the last bite of cake and scraped the crumbs from the saucer with his fork to answer. "I guess it can't hurt to tell you. She claims Ryan gave it to her."

I was dumbfounded, and that's not a word I ever thought I'd have the occasion to use. "That's . . . very odd."

Boots finished his tea and went to the kitchen to refill his glass. "I wish I could have one of your margaritas," he said when he returned. "This has been a tequila sort of day."

"I'll make you one. I have all the ingredients."

"No, unfortunately there's at least two hours of paperwork waiting for me at the office. Maybe one day this week?" he said hopefully.

"Sure. I don't leave town on another jewelry trip till next Monday."

He grinned. "Something to look forward to. You told me you and Caleb watched Stacey leave the party and walk home. Did you notice if she was wearing the pin then?"

I laughed. "We were hunkered down in the flower bed inside those gigantic azalea bushes, so everything was filtered through leaves. The lights in the parking lot aren't very bright, and she also had her back to us. So, no."

"I knew it was unlikely, but I did have to ask," he said, as he reached for the pin.

"Wait. Let me give you something besides a paper towel to keep the little guy in." I went through my supply cabinet and came out with a small hinged box, just the right size for a tiny salamander. After tucking him into his new home, I dropped the box into a metallic drawstring bag with Wyatt's Pretties stamped on the outside.

"The deputies are gonna laugh at me when I walk in with this," he grumbled.

"Better they should laugh than you lose or damage it. It's old and needs to be treated with care."

"Yes, ma'am. Thanks for the help."

I watched him go down the drive to the highway and turn toward town. I'd completely forgotten to tell him about the baby. What in the bejeebus had Valonda gotten herself into?

# Chapter Twenty-Two

I LOST TRACK of time after Boots left. Fell down an endless rabbit hole. Dropped off the face of the earth. I was distressed and depressed.

I couldn't reconcile the conversation I'd had with Valonda at the Magnolia Blossom the day after we found Ryan's body. Why had she come in to talk to me about a theoretical demantoid garnet salamander pin that she obviously already had in her possession? Why had she said she'd never be able to afford such a thing when she had one tucked under her dadgum pillow? Was she fishing for an appraisal? Did she hope to sell it? Should I have told Boots?

I felt used.

I heard a knock at the door and realized Caleb was there to watch a movie. Dating a month and already we were glued to the couch and TV. I still wore my bleach-spotted yoga pants with my hair pulled back in a messy ponytail.

"Come in," I yelled, trying to straighten up the place a bit before he made it from the door into the living room. Lost cause.

He had made an effort for the evening. He wore a soft brown henley and faded jeans that hugged his narrow hips perfectly, and his best pair of boots. Tennie wouldn't have a complaint about the way those pants fit. The sleeves of the henley were pushed up to the elbow, treating me to a view of muscled forearms and strong, capable hands. He didn't look like a guy who'd made a fortune writing specialized computer programs. He had a bottle of wine tucked under his arm and a six-pack of locally brewed beer in his other hand. Henry followed behind him, and promptly trotted across the room and stuck his nose into Montrose's ear.

He paused to take in my disheveled appearance. "Did you forget I was coming over? You're not quite your usual put-together self."

"Hold that thought," I said, running up the stairs. Soon I was back in leggings and a new rose pink cashmere tunic top that I'd ordered online but not yet worn. A spritz of Aunt Josie's Arpege finished off my efforts. "Better?"

"You look good either way, but this is nice. All you need to do now is take that stack of bracelets off before we start the movie." He had gone to the kitchen to open his beer and get a wine glass for me while I was upstairs.

I slipped the five bangles off and placed them on the mantle. "I suppose I should add your name to the list of people I drive crazy with my jewelry."

"Not crazy, but I'd rather not have the jingle jangle going on while I'm trying to concentrate on aliens invading earth."

"I thought we were watching Meryl Streep mangle opera."

"That's the third one. First aliens, then zombies, then Meryl."

"Something tells me we won't make it to number two, forget about number three."

Two hours later the earth was safe, and I was finally willing to bring up the subject of Boots' visit. Lafitte's head was tucked under his wing, and Pudge snored softly at my feet. Montrose had draped herself across Caleb's lap shortly after the movie started and looked as happy as I'd ever seen her. Henry slept on his back with all four of his short little legs splayed out wide, occasionally sneezing in his sleep. I hoped he wasn't allergic to the parrot.

"I hate to disrupt the peace and quiet, but Boots stopped by this afternoon. There's been some, shall we say, *unexpected* developments."

"More unexpected than a secret child?"

"So unexpected that the whole secret child story slipped my mind while he was here."

I told him everything I'd learned and was gratified that he was as puzzled as I was. Neither of us could come up with a scenario to explain the transfer of the brooch from Stacey to Valonda, much less produce a reason for Valonda to stab Ryan.

"Hey, I have an idea. Get your laptop. I ran into Merribeth Horton's husband at the feed store today, and he says there are pictures posted online from the party. Let's look and see if there's any interaction between Ryan and Valonda that we missed," Caleb said.

It didn't take long to find the photos. "It's funny how you can look at a picture and tell if someone is blotto. There's a look to the eyes that's impossible to miss," I said.

He stopped on a photo of the two of us and enlarged it. "Good. We look like we're alert and oriented."

"There's one of Merribeth hiding from Ryan," I said. "Wow, I didn't realize Christie's hair was the exact same color of blue as her dress. I wonder if she dyed her hair to match or found the dress after she'd gone blue."

"That question is beyond my pay grade, but we're definitely a motley crew. Steve looks like he's just come in off an oil rig. I think that's grease behind his ear," said Caleb.

We kept paging through, and suddenly I saw it. "Look at that. Blow it up. There, in the background of that picture of Christie Jenkins. Isn't that Valonda leaning against the wall?"

The picture was blurry at that magnification, but there was no confusion about the girl with the flirtatious smile. Caleb pointed to something next to Valonda. "Whose arms are those on either side of her? I can't see his face, but some guy is leaning in awfully close, and she isn't resisting."

"You're right," I said. "And I'll stake my reputation as a jeweler that the Rolex on that wrist belonged to Ryan."

It took us a half hour to pinpoint the time of evening when the picture had been taken and examine all the others. If the photographer posted them in order, it must have been shortly before we overheard the row between Ryan and Stacey. "I guess she did have a reason to get mad," I mused. "I'd have sworn Valonda spent the evening trying to avoid the guy."

"Should we tell Boots?" Caleb asked.

"No," I said. "I don't want to be in this any deeper than I already am. He has access to the same pictures. If I can misjudge something as thoroughly as I did Valonda's behavior at the party, then I think I'm not so reliable after all."

MONDAY MORNING BEGAN like Friday had, with the painters working on the second floor of the house. Gideon's estimate of finishing in a week had been optimistic. Though they weren't outside my bedroom, the location wasn't an improvement. I prefer to do my bathroom chores without an audience, and the scaffolding was right outside the bathroom window.

I brushed my teeth in time with Gideon's paint scraper, glad that I'd thrown on a caftan before leaving my bedroom. I went to the powder room downstairs to take care of the rest of my morning routine, and wished once again that the old farmhouse had more than one real bathroom.

The computer quietly booted up while I made coffee. I do a brisk number of online sales, and to my delight, in the middle of the night someone had purchased a fabulous beetle brooch set with diamonds and a cabochon star sapphire. There's nothing like an insomniac with a credit card to make my little heart happy. Those Victorian craftsmen were an imaginative group, and the sleepless woman in Denver who snatched this pin off my website was going to turn heads when she wore it.

I'd no sooner placed my coffee cup on top of the dinette, when there was a knock at the back door. Silas and Gideon stood on the porch with hopeful looks.

"Hi, guys. Want some fresh coffee?"

They handed me a bag of doughnuts and took seats at the table while I prepared two more cups. Neither spoke until I'd eaten my first doughnut.

"Have you heard the news?" asked Silas.

"You mean about your sister? Yes. I'm sorry."

"She didn't do it," said Gideon. "I hope you don't think she did."

I picked up a second doughnut. This conversation was pushing my eat-some-sugar buttons. "It's hard for me to believe that Valonda would hurt anyone. Have you talked to her since she was arrested?"

"My wife and I went to the jail yesterday to see her," said Silas. "She's supposed to be arraigned today. She's asked for a public defender; she doesn't have enough money to hire a real lawyer."

"I'm sure they'll assign someone real to her," I promised. "He or she may not be very experienced, but it's entirely possible to get someone competent."

"I'm worried about her being in jail till the trial," said Gideon. "She's already said she won't allow either of us to post bond, because she doesn't want to cause problems with our wives."

"Do your parents know?"

"I called them," said Gideon. "All it did was set Dad off on a rant about sin and damnation. As far as he's concerned, Valonda's so wicked anyway that a little old thing like murder doesn't surprise him at all. I didn't get the chance to talk to Mom, but she usually toes his line."

Just as I was wondering why they were sharing all of this with me, they got to the point.

"Annalee, we heard about that thing that happened with the Sessions last month, and how you figured out who the bad guys were. Do you think you could do the same for Valonda?"

Silas asked the question, but he and Gideon both looked at me like puppy dogs waiting for a treat, all eager expectation and blind hope. I choked back the response that came naturally to me, you know, the one where I asked if they were nuts. "Guys? You know I'm not a detective, right? I sell jewelry for a living. I have an *art history* degree, for gosh sakes."

"We know. And we can't afford to pay you except to give you a discount on your bill."

"I can't imagine that I could do a darn thing that would merit a paycheck." They looked so disappointed. I sighed and made an offer I was sure I'd regret. "Okay, I'll do some minor checking around, but don't get your hopes up. And don't tell anyone," I emphasized with a pointed wag of my index finger.

LATER, AS I packed the late-night-buyer's brooch for shipping to Colorado, I wondered what I'd gotten myself into. How do detectives plan their detecting? I decided to begin with Christie.

Since she cuts my hair, I had her number in my contacts list, but it was too early to bother her on her day off. I spent another couple of hours listing items online. It's not hard to do once you get the hang of it, but I've been known to make mistakes when I'm distracted. The worst mistake I've ever made was pricing a $500 dollar item at $500,000. It could have been bankruptcy-worthy if I'd reversed the error.

The clock hit eleven, and I texted her. Just as I hoped, she jumped at the suggestion of meeting for lunch.

# Chapter Twenty-Three

I PARKED UNCLE Raine's old pickup under an overhanging live oak tree. Even though it was November, that Southern thing of looking for some shade all summer long makes it hard to bypass at any time of year. Christie was already in line inside the Dairy Kreme, and I joined her there and ordered a burger basket with onion rings. I'm capable of overdoing the calories anywhere; I don't have to be at Katie's Kitchen to eat too much.

We slid into one of the pastel Formica booths, and the first thing she did was lean over and grab a hank of my hair. "Those ends are starting to fray. You'd better get in for a trim," she said. "Plus your light streaks from the summer sun are going to fade, so maybe you'll let me put in some highlights this time. I'm thinking green."

"You just keep thinking. It's as close as you're going to get to doing the Crayola box dump on me," I said. "You can carry it off, but I'd just look silly. By the way, your blue hair and your blue dress were great together at the party. I would have expected it to be too much, but you rocked the look."

"Thank you. That was a fun party. I love to dance, and so does Sid. I think everybody there had a good time. It's so weird to think that Valonda killed Ryan right afterward."

Here was my opening. "That makes no sense to me at all. Can you think of any reason for her to do that?"

She went to the counter to pick up our orders and answered on her return. "Stacey claims they were having an affair."

"When were they supposed to be doing the deed? I've seen Valonda around town smooching a couple of different guys over the last few weeks. How would she work someone else into the lineup?"

"Well, she and Ed have stayed conveniently friendly since their divorce, and I know she's had an on-again, off-again thing with one of the salesmen at the equipment dealership, but I think both of those guys are just entertainment, if you know what I mean. She would probably drop them in a hot minute for Ryan."

That explained the PDA by the bulldozer, but it still didn't make me believe she'd been bonking the murder victim. "Okay, what if you add this to it: I saw Ryan put the move on her at the party, and she was visibly grossed out. Caleb and I stayed fairly late, and we both saw her darting and dodging around the room, trying to stay out of Ryan's reach. Did you even see them talking to each other?"

She paused, the French fry in her hand dripping ketchup down her forearm, and thought. "Yeah. I did. A couple of times, but the last one was toward the end of the party. I have no idea what they were saying, but she wasn't running away from him then. I mean, they weren't doing anything inappropriate, but I remember her smiling at him sorta flirty-like. I didn't see Stacey around."

"I think she left about the same time Caleb and I did," I volunteered, not mentioning the circumstances of the departure.

"He was sooo drunk. I wouldn't have been at all surprised to find out he'd passed out on the way to Stacey's parents' house and gotten run over, but getting knifed? That was crazy." She dipped her napkin in her tea and wiped the ketchup off her arm. "Valonda's not crazy. I know they arrested her, but I guess I don't really think she did it."

I agreed immediately. Inside, though, I was not as sure as I'd been before the unexpected appearance of the jeweled salamander the previous afternoon. Something precipitated Valonda's expression in that online picture. That flirtatious smile had just been corroborated by Christie's observations. What information was I missing? If I learned more, would it establish Valonda's innocence or lead me to believe Boots had the right suspect after all?

SET-UP HAD BEGUN for a fall festival along Main, so I took one of the side streets out to the highway. It carried me by Tennie's long, low ranch-style home, and she was out in the front yard watering the mums with a garden hose. I waved, and she sprang into action, gesturing and yelling at me to stop.

I got out of the car and said, "What's going on? This is an Ernestine Greener's caramel cake level of excitement."

"You're not going to *believe* what just happened." She stopped and looked at me expectantly.

"Am I supposed to guess?"

"You'll *never* guess."

"Any chance you're going to tell me?"

"Dinah Morrison was *murdered*. They've just identified her body."

My stomach did a nasty flip and landed at my feet. "Oh my gosh, that's horrible. How awful for her parents and her little boy."

"I know. All this time people thought she'd done another runner, and the poor thing was lying dead in a swamp. I guess we're all too willing to believe the worst," she said. "Well, the worst would have been that she was dead, I suppose, and we didn't think that, but it was unkind to believe she left her little boy. And I was unkind along with everybody else; I'm not a bit better."

She turned and got me with the hose. "Sorry. I guess I'm distracted."

I took off my loafer and poured water out of it, balancing on one foot until I could slip it back on. "That's okay. I'll dry. Do they have any clues yet?"

"Not that I've heard. It must have happened right after she went out of town. They found the body over a week ago but have just been able to identify it. Her parents had delayed reporting her as missing, because they thought she would turn up back home. I think they're feeling awfully guilty."

"That's understandable, but it probably wouldn't have made a difference. Now neither she nor Ryan are here to tell the truth about Danny."

THE FIRST CHURCH of the Devil's Destruction sported a new message on its sign, and I noticed an electrician out front installing flood lights. I guess the preacher decided we needed to read his missives at night, since the daytime instructions weren't working so well.

## A HALF TRUTH IS A WHOLE LIE

That one could be subject to argument in my opinion, but I couldn't help but feel that the Reverend Nelson's latest bon mot might be easily applied to his daughter. I didn't think I'd heard the truth about that brooch, and most likely Boots hadn't either. If Gideon and Silas were counting on me to help, then I had to talk to their sister. Since I knew the jail didn't let just anyone waltz in to see the prisoners, I'd have to come up with a way to get in, short of getting arrested myself.

I spent the rest of the drive home mentally going through old "I Love Lucy" plots but was unable to some up with anything that could be adapted to gain entrance to the Sebastian Parish jail. Tennie is the closest thing I have to an Ethel Mertz, but I didn't dare call her for suggestions. She might tell me to scale the brick wall at midnight, and I'm afraid I'd do it. She's very persuasive.

Since I didn't know the motive for Valonda's supposed crime, I decided to look for someone else with a motive. Where to start? It had to be someone who was at the dance. Proximity taken care of, I thought of motive. Ryan had made so many people angry that night. I could hardly start calling everyone who'd attended and asking just how mad they'd been on a scale of one to ten.

Parker Burns made the comment that guys might line up outside the dance to punch Ryan on the way to his car. What if there was someone whose anger wouldn't be satisfied with slamming a fist into his jaw?

I MADE MYSELF a real dinner. No cereal, no peanut butter and jelly sandwich, but a healthy meal that I wouldn't be ashamed to admit I'd eaten. I roasted a farm-raised chicken (not my farm), with garlic and onions and threw some new potatoes into the bottom of the pan. Clotille had made a pot of fresh mustard greens from her garden and brought me some, and I broke down and baked a small cast-iron skillet of cornbread. It's about as fattening as Clotille's biscuits, but you can't eat greens without cornbread in this part of the country. Once again I thought of eating such a meal in Houston, and figured not only had I just saved thirty dollars, I also had chicken left over for enchiladas later in the week.

By the time I cleaned the kitchen and swept the floor, I admitted that the process of eating in a restaurant and walking right out the door afterward just might be worth the thirty dollars. Montrose and I went to the living room and snuggled together on the couch while Lafitte muttered to himself. I put Wheel of Fortune on mute and called my boyfriend.

"Caleb? Could I talk you into doing me a really big, important favor?" I used a voice that I hoped was persuasive, but probably just sounded wheedling and whiney.

"I don't know. The tone of your voice is setting off alarm bells. Maybe I should hang up."

Okay, definitely not persuasive. "Do you ever talk to Parker Burns?"

"No, but we discussed playing tennis when we were at the party. Why?"

This could work. "Did you set a date to play?"

"And that brings us back to why."

"You have a suspicious nature. I never realized that about you; it's been hidden for a whole month."

"I'd prefer to call it an instinctive masculine sense of self-preservation. Now tell me, what sort of information do you want me to extract from Parker?"

"You're either too smart for feminine wiles, or I'm not experienced at using them, so I'll just go ahead and ask. Do you remember what Parker said at the party about guys being lined up in the parking lot to punch Ryan?"

"I do remember, but he said 'punch'. He didn't say anything about anyone stabbing him," said Caleb.

"But maybe there was someone there who had a real grudge against him, more than the guys who were mad about him hustling their wives and dates. Maybe he knows who it could be, and you could sort of casually get it out of him. That would be extremely helpful."

"Extremely helpful to whom? Did Boots deputize you? Did I miss the ceremony? I want to see the badge."

"I'm not official, but I did promise Silas and Gideon I'd try to help. I can't get into the jail to talk to Valonda, so I'm reduced to following tiny little leads that Boots might not consider."

Caleb cleared his throat. "Tiny little leads. I didn't know they made a Detective Barbie."

"In case you meant that as an insult, I'll admit to having a Barbie collection that Mattel would be proud of. Will you do it?" I asked.

"Okay," he said, without enthusiasm, "if I can come up with a way not to sound like an idiot, and if this is the only thing you're going to ask me to do."

THIRTY MINUTES LATER my phone rang. I looked at the caller ID before answering, as I still hadn't assigned a ringtone to Caleb. That was a two months of dating thing, not one.

"Hey, you wonderful guy, did you already talk to him?"

"Yeah, and thanks to you, I now have a tennis match set up for Sunday afternoon. So much for spending the day in your swing with a glass of tea and the New York Times online," he said.

"There's a cold front coming in," I answered. "Perfect weather for tennis, not so much for porch-sitting. Come on, get to the point. What did he say?"

"Parker adm\itted he may have overestimated the number of potential assailants. He and Jason were probably the only people there who were really mad enough to punch him, and he overindulged on beer, too, just like the victim. His wife took him home and tucked him in before Ryan even left the gym. Jason left early to drive back to Shreveport so he could take the kids to Sunday School the next morning. You're gonna need to take your tiny little magnifying glass and search for more tiny little clues elsewhere."

"Thanks for your alibi-gathering. I'll feed you Mexican food and a tiny little margarita later in the week."

His mood perked right up. "Great, I can be there at a moment's notice. And make mine *grande*."

# Chapter Twenty-Four

My room is perfect for reading in bed. The bed itself is antique, and if I wasn't so tall I'd need those old-fashioned wooden steps to get up into it like my Aunt Josie did. I have lots of down pillows, and the bedside table has a coaster to protect it from my water glass, or wine as the case may be. Then there's the lamp. Do you know what a Gone with the Wind lamp is? It's one of those Victorian kerosene lamps with the painted glass globes on the top and the bottom. This one has pale pink glass with purple Louisiana wild irises painted on it. It's been electrified, of course, and the bulbs cast a soft glow through the glass. Like I said, the room is perfect for reading. I looked out the window to watch Repentance walking through the pasture, then climbed between the sheets.

The night's choice was a detective story. The newspaper reporter protagonist finagled access to police reports, the coroner's office, and even broke into a suspect's apartment, none of which were likely for an antique jewelry dealer. Oh, and she was dating a police captain, not a computer-whiz goat-farmer. My goat farmer had stepped up to the plate when asked, but he was unlikely to take me on a car chase with sirens and flashing lights. When Ms.

Reporter had someone shoot through her front window, I electronically marked my place and switched over to my custom comics page to clear my mind with a few laughs before I tried to sleep. Having recently had a bit of death-defying excitement myself, I found I didn't like a reminder.

TUESDAY DAWNED CLEAR and sunny. I compensated for my heavy dinner the night before with a bowl of yogurt and a banana. Thirty minutes of yoga and two cups of coffee later I was ready to start work.

People (Frankie) think that my life is free from work because I don't go to an office every day. I guess I'm supposed to be lying around watching soaps and eating Oreos, although I'd prefer popcorn. It's true that I set my own hours, but I can be busy all day long. My internet sales have to be photographed and listed, and require frequent monitoring for questions, or, if I'm lucky, purchases. I look at estates online and make bids myself. There's always new jewelry to be checked and sometimes repaired, and everything has to be appraised and priced.

Those are my excuses for not doing any sleuthing all day, although to be honest, I didn't know where to look next. The Nelson brothers offered no help. Neither Silas nor Gideon could suggest anything I should check out or another possibility for the murderer. They left at dusk, and I wandered into the back yard to watch the stars come out, one of the perks of living in a place without city lights.

I'd just returned to the house when I heard a loud banging on the front door. Unexpected and unnerving, my first instinct was to hide and pretend no one was home. The pounding was then joined by a gruff voice calling my name, and I pulled up some backbone and went to answer.

I opened the door to Reverend First-Church-of-the-Devil's-Destruction Nelson and had a brief, instinct-fueled moment when I almost slammed it in his face and ran up the stairs.

"Miss Wyatt? I'm Terry Nelson. May I come in and speak with you for a moment?"

He sounded normal, but my hand automatically went to my neck. I felt a platinum filigree camphor glass necklace and not the offending cross, and swallowed nervously. I must have been staring at him, because he took pains to be pleasant. It didn't sound like it came naturally. Was this an evangelical visit? I began to tell him I was quite satisfied with being an Episcopalian, but he interrupted.

"I know I got off to a bad start the other day, but I need to talk to you about something important. My wife and I are worried about our daughter."

Well, slap me upside the head with a feather; the surprises just kept coming.

Unlatching the screened door, I ushered him into the living room. I removed the cat's blanket from Uncle Raine's leather recliner and offered him a seat, then ran to the kitchen and brought back two glasses of iced tea. As I handed one to him, I pretended not to notice that he'd flipped the table-top issue of Rolling Stone over to hide the cover picture of Katy Perry. Not a fan, I guess, and the fact that she was a preacher's daughter no doubt lowered her even more in his estimation.

After taking a seat across from him, I said, "Please, Reverend Nelson, tell me what you think I can do. I'm sure you and your wife are sick with worry about Valonda's situation." I wasn't sure at all, in fact; Silas and Gideon left me with the impression that their father had written his daughter off as a bad seed.

He ran his hand through his slicked-back hair and shifted his hefty behind in the chair. I was wearing leggings and a fitted T-shirt, and he averted his eyes from my body. I suddenly wished I was wearing a floor length choir robe, but shook the idea off. I am who I am.

"My daughter is a sinner," he said abruptly. "She strayed from the path of righteousness at an early age. I tried to beat Satan out of her when praying didn't work. All the whippings did was make her more determined to disobey me. She's stubborn as a bulldog, and has been since she was old enough to say 'No'.

"My wife has pointed out to me many times that Valonda has my temperament. I was a rebellious young man until I met Margie, but I didn't truly come to know the Lord until my child was born with a heart defect. God punished me for my wrong-doing, but he saved my baby when I promised to change my life."

I was semi-horrified. "Surely you don't believe God caused a little baby to be born with a life-threatening problem in order to punish you. Surely He would have smitten you more directly, oh, maybe not with something as biblical as leprosy, but, you know, a broken arm or something."

"My wife says that, too." He glared at the floor. "I am guilty of the sin of self-righteousness, but even worse, I've been a bad father."

I didn't know how to respond, but I didn't have to. A beatific smile appeared on his face.

"No more, praise the Lord! Margie and I scraped together the money for Valonda's bail, and she will be free tomorrow. I just need you to agree to help her get out of this pickle. My child may be a sinner, but she did not commit murder. I believe God has delivered you to us so that she can prove her innocence and take up the path of righteousness. There is still time for her to repent. "

Omigosh. Really. Omigosh. Why does this family think I'm Sherlock Holmes? Has anyone anywhere seen me in a deerstalker hat or even a Murder She Wrote pastel suit and scarf? "I sell jewelry, Reverend Nelson. I'm not qualified to clear suspicion from your daughter. That's a job for law enforcement."

"Girl, you got your own self out of a mess last month. You told Silas and Gideon you would help. I'm offering to pay you whatever it takes."

That addition was really upsetting, as was the look that implied I was trying to pull a fast one on him. Surely Louisiana has laws regarding private detectives, maybe even including training and qualifications, two areas that were not covered in my art history degree. I'd have to Google that.

"I won't take a penny. I'll ask around, and perhaps I'll turn up some ideas. Nothing more," I said firmly. Maybe I could get him out of my living room with a vague promise. "One thing in her favor is she's too tiny to stab someone as strong as Ryan. I can't imagine a jury believing she was capable of committing that particular crime."

He thought about it for a minute, then said, "A lot of folks around here will remember the article the Shreveport paper did about her when she was ten and killed an eight point buck. The reporter was more surprised that she field dressed it herself than he was that she'd shot it. The girl can handle a knife."

I'm pretty sure I just stood there with my mouth hanging open; I can't recall saying a word in response. He gave me a thin smile.

"Well, Miss Wyatt, we'll be grateful for anything. She's our girl, and we love her." He stood to leave but paused with his hand on the doorknob and a smarmy smile on his face. "And by the way, I do apologize for my harsh words about your fancy necklace."

I watched his taillights vanish down the driveway and marveled at his seeming transformation. I remained skeptical of the depth of his regret, however, even though the Lord does truly move in mysterious ways. I'd think about Valonda's knife skills later.

# Chapter Twenty-Five

I MET VALONDA in her half of a small duplex the next afternoon. She lived in an older, well-kept neighborhood of modest homes. The wood-framed house sat close to the sidewalk, its cherry red shutters almost hidden by overgrown holly bushes. I noticed a white-haired woman peeking out the window in the other half of the house. She jerked the curtain closed when our eyes met, and I gave an inadvertent smile. She probably went directly to her phone to spread the news that her neighbor had an unfamiliar visitor. I glanced at the house across the street and saw another face duck out of sight.

"Annalee. Come in; Daddy said you might be by today."

I stepped into a tastefully decorated living room and once again found myself surprised by how little I knew about my hostess. Mid-century modern, a la Mad Men, was an unexpected find in Berryville, unless it was in a home that just hadn't been redone in sixty years. "I love your furniture," I said, as I sat down on a turquoise sofa that looked like it came out of George Jetson's outer space abode. A blonde wood sculptural coffee table held a Murano glass candy dish, and the lamp on the end table was teak and bronze and about four feet tall.

"Thanks. It belonged to my grandmother, and I'm the only grandkid who liked it," she said. "It's comforting. I used to ride my bike to her house when I got in trouble with my dad."

She brought me the ubiquitous iced tea in a cool sixties glass with swirly gold medallions on the side and sat across from me in an apple green armchair. I'd never seen her without overdone makeup and was struck by how simply pretty she was in her own skin. Ancient looking cut-offs and a faded blue work shirt suited her in a way that a tight, short dress didn't.

"My family thinks you can help get me out of this mess," she said, giving me a doubtful look. She obviously shared my own opinion of my skills.

"Yes, I've gotta say I'm baffled by their opinion, but here I am. Do you have an attorney yet?"

"Someone was appointed by the court, but I haven't seen him since bail was set. We're supposed to meet next week."

"Maybe if we talk things through now, you'll be better prepared to work with him. For starters, do you have any idea why you're even a suspect?"

She slid down in her chair and propped her bare feet on the coffee table, her iridescent red toenails gleaming brightly in the dim afternoon light. "There's no mystery. Stacey hates me. She's had it in for me since high school. She's been blaming other people for Ryan's faults since we were teenagers."

"What kind of faults?" I'd seen evidence of several in my own short acquaintance, but it might be telling to know what others thought. I might have missed some.

Valonda was willing to share. "Bad people made Ryan drink too much, bad teachers gave him grades he didn't deserve, and of course, the biggie: bad girls made him chase them around and cheat on his loyal girlfriend. She never believed that I didn't sleep with him." She scowled. "Maybe I would have if we hadn't gotten so drunk, but I didn't. The coach punished him because he was underage and drinking, not because he was making out with me."

In actuality, the state of undress I saw them in that day ruled out the idea that no hanky-panky at all took place, but I kept my mouth shut. "Was there anything that night at the party that made her jealous?"

Valonda sat up abruptly and leaned across the table toward me. "You were there. You saw what he did to me while she was standing right next to him!"

"I saw it, but it was pretty obvious that you weren't happy about it. I didn't see you trying to entice him with your charms at that point," I grinned.

She grinned back at me. "That would have been a jerk move in high school. I wanted to barf. Why the heck would a thirty-year-old think that was sexy?"

"Arrested development?"

"After my weekend, I don't like the word 'arrested.' We'll just call him a creep. He hustled every girl at the dance, so there should be plenty of murderer possibilities besides me. I saw some husbands who weren't looking at him so friendly."

"People who were at the party posted pictures online. Have you looked at them?" She shook her head. "I have. There's a shot of you and Ryan taken later in the evening, after the kissing incident. I can't say you were enticing him with your charms, but you don't look unhappy at all." All that got was a scowl. No excuse or rebuttal.

I pushed on. "Do you think Stacey saw the two of you? Or perhaps someone told her?"

"There's no crime in talking to someone," she snapped. "That hardly shows that I killed him. In fact, it shows that we were, what you call it, convivial. We were friendly. I thought you were supposed to be helping me, not agreeing with Stacey."

"I am trying to help. You need to take a realistic look at how things appear. If people think the two of you snuck off together it makes you the prime suspect." That sounded detective-ish. Prime suspect. I reminded myself that I sold jewelry in my other life. "*Did* you sneak off together?"

"No, but whether we did or didn't, I didn't kill him!"

That sounded like a yes to me. Stacey's suspicions were unfortunately sounding more legitimate.

As Valonda continued to sulk, I set my glass on a coaster and steepled my fingers together under my chin. Things were about to get serious. "Why did you come into the Blossom and ask me about Stacey's pin?" I raised my brows like an actress for effect.

Her blue eyes narrowed and her expression took on a speculative cast. I'd taken her by surprise.

"I thought it was pretty. I just wondered how much it would cost to buy one."

"Buy one?" I asked. "Or sell one?"

*Now* she was surprised. "Where would I get a pin like that to sell?"

"That's an interesting question. Boots brought one to me for identification and appraisal the same day he took one from under your pillow. I'd stake my reputation on the fact that it was Stacey's."

Her face blanched magnolia white, then flushed as red as the Murano candy dish on the table. I wondered how green she could turn if she was nauseated and hoped I'd never find out. When she realized I wouldn't make things easier for her, she finally began to talk.

"Ryan gave it to me, like I told Boots. We were standing in the middle of the dance floor; I'm sure someone must have seen us," she said, with an outward thrust of her chin. "Unless you can find them, you'll have to take my word for it."

"And he got it . . . how?" I asked. "It was pretty firmly attached to Stacey's dress earlier in the evening."

"He said she didn't want it anymore. Maybe she only needed it for the reunion."

This time my brows rose of their own volition. "Even the Dawsons wouldn't spend $3000 on a piece of jewelry to wear for a few hours. How did it really wind up in your bedroom?"

"I found it on the floor of the athletic building, near the gym door." There went that chin again.

"And you never even spoke to Ryan about it? He didn't know you found it?"

Silence.

"Why on earth would you claim he gave it to you?"

"Because if I said I found it, they'd have made me give it back," she yelled, as if it were the most obvious thing in the world.

I closed my eyes and rubbed my temples. I could feel a major headache approaching like a March tornado. "So instead you implicated yourself in something that suggests a close relationship with a murder victim. Did you think about that when Boots pulled the box out from under the sheets?"

Silence.

"What did you plan to do with the information I gave you? You played a poor, pitiful jewelry-deprived girl that day. 'Woe is me, I'll never have anything pretty', and you'd had her pin since before her husband was murdered."

"That is *not* nice."

"You're right, it isn't, but I told you I was an amateur from the beginning. Now tell me why you wanted all the details the day after Ryan's body was discovered."

She ran her fingers through her hair and pulled it down to partially cover her face. "I wanted to know if I could ever afford to buy one for myself," she said, from behind a curtain of tangled locks. "If I could, then I thought I'd return it to Stacey. But I'll never make enough money to spend $3000 on something to wear once in a while just because it's beautiful, so I talked myself into keeping it even though I knew I shouldn't."

"Oh, Valonda. Not a good move." I sank back into the couch, relieved at her confession. Her thinking was convoluted and decidedly wrong, but understandable, at least to me. The pull of the pretty is a strong thing.

# Chapter Twenty-Six

IT WASN'T EVEN two o'clock when I left Valonda's house, so I decided to head into the big city for a Target run. I was low on foundation and sunscreen, plus I wanted some granola for my yogurt. I ran by the pet supply store first to get food for my menagerie, then drove across the street to the Super Target.

Thirty minutes later I'd acquired a basket full of impulse items, in addition to oat and almond granola and 70 SPF sunblock, and I steered my shopping cart into the clothing aisle. My stock of long-sleeved T-shirts was looking frayed around the edges, and with the cooler weather, I realized most of them needed to be moved into the "at home only" section of my closet.

I walked around a standing display and ran face-to-face into Stacey Dawson.

"Oh, hi, Annalee," she said listlessly.

"Hi, Stacey. This is probably a stupid question, but how are you doing?" I was sincerely concerned, because the contrast between how she looked at the funeral and how she appeared today was striking. The face that on Saturday reflected unimaginable sadness now looked disinterested in life.

"Not good. My mom just about forced me to come up here today and get some clothes. She said I've been wearing the same things for over a week, and she needed a change of scenery. She's over in the grocery section. She didn't trust me to drive myself."

I noticed she had some slacks, underwear, and a pair of shoes in her basket. "Are you planning to stay in Berryville?" I asked politely.

She gave a long sigh. "I'll have to go back to Nacogdoches eventually, but I don't know when I'll be able to stand it. My next door neighbor is keeping the dog for me; he was Ryan's hunting dog anyway, and he probably doesn't miss me at all."

"All of the out of town visitors are gone?"

"Finally," she said emphatically. "I was so tired of having to talk to people when all I wanted to do was lock myself up in my room. I didn't think the Crocketts would ever leave. They're nice people, but we aren't close enough for me to want to be around them all week long."

So count the widow as one of the folks who thought the Crocketts were too attentive. I felt guilty about what I was about to ask, but I might not get another chance. "I know you won't start healing until they figure out who committed this awful crime. I heard they'd arrested Valonda Nelson. Do you really think she did it?"

Suddenly she had some color back in her face, and her eyes flashed with conviction. "I don't have any doubt at all. She's been after him for years—she got him drunk in high school and the coach wouldn't let him play the championship game. You remember, you were there! You saw the two of them together."

So someone did remember my role in the scene, after all, even if that someone put a weird spin on who was at fault.

She continued. "I saw her flirting with him at the homecoming party. You were standing with us when she enticed him to kiss her right in front of me."

"You mean when he turned around and saw her and kissed her on the ear?" I asked carefully.

"Exactly! She gives off pheromones," she said, as if it were a medical fact.

"Is there any other reason that you think she's guilty?"

"I found out yesterday that she had my pin. The alligator with the emeralds. Sheriff Lacasse said it was in her bedroom, and she had the nerve to claim Ryan gave it to her. Boots called me into the office to identify it."

I busied myself searching the stacks of shirts for a black one in my size, as if I weren't hanging on to every word. "I don't understand. You were wearing it that evening, not Ryan. Does she claim he took it from you and gave it to her?"

A tear formed at the corner of her eye. "We had a fight before I left. I took it off and made a big deal of pinning it to his lapel; I only bought it to please him, anyway. If he did give it to her, it was for services rendered," she insisted.

After a few more words, we parted ways to finish our shopping. I was more confused than ever. One five-minute conversation with Stacey left me wondering if anything Valonda told me that afternoon was true.

MY PHONE RANG on the drive back home, and I saw Tennie's name on caller ID.

"Hoyt's still out of town. You want to come over for an early dinner? We can have wine and pimiento cheese sandwiches in the sunroom."

"Your famous home-made pimiento cheese?"

"I'm not going to serve you store-bought. I got tired of eating cereal for dinner, so I whipped up another bowl after the funeral yesterday."

"I'll be there in twenty, but I'll need to put my ice cream in your freezer."

Tennie and Hoyt live in the middle of Berryville, which, considering the size of our town, means they're also close to the outskirts of Berryville. The brick home is painted a pale celery, and the lawn is bordered with neat flowerbeds, mostly in tones of red, interspersed with precisely placed shrubbery. It's on a generous two acre lot, as are most of the surrounding homes. I know from past comments that she expects her neighbors' horticultural efforts to meet her own high standards, and is willing to let them know when she feels they've failed. Much as I like her, I'm glad there are a few miles between us. My yard might drive her nuts.

She's such a vibrant character that you'd expect crazy patterns and intense colors when you step through the front door, but the home is decorated in about ten different shades of cream, with a little beige thrown in for excitement. I slipped off my shoes before I stepped onto the ivory carpet, then walked through to the kitchen where I put the ice cream away.

My hostess placed a glass of wine in my hand, and I followed her into the sunroom. I'd never seen it before, and was startled to observe bold Hawaiian style upholstery in shades of red, orange, and bright green. A three foot tall papier-mâchè macaw hung amid a thriving group of tropical pot plants, as if in his native jungle habitat. I dropped into a lemon yellow glider and put my wine on a glass-topped table.

"I'll bet your parrot is quieter than Lafitte," I said.

"He doesn't molt feathers all over the room, either," she answered, "although I dare say Lafitte is more entertaining."

"What's the news? And did Hoyt get lost at sea? I thought he was coming home Sunday."

"He called and asked if he and Hubert could stop at Toledo Bend for a few days and do some freshwater fishing. I guess they caught all the ones that were swimming in the Gulf of Mexico. The two of them are trying to make up for all the fishing time they've missed through the years. Neither one of them would ever take a vacation from work, but now that Hubert's son-in-law has signed on at the stockyard, those two old men are ready to cut loose and have some fun. As long as it involves fish, that is."

"Good for them."

"I can't believe I'm saying this, but I'm ready for him to come home. My sister-in-law even misses Hubert. They're only an hour away now, but the fishing camp they're staying at will clean, fillet, and freeze their catch, which we wives refuse to do. I'll share some with you when they get back to town."

"So I'm here because you're lonesome?"

"That, and for a little gossip. I thought we could trade information. I heard you were at Valonda Nelson's this afternoon," she said. A satisfied grin spread across her face when I looked at her in astonishment.

"Don't tell me you're surprised that I know. I won't believe you."

"It was just four hours ago. How on earth did you find out about it?"

"Hoyt and I own the duplex she rents. Her next-door neighbor called me the minute you went in the door. She's convinced Valonda is a cold-blooded killer, and was worried you wouldn't come out alive. She's been trying to get me to evict her since the arrest on Saturday."

"She was worried about my safety? Even though I'm twice Valonda's size?"

"Heck, Ryan was three times her size. If she could do him in, you'd be easy."

"Maybe not, since I was sober at one in the afternoon."

"There's that," agreed Tennie. "But I am dying to know why you went over there."

I debated whether or not to tell her the truth. I felt a little ridiculous admitting I was acting as an amateur detective. If anyone knew I wasn't qualified, it was the diminutive woman sitting across from me. Our efforts at sleuthing the previous month had gotten me into a mess of trouble. Then again, I could use someone to bounce ideas off. I made a quick decision to come clean.

"This will sound crazy, but Valonda's brothers asked me to look around and see if I could find out anything that would help her." I waited for her reaction before telling her about the Reverend Nelson.

"Silas and Gideon are good boys. I'm glad they came up with the money to bail their sister out of jail."

Strange, but she wasn't shocked by their request for my assistance. I continued. "They didn't post bail. Their father did, and he showed up at my place last night with the same purpose as his sons. They all seem to believe I can help."

"You gotta be kidding me."

Now she was shocked. "That's how I feel, too. But there is a jewelry tie-in, so at least I'm qualified for that part." I then gave her the basics on the demantoid brooch.

"So how did she really get the thing?" she asked when I finished the tale. "Somebody is lying."

"It's wacky. She tells me that she found the brooch and lied to Boots about Ryan giving it to her, because she thought she'd have a better claim to keeping it. But now I've found out it had really been in Ryan's possession at the dance, and I don't know what to believe. She skittered around the suggestion that the two of them had spent some alone time together that night. Maybe he did give it to her, in private rather than on the dance floor. That admission would put the two of them together, possibly outside, at some point. I've been so convinced she isn't the guilty party, but maybe I'm wrong."

"This is giving me a headache," said Tennie.

"I had one by the time I left Valonda's. My conversation with Stacey didn't cure it."

"You interviewed Stacey, too?"

"I didn't interview her," I said, defensively. "I saw her at Target, and we spoke to each other. That's how I found out she'd given the brooch to Ryan before going home. She said she pinned it to his lapel when they had a fight about him drinking too much and chasing all the women at the party. I think Caleb and I listened in on their argument from somewhere in the middle, because we didn't overhear anything about the pin."

"Wait a minute. This is the first you've told me about a fight. Don't hold out on me. Did Stacey sound mad enough to get violent?"

"That's the big question. I don't know. We watched her walk home alone, but I suppose she could have left the house and come back to the school. Perhaps her insistence on Valonda's guilt is a means to deflect attention away from herself, and maybe she's been so torn up about the death because she regrets her actions. It sounds far-fetched, but it's a possibility."

# Chapter Twenty-Seven

We moved to the breakfast room table for our dinner of pimiento cheese on whole wheat, thinly sliced apples, and carrot sticks. A cut-glass plate covered with lemon teacakes sat within easy reach. I'd made the switch from wine to a tall glass of water, poured from a crystal pitcher. I loved the touch of refinement and wished I was willing to put out the effort at my own home. "Tennie, do you put the milk for Hoyt's cereal in a pitcher every morning?"

"Of course. That's the way his mama did it. I learned a few things from her, including how to be a good mother-in-law."

"You were lucky to have a nice one. You hear horror stories."

"Who said she was nice? She was a witch till the end—she died still believing he married the wrong woman. No, I do most things completely opposite from the way she did, and it's worked out fine."

She took a bite of sandwich and dabbed her mouth with a monogrammed linen napkin. "There's news about Dinah, although most of it's still a mystery."

"What did you hear and who from?"

"I played bridge with my usual group today, and Pete's wife, Hildy, told us Dinah's parents had been in touch with the Dawsons. They sent some baby pictures of Ryan to them, and everyone agrees the resemblance is unmistakable. They plan to do DNA tests; the Dawsons sent them some of Ryan's hair by overnight courier."

"Gosh, they're moving fast. Stacey didn't say anything about that today."

"It's a messy situation," said Tennie. "Hildy doesn't think anyone has told Stacey, but she herself sat there and spread the news to seven women this afternoon. I'd call it ill-advised, but that cat's out of the bag now. It won't be long before it's scratching at the Sawyers' front door."

I RETURNED HOME to find the painters had finished their work. The scaffolding was dismantled and gone, and an envelope containing the final bill was folded and tucked through the door handle. I opened it and was surprised to see a ten percent discount from our agreed upon price. As that was certainly connected to their request for my non-existent sleuthing abilities, I resolved to pay them the full amount I'd been quoted. I'd taken on their challenge willingly with no expectation of remuneration. Plus I still hadn't looked at state licensing requirements for private investigators, and according to Valonda, jail wasn't a place I'd like to visit.

The first thing I did upon entering the house was head to the kitchen and chop some vegetables for Lafitte. I placed some carrots and raw collard greens in his bowl, and he responded with an out-of-tune version of R-E-S-P-E-C-T. Aretha Franklin needn't worry about the competition. Pudge yodeled in anticipation as I filled his bowl, and Montrose merely gave me her usual look of condescension before lowering her head to nibble her kibble.

An email check came next on the agenda. Most of my friends do everything on their phones these days, but since so much of my correspondence involves pictures of jewelry, I prefer to rely on my laptop, or if I'm traveling, a tablet. One of the first messages I opened was from Janice Smith, the jewelry saleswoman in Nacogdoches. She sent multiple photos of a local estate she'd been asked to appraise, and asked if I wanted to look at any of the pieces.

Did I ever. The photos weren't of the best quality, but I could tell at a glance it would be worth my time to drive over and see the items in person. I shot her a reply asking if I could come the next day, and she quickly responded in the affirmative.

I then contacted Caleb and the Lacasse duo. It was time for me to come through on my margarita promises, and I remembered driving past a great-looking Mexican grocery when I was last in Nacogdoches. I could pick up some fresh tortillas and make enchiladas with my leftover chicken. If I plied Boots with Mexican food and tequila, there's no telling what I'd learn about the investigation.

My first cup of coffee the next morning gave me the bright idea to take Tennie with me to the jewelry store. She would provide lively company for the drive, and the trip would help her pass the time till Hoyt came home. She sounded sleepy when I called, but agreed to be ready in an hour.

Clotille waved from her living room window as I drove past, and I could see the TV flickering in the background. Now that the weather was cooler, she spent her mornings watching game shows. I'm glad she wasn't out in the yard like she usually is. I'd have stopped to talk to her and might have let slip that Tennie and I were going on the road. She considers Tennie a bad influence. When she and Aunt Josie got into trouble together, Clotille was loyal enough to cast all the blame on Tennie. I'm not sure that was accurate, but I can't deny she and I have had our moments already in our relatively short friendship.

It was a chilly day with the promise of rain. The first drops fell as I rounded the curve into town, and as I passed the First Church of the Devil's Destruction, I saw Reverend Nelson putting the last letters of a new saying on the sign. Maybe Valonda would take the message to heart.

FREEDOM IS NOTHING BUT A CHANCE TO BE BETTER

I slowed for the school crossing even though it was less than five minutes till the flashing yellow lights turned off. The pile of leaves that had hidden Ryan from view was long since cleared away, and there was no outward evidence that any crime had taken place there. Maybe I would eventually be able to drive past without remembering that afternoon.

Tennie was not watching at the window for me as I'd expected, so I parked the car and went to the door. I wasn't prepared for the sight that greeted me. The older woman was dressed more casually than I'd ever seen her, in neat jeans and an LSU purple and gold pullover sweater, but the shocker was her hair. Her black, shot-with-silver tresses hung long and thick down to her shoulders.

"I've never seen you with your hair down, even on that day last month when you showed up at my door in camouflage. I guess I thought you were born with a French twist."

She giggled. "I'm having trouble getting myself together this morning. Hoyt came in late last night." She giggled again. "I'm going to send him off more often. We were awfully glad to see each other."

"Too much information," I grinned. "Throw a scrunchie around it, and let's hit the road."

A LITTLE OVER an hour later we pulled into downtown Nacogdoches, and I drove straight to the jewelry store. "I didn't expect to see you so soon, Janice, but I appreciate the opportunity to look at what you have. Thanks again for calling me." I introduced Tennie and began to examine the jewelry.

"The Crocketts are back in town," Janice volunteered. "I saw him walking into the courthouse this morning. I imagine he has a lot of work to catch up on."

I'm afraid I barely acknowledged her comment, because I couldn't tear my eyes or my attention away from the estate pieces arrayed before me. The quality and variety of the jewelry was mind-boggling. "Who did these belong to? Your email just mentioned a local owner, but these certainly weren't purchased locally, and not even in Texas, I'd guess."

"You've heard of Spindletop?"

"The old oil field down around Beaumont?"

"That's the one. Texaco and Gulf Oil both got their starts there around the turn of the last century. This elderly woman's father was tied into the discovery in some way. The wells didn't produce for more than thirty-five or forty years, but my goodness, they made some people rich. Her mother supposedly took off for Europe and spent the money just about as fast as the oil was pumped into the barrels here in Texas, and for a small town girl, she had excellent taste."

"No kidding." I picked up an Edwardian cat's eye, or chrysoberyl, brooch. The central green stone was surrounded by six diamonds of at least a carat each, interspersed with smaller ones. "This was made in England; you can see the British hallmarks," I said, for Tennie's benefit. Next my eye was drawn to a retro rose gold bracelet set with one ruby per link. "This is French, from the 1950s." The whole thing probably weighed four ounces. You'd build muscle just wearing it while you ate dinner. These bracelets were nearly always hollow, but this seemed to be solid. My hand lingered over a ring with a trio of two carat diamonds set in platinum, then moved unerringly to an enamel and pearl choker.

"My gosh, Janice, this is a Lalique *collier de chien*, or dog collar necklace, from the early 1900s. The last time I saw anything this fine it was in a museum." I held the choker up to my neck and admired myself in the mirror. The central piece, made of intricately modeled gold roses set among green enamel leaves, was perhaps two inches tall and several inches long, and curved to fit against the neck. Ten strands of seed pearls were attached at either side to form the remainder of the necklace.

"Women were thinner back then," said Tennie. 'You'd have to be a tall skinny model to wear that now. You could maybe pull it off."

"I'm not sure that was a real compliment, but for enough money a removable extender could be added to the back without hurting the value of the piece. Or the central piece could be placed on a wide velvet ribbon; that's also traditional." I placed it reverently back in its box. "I can't get over walking into a store in the Piney Woods of east Texas and finding such a collection of showpieces."

"You'd be surprised," said Janice. "There's no telling what's in safe deposit boxes and under beds and in cookie jars around here. I'll bet Bonnie Everett has a lot of real nice jewelry that never gets worn. She is the only child of an old pioneer family that made its money in cotton and timber. Everett grew up poor and proud, and still carries a chip about it on his shoulder. He only wants her to wear things that he bought her. Isn't that stupid? And to make matters worse, I don't think he's bought her very much."

"Somehow I'm not surprised by that," I said.

"That man's got terrible taste in clothes," Tennie chimed in. "I'd hate to see what he thought was pretty in jewelry."

I made an offer for the lot, which included taking many of the pieces on consignment. I also suggested that the family might want to consider contacting one of the big auction houses, considering the rarity of some of the items. Janice steered us to a nice restaurant on the square for lunch while she called the family, and Tennie and I went back out in the rain.

# Chapter Twenty-Eight

THE RESTAURANT WAS a pleasant surprise. The owners had turned an old pharmacy into an upscale casual eatery. A polished bar made use of the wooden counter behind which a pharmacist once compounded and dispensed medicine to the local clientele. Original Hunter fans hung from the ceiling, and cozy booths lined in striped blue linen ran alongside red brick walls. We were ahead of the lunch crowd and were shown to a booth near the front window, where we could see out to the drizzly square.

Our waitress was an older woman, friendly and competent. We chose hot soup as starters and relaxed into the warm comfort of the restaurant. Since I was facing the window, I was first to see the young couple that came in and sat in the booth behind us. Tennie cocked her head to the side and peeked as inconspicuously as she could manage.

"What do you think?" she asked quietly.

"The same thing you do," I answered. "The resemblance can't be coincidence."

Just then the waitress approached their booth, and our suspicions were confirmed. "Well, if it isn't the Crockett kids. I haven't seen the two of you in here together without your parents in years. Iced tea to start with? Sweet for you, right, Neill?"

She went off to get their drinks, and I heard the woman say, "It won't be long till the folks find out we had lunch together."

"Don't worry about it. Mom will be thrilled, and Dad won't be interested."

Tennie mouthed "*Can you hear?*" from across the table. I nodded yes.

The woman replied. "You're probably right. It isn't like we have to skulk around, but I didn't want to have this conversation over the phone, or, heaven forbid, by text."

"I'm still not sure what you're upset about. They seem like they're just rocking along as usual, Dad at work and Mom with her volunteering. What's different?"

"Something changed around the time they came back from the Dawson funeral. Mom's more unhappy than usual."

"You don't think it's just because her favorite son's dead?"

"Now, Neill, don't say favorite. You know she loves you a little bit more. But I have wondered if it's because she's afraid her favorite *daughter* will move out of town." I could almost hear the grin in her voice and decided I'd like to know her. She must take after her mother.

The waitress brought their tea and our soup, and left after taking their order. I devoted more time to eavesdropping than I did to eating.

Neill continued. "How did this happen, Tina? Why did they get so attached to those two? It's odd enough that I've had several people mention it to me."

"You and I are busy with our lives and families, and Ryan and Stacey moved to a town where there was no one they knew. I think our parents were flattered that a young couple was willing to spend a lot of time with them. It wasn't up to me to say they were using Mom and Dad for social climbing. But something must have happened, because Mom is absolutely furious at Dad. I went by the house yesterday afternoon and found her moving all his clothes into your old room."

"Did you ask her why? Maybe she just needs more space in her closet. Heck, maybe he needs more room; he's bought a lot of questionable clothes lately."

"That's what she said, but she put his pillow in there, too. You know he hauls that nasty old thing with him every time he leaves town. Also, all his toiletries, including some gosh-awful new cologne, are now in your bathroom. Mom was outwardly calm, but she had that look in her eyes, you know, the one that sent us running to our rooms when we were little before she said a word."

"She'll probably get over it. He'll be in the doghouse for a few days and then argue himself back into her good graces."

"I've saved the worst for last. As I left, a locksmith drove up. He said he was there to install a deadbolt on the master bedroom door."

"Wow." There was silence for a long moment before he continued. "You've got me there. I can't explain that one."

"Do you think she caught him in an affair?" asked Tina.

"That self-righteous prig? Every time it happened with a couple they knew, we were treated to his sermon about the sanctity of marriage and family, not to mention the financial fallout that results. He won't even take on divorce cases. If anyone has kept his khakis zipped, it's Mr.

Self-Control. But, I'll go by this afternoon and visit Mom and report back to you. Now tell me how the kids are doing and how you managed to sneak away from work for lunch. And we'll hope that if there's an affair going on, it's Mom's. She deserves some fun."

TENNIE AND I finished our salads and returned to the jewelry store. I was pleased, and quite frankly astounded, to find that the deceased woman's family had chosen me to disperse the entire estate. We tucked the items into the hidey-hole under the floor of the BMW cargo space, and I prayed our trip home would be uneventful.

"Do you realize that we're traveling with hundreds of thousands of dollars' worth of jewelry?" I asked Tennie, as we left the parking lot of the Mexican grocery a few minutes later.

"I wondered why you were grabbing things off the shelves in that store like you were afraid you'd never see another tortilla in your life. You didn't want to leave the car unattended. I'm surprised you didn't make me stay in it to guard the goods."

"You're mean enough, but not big enough, and I don't think you're carrying today."

"Nope, all the guns are at home. Speaking of mean, it sounds like Bonnie Crockett can hold her own with that man she's married to. I've been plenty mad at my husband before, but I never thought to put a bolt on the bedroom door."

"What do you make of that conversation?" I had filled her in on the things she couldn't hear as we drove to the market.

"Eh, I don't believe she's having an affair. She was too patient with him, too concerned with his comfort and well-being. And I can't see him having one because, well, heck, for the same reasons. Who else would treat him the way she does? He's spoiled, although he's probably too self-centered to realize it. Add that to the thought of what his skinny caboose looks like naked, and I'd say the chances are slim to none."

WHEN I GOT home, I immediately put the jewelry in the safe, then went to the kitchen to begin dinner. The weather hadn't improved, but I like being inside my house when it's rainy and cool. It makes me feel snug as a bug. I began prep by weaving my long hair into a braid and donning an apron.

After squeezing a dozen limes, I added most of the juice to equal parts triple sec and white tequila, then put the mixture into the refrigerator. Inspired by Tennie's habits, I opened a jar of salsa and put it in a pretty bowl from the dining room china cabinet, rather than dumping it into a cereal bowl as I usually would. I'd wait and put the chips into a basket right before my guests arrived; the humidity would make them foldable instead of crunchy if I did it too early.

Garlic, onion, and coarse salt went into my molcajete, and I pummeled it into a paste with the stone that acted as a pestle against the volcanic rock mortar. After smashing tomatoes and avocado into the mixture I added the rest of the lime juice, tasted, and put the finished product into the fridge. I'd serve the guacamole straight from the molcajete at dinner.

I can throw together a skillet of Spanish rice with my eyes closed, but for the life of me, I've never successfully produced a decent looking pan of enchiladas. I continue to try, but I never improve. I shredded the leftover chicken and warmed it in a little bit of broth, then prepared to roll the corn tortillas around it. Forty-five minutes later I had a pan full of shredded chicken and shredded tortillas, ugly and unfit to serve even to close friends. I didn't know what to do.

I had a flashback to Saturday afternoon's parade of home cooked food. Chicken enchilada casserole. I mixed in the tomatillo sauce I'd made and covered the whole thing very liberally with Monterrey jack and queso fresco, the Mexican cheese I'd gotten at the Nacogdoches *mercado*. In lieu of funeral food cornflakes, I topped it with crushed tortilla chips. By the time it was out of the oven, I'd have a dish worthy of a church fellowship hall.

# Chapter Twenty-Nine

CALEB WALKED THROUGH the kitchen door as I was stirring Kahlua into melted chocolate for an ice cream topping. I rapped him across the knuckles with my spoon when he tried to stick his finger into the bowl.

"Ouch, woman. I write code with those fingers," he yelped.

"Who's injured?" asked Frankie as she and Boots walked in behind him. "Wait, don't tell me. I'm here as a civilian tonight."

"I just want a margarita," said Boots.

"You got it, Sheriff." I passed around the drinks that were waiting in salt rimmed glasses in the refrigerator. "Let's sit in the living room and socialize until dinner's ready."

Boots claimed Uncle Raine's overstuffed armchair and swung his feet up onto the ottoman with a sigh of relief. "How many of these can I have tonight, Annalee? Frankie is my designated driver."

"As many as you want, but I suggest that you want no more than two. Studies have shown that excessive tequila intake leads to serious regrets."

"This week I've regretted I didn't go to dental school

like my dad wanted. Or become a priest like my grandma wanted."

Frankie reached over from her chair and pinched his cheek. "You weren't cut out for the celibate life, dear."

"What can you tell us about Ryan? Anything?" Caleb picked Pudge up and put him on the couch beside us, and the dog looked mournfully at Boots.

"Other than we made an arrest? What do you want to hear?"

"Do you really really truly think Valonda killed him?" I asked. "Stop scowling at me. You know it's a legitimate question."

Boots cleared his throat and looked at me over the rim of his glass. "I will not tell you if I think she murdered him. I will share the evidence we used to prepare her indictment."

"We're okay with that," said Caleb. "In return, maybe Annalee will tell you what she's found out on her own."

That got me a sharp look from the sheriff, and I got a little hint of how it would feel to be under suspicion. I gave him an innocent smile.

"Valonda was seen leaving the gym with Ryan at the end of the party, and the coroner says the time frame is within the probable time of death."

"I *knew* it," I crowed.

"You knew what, specifically?"

"Never mind. I'll tell you when you're finished."

"Okay. That's opportunity. Next is motive. There are several things that could be part of the equation. They have a history together dating back to high school. Both of them are known for their extracurricular activities involving the opposite sex although there was no forensic evidence to suggest intercourse had taken place before the murder."

Caleb interrupted. "Are you saying you know Ryan messed around after his marriage?"

"Yes, Stacey admitted to me that he had at least one affair during law school. Next there's the piece of jewelry. She says she securely pinned it on Ryan's jacket during their fight before she went home. The clasp is well-made, and has a safety catch to prevent it from coming loose. Quite frankly, she says he was too drunk to undo it himself and too cheap to give it away even if he managed. She thinks Valonda killed him and took it."

"The working scenario has them leaving together, things getting out of hand, and Valonda stabbing him and taking the pin. The murder weapon was a knife with a long, thin blade, possibly a filleting knife, and as I've been told by several people, she's no stranger to the use of a knife."

"It's one thing to be skilled, but quite another to put a fish knife in your purse before you go to a dance," I said.

"True, and that's why we checked out the purse she carried that night. It's not very big, but it's long. I know nothing about handbag fashion, but one of the female deputies says it's called a baguette, like the bread loaf."

"Do you have the weapon?" asked Caleb.

"No. We're still looking. We've searched the area of the murder and turned her house inside out. Nothing has turned up yet."

I decided it was time to bring up the baby thing. "Do you know that Danny Morrison may be Ryan's son? That could be a motive for murder."

"A motive for whom? Dinah was already dead by then, and her parents didn't know. Even if they had, that provided no reason to kill the child's father. It's my understanding Dinah was receiving child support each month."

"Stacey," Caleb and I said in unison, then looked at each other in surprise. If he thought it was possible, I didn't feel so awful saying it out loud.

"Stacey? I have nothing that incriminates her. She's been genuinely grief-stricken, and the two of you are her witnesses that she left without him and went home alone," said Boots.

"Maybe she's grief-stricken because she killed him. And her folks' house is within sight of the gym. She could have gotten a knife from the kitchen and walked back over," I said. "After all, she does think the two of them were having an affair. And who's to say she didn't know about Dinah's baby?"

"I'll admit it's a possibility, but there's no evidence that's what happened," he answered.

Caleb wasn't satisfied. "How about other enemies? Ryan made a lot of people mad that night. Plus he told us about some of the cases he's taken to court, and he represented some real dirt bags. Maybe it was someone mad about that."

"The only person from the party that I can tie to him is Valonda. As for someone affected by his law practice, it's pretty far-fetched that they'd come all the way to Berryville to get revenge."

Caleb's face took on a look of resignation. I knew how he felt. Neither of us wanted it to be Valonda, but we were failing to make a case for another murderer. I heard the oven timer go off and steered the group to the dining room.

"WE'VE SPENT A lot of time talking about Ryan, but what happened to Dinah?" asked Caleb. "Does anyone know why she was so far from home and in such a remote location?"

Boots sipped from his second margarita, then refilled his plate from the Pyrex casserole dish. "I don't know what you call this stuff, but it's good."

"Deconstructed enchiladas. Mexican food as modern art," I said. "Eat some more rice, too. You'll need something to soak up that tequila."

"Works for me. Regarding Dinah, I'm not in charge of that investigation, although the south Louisiana guys are trying to keep me informed. They've also been up here to talk to her parents. So far they think she was killed somewhere in the vicinity of the recovery site, and the body was moved there shortly after death. There are several hunting camps in the area, but the one where she was found isn't in current use. The owner passed away last year, and the heirs are arguing over whether or not to sell the property, because only one of the grandsons hunts. If he hadn't gone by to check on things, she might not have been discovered for months."

"I understand her parents had no idea she'd gone there," I said.

"Not a clue. She told them she was visiting a friend and would return early in the week. It was the first time she left the baby overnight. She drove off in jeans and a sweater, but she was found in some sort of slinky dress with a pair of high heels nearby."

"That's so bizarre. Do you know what day the body was found? I think I might have been in the area." I recounted the experience I had on the drive home from New Orleans, and Boots affirmed that I'd no doubt been there when the recovery effort was proceeding.

"She's believed to have been killed the same day she left Berryville. Law enforcement contacted the friend she was supposed to see, but she says they had no plans to get together that weekend."

I was puzzled. "Where on earth could she have gone in nice clothes in that area? There's no place to dress up. There's nothing down there but small towns, farmland, and swamps."

"Honkey-tonking," said Boots. "Juke joint. There's all kinds of dance halls in that part of the state."

"Spare us the stories of your childhood, bayou boy," said Frankie. "Can they place her at any of them?"

"Yeah, she was at Big Cypress Lounge for an hour that evening. The owner says she was obviously waiting for someone who never showed. She left by herself around ten after getting a text, but her cell phone is missing."

"He remembered all of that? They must not have been very busy," said Caleb.

"Dinah was pretty, and she sat at the bar by herself and made chitchat with the bartender. She was probably the best part of his evening."

Caleb helped me clear the table, and we reconvened in the living room with ice cream and fudge sauce. Lafitte woke from his nap and began to hustle Frankie. "Hey, baby, just a little kiss," he squawked, shuffling back and forth on his perch and bobbing his head in time to imaginary music. "You're lookin' hot! You're makin' me crazy!"

"You haven't put the moves on me like that in years, Boots Lacasse. Listen and learn," she instructed.

"When we finish our desserts, we'll go into the study," I said. "I forgot to tell you about my trip to Nacogdoches today for some prime jewelry-buying. You may never have the chance to see anything of this quality again. There are a couple of pieces that belong in a museum."

"Nacogdoches?" asked Boots. "That reminds me; what have you found out?"

I told him the whole story of Valonda coming into the Magnolia Blossom to query me about the pin she already had in her possession. "So you can see how I would be surprised when you brought it over here for an appraisal."

"That's all?"

Caleb gave me a stern look. He knew I didn't want to admit any other involvement. I had to come clean. "No, that's not all. Valonda's brothers and her parents asked me to see if I could find out anything to exonerate her of murder charges. Don't give me that look, I know I'm not qualified, but I felt sorry for them. After I agreed, I seemed to find myself in situations where people just talked to me with no prompting."

Boots looked skeptical, but allowed me to continue. I told him about Janice Smith's comments about the couple the previous week, then about my visit with Valonda the day she was released from jail on bond. As I related the story she'd told me about finding the brooch on the floor, followed by her unconvincing insistence that she had not spent any time alone with Ryan, I realized how bad things looked for her.

"Then the same day I ran into Stacey. I didn't learn anything new from her, but she does believe her husband and Valonda were having an affair. She gave me no evidence to back it up, but she's convinced it's true, just like she's convinced Valonda killed him."

"Is that all?" asked Boots.

"Pretty much." There was no reason to tell him about the Crocketts' marriage problems; he was working a murder case, not a domestic dispute.

"I'm glad to hear it. I don't want any reports of you sneaking around, listening at doors or peeking through windows. I understand that the Nelsons are concerned, but you're hardly qualified to investigate. Someone was murdered; this isn't a search for lost jewelry."

"Yes, sir. I promise. Now come see my new acquisitions. I'm so excited about them that I'll probably be up all night long doing research."

# Chapter Thirty

AND I WAS. Up all night, I mean. At my age, three a.m. qualifies as all night. I crawled out of bed at nine, having put Pudge out before I crashed, in anticipation of sleeping late. I made a cup of coffee and took some of the new jewelry down to Clotille's house.

She was suitably impressed. "I think you should keep it all. I don't know how you can bear to sell a piece of it."

We were seated at her maple dining table, and she'd thoughtfully refilled my coffee cup and put a lemon tea cake in front of me. "Can you imagine finding these things in a small east Texas town? Where would the owner have worn a Lalique necklace a hundred years ago?"

"Probably not in Nacogdoches," Clotille laughed. "I'll bet the person who spent that much money on something to hang around her neck would want everyone to know what she was wearing. It's not likely her neighbors would realize how special it was. Kind of takes the joy out of flaunting."

"Heck, I'd wear that sucker every day. I'd wash the car in it if I didn't have anywhere to go. Then I'd go inside and stand in front of a mirror."

"Is there any way you can keep it?" she asked.

"It's too much for me. Too much money and too much history. It belongs in a museum, or at least it should be in the collection of someone who wears it once a year. Besides, my demantoid ring is my splurge for the foreseeable future. I'm going home to call my friends in New Orleans. If they don't want it, they can steer me toward the right buyer."

I TEXTED FINN and told him to Facetime me when he had a moment, then returned to my desk in the study. Setting up a lightbox near the window, I prepared to photograph the new pieces. Two pairs of earrings and one pendant later, my computer pinged, and I clicked on accept to take Finn's call.

"Hey, Annalee, what's up; what the HELL is that around your neck?"

"Just a little something I picked up a few days ago," I teased, watching his face come into close-up as if he could peer through his computer camera to see me better. "I couldn't resist putting it on for this conversation."

"Give me the full details," he demanded.

We talked for half an hour, and by the time we finished I'd shown him most of the things in the estate. He was suitably impressed.

"The thing that's most surprising to me is that the estate was intact. It's a wonder it hadn't been split up and sold a long time ago, because most of those items look like they've hardly been worn. You know, we sold something to a woman from Nacogdoches within the last couple of months."

"Would that be the demantoid salamander you mentioned to me when we went out to dinner?"

"How did you know?"

I gave him the whole sorry story, including my role in the discovery of the victim. I then followed with the saga of the brooch itself.

"I remember the woman vividly. She wore enough gold chains to hang a giraffe, and she popped out her credit card like she was purchasing a strand of plastic Mardi Gras beads. There wasn't even a request for my best price. Plus she kept calling it an emerald alligator, and after correcting her three times I just gave up. She bought it; she could call it whatever she wanted. I was surprised the guy with her didn't pay, though. In my experience, when you have a disparity in age and looks like that, money is changing hands in some form or another."

My heart rate picked up. This sounded exceedingly suspicious. "Is there any chance you remember what the guy looked like?"

"An idiot. He was about her height, skinny, early sixties, white hair swooped back from his forehead, and wireframe glasses. His clothes looked like his momma picked them out for class picture day."

"Let me guess. Tight blue jeans, some sort of overdone sports shirt, and boat shoes or perfectly polished leather sneakers without socks."

He whistled. "You got it nailed. How'd you do that?"

"Was he a sour puss? That would complete the picture."

"Totally. He was even whiney with her, and he acted like he knew everything. He must have some redeeming qualities, but they're hidden behind a boatload of annoying ones."

"Stacey, your alligator customer, is the murder victim's wife, and Everett Crockett, the old grouch, was his law partner. Did you see a tall, used-to-be athletic thirty-ish guy or a petite blonde in her early sixties with them?"

"No, they were alone as far as I could tell. There were no obvious displays of affection between the two of them, but I got couple vibes."

"Thanks, Finn. This little bit of information makes a complete muddle of my suspicions."

"Glad to help," he laughed.

LUNCH WAS A peanut butter and banana sandwich, heavy on the local honey. As I was pouring another glass of tea, a text came in from Janice.

*The client found a couple more pieces of jewelry. One is Boucheron and the other is Cartier. Are you interested?*

I spilled tea all over the counter. *Yes! Will be there by three this afternoon!*

Lafitte and Montrose watched me dance through the living room and up the stairs.

IT WAS NEARLY five o'clock by the time I finished my business with Janice, and I had nothing at home for dinner. My company the night before consumed the entire pan of ugly enchiladas, and I wasn't in the mood to cook or eat cereal. I made my way across the town square to the restaurant Tennie and I visited only the day before.

Happy hour was cranking up, and on the way to my booth, I passed behind a line of early drinkers at the carved oak bar. I ordered an arugula salad with grilled shrimp and some tea. I'd peeked at the desserts the day before and planned to save some calories for the caramel banana pudding.

I scrolled through the news on my cell phone, then switched to a fashion site after the political craziness of the day started to get to me. A large, carefully composed salad appeared before me, followed closely by a small, somewhat inebriated Bonnie Crockett. She slid into the booth opposite me without waiting for an invitation, and I immediately noticed the large black opal on her right hand. That hadn't been there at the funeral.

"You look familiar," she said, her speech slightly slurred. "Do I know you from somewhere?"

I smiled. "We met in Berryville. I'm Annalee Wyatt."

She grabbed the linen-wrapped silverware on her side of the table and pointed it at me. "Did you come here to see my hushband?"

Startled by her question, I quickly assured her that my visit to town had nothing to do with Everett Crockett. "I'm an antique jewelry dealer, Mrs. Crockett. I purchased a local estate and came to town today to pick up some more pieces."

"Call me Bonnie," she said, returning the weaponized cutlery wrap to the table. "I have a lot of jewelry."

She extended her right hand for me to more closely view her ring. It was a beautiful 1960s creation with an exceptional opal surrounded by bright emeralds and diamonds. Leaning over the table, she gave me a view of her cleavage that I'm sure she wouldn't have shared if she was sober. She wore a pendant that matched the ring. My favorable comments were met with unasked-for revelations.

"I think I'm going to divorce my hushband. He doesn't like me to wear my jewelry. Jus' a minute." She left the booth and returned with a full wineglass and a friend named Brenda who shared her talkative mood.

The next ten minutes I spent eating my dinner and listening to the two older women trade gossip and jokes about people I didn't know. When I ordered dessert I got their attention once again.

"Oh, what I wouldn't give to eat dessert," sighed Brenda. "I haven't eaten anything sweet since I turned fifty."

My horrified look brought a giggle to her lips along with a confession. "Not really. I should have said I haven't eaten anything sweet without feeling guilty since then."

"Annalee's tall and skinny," Bonnie grumbled. "And she isn't married. I've had someone comment on every bite that went into my mouth for over thirty years."

"You're beautiful, Bonnie. I can't count the number of people in Berryville who said so last week," I answered.

"Everett doesn't think so."

"Okay, this isn't very nice, but I also can't count the people who made negative comments about him. He isn't handling the aging process very gracefully."

Brenda hooted and gave the other woman a high-five. "Order this girl a glass of wine on me!"

I asked for a tea refill instead and questioned Bonnie about her jewelry. "Did I hear you say your husband doesn't want you to wear your beautiful baubles?" I'd already heard that from Janice the previous day, but it was odd enough to warrant further questions.

Bonnie pointed to a perfectly serviceable Seiko watch. "This is the last thing he bought me, fifteen years ago. I have a safe full of gorgeous things I inherited from my mother, but he says a woman's husband should provide her jewelry. It doesn't matter if he's cheap and has bad taste."

"That's a shame," I said. "I get a lot of joy out of wearing my things."

"I think Everett has been providing some joy for another woman, and he thinks little old me is too dumb to figure it out," Bonnie said. "On Sunday I found credit card receipts from a jeweler in Houston. They're for expensive things he hasn't given to me. It's hard to divorce a lawyer and not get screwed over in the process, but I'm getting ready to give it my best shot. There's not a darn thing he can say to make me keep him around if he's been cheating."

She let out a deep sigh. "I wish Stacey would come back to town. Ryan probably knew about it, and maybe he said something to her. She's too sweet to tell me herself. If she does know, I'm sure it's been hard on her to keep quiet."

# Chapter Thirty-One

DUSK WAS FALLING fast when I left Nacogdoches, and I kept my eyes open for deer as I followed the winding country highway. I thought about Bonnie all the way home to Goat Hill. It was uncomfortable to think I might know Everett's jewelry recipient. If Finn's description was accurate, Stacey and Everett had been in the French Quarter together, and my guess was that Ryan and Bonnie were not in the praline store next door to the jewelry shop at the time.

But what if the bits and pieces I'd learned today amounted to a simple coincidence rather than a grand collusion? Everything else pointed to nothing more from Everett than a fatherly interest in both Ryan and Stacey. Only a nutcase would move his wife into his mistress's home for a week after the other woman's husband was murdered. Everett had a successful law practice and a solid professional reputation, and those things weren't associated with bad judgement. I wouldn't be surprised if he was having an affair, but realistically, it probably wasn't with Stacey.

The road from Texas brought me in on the west side of town and required a left turn by Reverend Nelson's church.

## FEAR: FALSE EVIDENCE APPEARING REAL

I resolved to take a very skeptical look at the evidence I'd collected, and considered sending a picture of the signboard to Boots.

A few minutes later I turned into the Goat Hill driveway, dodging mud puddles from yesterday's rain as I drove up the gravel drive. Not that it made any difference; my car was filthy. There was enough dirt on the back windshield to hold a large finger-drawn "wash me."

The lamp left on in the living room spilled a glow out the window and revealed an unusual sight. Repentance stood on the front porch as if awaiting my arrival. When I turned off the engine, he seeped through the screen and disappeared into the darkness. I barely had time to wonder what brought him so close to the house when I heard Pudge moaning his I-have-to-go-right-now noise.

"Sorry, doggy," I apologized, opening the door. "I didn't plan to be gone so long. Repentance was worried about you." I heard my text tone and saw a message from Tennie requesting a phone call.

Tennie has been known to talk for excessive periods of time, so I settled into my favorite chair. My index finger was about to push the call button when my phone rang. "Hi, Gideon. What's up?"

"I was hoping you'd have an answer to that, Annalee. Any news on Valonda's situation?"

"Gideon, I'll be honest with you. While I still don't think she killed Ryan, she's not been truthful with me or the investigators. I've caught her in some outright lies. It doesn't make sense that she's trying to protect the killer, and she's hurting herself by not being truthful."

"I was afraid of something like that," he sighed. "I remember Daddy spanking her and saying she'd tell a lie when the truth would serve her better. I never thought she was perfect, but she isn't a murderer."

"I'll keep looking," I promised, before ending the call. The phone rang again, and this time it was Tennie.

"Where were you today?"

"I went back to Nacogdoches for some more jewelry," I said. "Why do you ask?"

"I saw that car of yours heading west at about two-thirty."

"I have to remind myself how small Berryville is. Of course, the New Orleans area is over a million people, and today I managed to get some interesting information about two tourists that were there a few weeks ago." That statement required a complete explanation, but she moved on to another topic quickly.

"Too bad you didn't stop by the drugstore on your way out of town."

"What did I miss?"

"Valonda and Stacey ran into each other on the hair care aisle. They picked the same day to buy shampoo."

"Don't keep me in suspense. What happened? Were you there?"

"I ran out of hair spray yesterday morning, which is an emergency in our humidity. Lucky for me, it's stocked opposite the Pantene. The two of them were talking low to each other, but I heard every word." She paused, and I heard her open the oven door.

"Sorry, I'm checking on Hoyt's dinner. The rolls aren't quite done yet. Where was I? Oh, yes, I was pretending to read the ingredient list on the L'Oréal can when I heard somebody say, 'You bitch!' and I thought that was strange, because I don't think I've made anyone mad lately, and then I heard 'Don't you call me a bitch, you tramp!' and I thought nobody could accuse me of being a tramp, and then—"

"Wait," I interrupted, confused but fascinated. "Who was calling who which name?"

"Valonda called Stacey the B-word. After Stacey called her a tramp, she also said Valonda killed her husband, and that was a lot worse than just being a tramp. But she upgraded the word 'tramp' to something really vulgar, which I will not repeat, because I am a lady.

"Then Valonda said Stacey probably killed Ryan herself, because she knew about Ryan and Dinah, and then Stacey said that was a dirty lie, that she loved Ryan more than anything and that women were after him all the time and that he didn't have a thing to do with Dinah and she was tired of people whispering about Dinah's little boy and it was all lies, lies, lies." She finally stopped to take a breath.

"I can't believe Valonda started it. She was so reserved around Stacey at the reunion," I said.

"I guess being arrested for murder has toughened her up. Hoyt, dinner's ready!" she called. "I gotta go. I'll talk to you tomorrow."

I WANTED TO call Caleb and ask him over, but it was his turn. Also we weren't at two nights in a row in our dating relationship. I was spared the dilemma when he called me.

"Mom said she saw you driving west out of town today. I just wanted to make sure you came home."

"Your mom should join Tennie on the Homeland Security payroll. I can't make a move without that woman noticing."

"No need for that; they're both on my payroll. I'm worried that you're partaking of the Sebastian Parish wild lifestyle. Lafitte's reports only apply to what goes on in the house."

"The news of me heading toward Nacogdoches hardly merits a press release, though it's flattering you're interested."

"Mom said you missed a to-do in the parking lot of the drugstore."

"Let me guess; it involved Stacey and Valonda."

"The Berryville grapevine strikes again. How did you know?"

"Tennie. She overheard a disagreement between the two of them in the store. It must have carried out to the parking lot. Did your mom hear anything?"

"They were trading accusations of murder and infidelity. Mom said they both looked like hell, not her words, of course, and they were mad enough that she thought it might get physical. She'd never admit it, but I think she enjoyed the spectacle."

That made me laugh. The thought of sweet, always pleasant Sarah Bright watching in anticipation of a thrown punch was totally out of character.

"Oops," he said, "the file I've been waiting on just came through. Talk to you tomorrow?" and he was gone.

I HEARD THE sound of tires on gravel and looked out the study window to see an approaching white Toyota. It was old and battered, and the face that narrowly cleared the steering wheel belonged to Tennie Martin. I rose from the desk and walked to the front door, where I greeted her as she exited the car.

"It's a bad sign when you show up unannounced in the Toyota. Where's the GTO?"

"You know I don't drive it when I want to fly under the radar," she answered.

I looked her over. "At least you aren't in camouflage, like you were the last time you popped in. Those are normal slacks, and your jacket still has a tag hanging off the sleeve."

She frowned and yanked the price tag off with a quick jerk. "Go change out of those yoga pants. We're going to the lake."

"Which lake and why, if it's okay to ask," I said, as I showed her into the living room. "And can't I drive? You scared the heck out of me the last time I got in that car with you."

"You don't know the Toyota's quirks," she answered. "We need to be inconspicuous. Toledo Bend isn't a BMW sort of place."

"We could go in Uncle Raine's pickup." She looked at me doubtfully. "It runs. I just had it tuned up a couple of weeks ago. Here comes Montrose. Sit down and entertain her while I change."

As I ascended the stairs I questioned my sanity. Was it deteriorating since I moved to Louisiana? I slipped into some khaki slacks and a pullover and ran a brush through my hair. I'd never been to our destination, but I was pretty sure it didn't call for much in the way of primping.

# Chapter Thirty-Two

"There's no navigation system on this thing, so I hope you know how to get there," I said, as we left the driveway.

"Go south toward Logansport, like you're going to Nacogdoches."

"Great, this is the third day in a row I've made this trip. I wonder how many people will recognize me in the truck."

"As slow as you drive, they'll be able to paint pictures," she muttered, not quite under her breath.

"Well, excuse me. This old diesel engine won't go much faster. I know you're accustomed to leaving a trail of wind damage behind you," I said. "It's time for you to tell me why we're going on this unexpected jaunt."

"You'll never guess—"

"Don't start this, Tennie. We both know I won't guess. Just tell me."

She gave me a self-satisfied smile. "Bits and tidbits. That's how we'll solve the crime."

"You've been talking to the Nelsons. I don't anticipate solving this, but I'm happy to listen to what you've got."

"Hoyt is not the talkative sort, but I gave him such a good dinner last night, including homemade rolls. I started it off with a Sazerac when he walked through the door, and that always makes him happy."

"Hold it right there. You aren't planning another update on your sex life, are you? Because as I told you before, that's Too Much Information for me."

"You should be so lucky, youngster. No, he actually listened to me when I told him about the drugstore argument yesterday, then he asked for a description of Stacey. He hasn't seen her since she got married. And guess what?"

"Tennie!"

"Sorry. It's a habit. Hoyt and Hubert stayed at a motel at the reservoir last weekend. It has what passes for a nice restaurant in those parts; I guess they serve the fried catfish with a sprig of parsley. Anyway, the waitress went to school in Berryville for a couple of years, and she asked about the Dawson murder when she found out where they lived. She's pretty sure Stacey has been in the restaurant a few times with an older man."

"No! Do you think it was Everett?"

"That's what we're gonna find out. Let's hope she didn't just go fishing with her daddy."

A LITTLE OVER an hour in the truck brought us to the shore of the muddy green lake. The T-Bend Bistro wasn't difficult to find. I turned into a parking place that provided plenty of room for the big pickup and stepped down into the ubiquitous gravel parking lot.

The exterior of the building was rough, board-and-batten cypress siding, weathered to a light gray. A deep porch lined with picnic tables stretched across the back facing the lake, and the neon beer signs in the windows all proclaimed in-state craft brews, except for one that glowed red and advertised Bud. I held the door open for Tennie, and we walked inside and found a table by the window.

It smelled salty and greasy and good, and my eyes wandered to the list of daily specials on the chalkboard behind the bar. Fresh bass baked with tomatoes, Greek olives, and garlic caught my eye, and I had no need to look at the menu that was folded between the napkin holder and the ketchup. "I have to say that I wasn't expecting much from this place, but we might get a good meal here."

"Hoyt said so, and he's accustomed to my cooking. He knows food," said Tennie absent-mindedly as she perused her choices. She put her menu down and looked around the room. "I only see one server. I hope she's the right one."

A pleasant looking woman in her mid-twenties approached our table bearing glasses of water. "Hi, my name is Lou. Do you ladies know what you'd like?"

Tennie greeted her with the news that her husband and brother-in-law had been there on Saturday and reported that "The food and the service were both first-rate." This elicited a pleased smile, and she left our table to turn in the order with a promise to be back soon.

"Do you think she remembers them?" I asked.

"Hoyt's a great tipper, in addition to being charming without being creepy. I'm sure she does. When she brings our tea, I'll ask her about Stacey."

Soon Lou was back with tall glasses of iced tea and a basket of hush-puppies. I picked up one of the cornmeal nuggets and immediately dropped it back in. It was fresh from the fryer and hot as the dickens.

"Lou, Hoyt said you knew Stacey Dawson from high school. Did you grow up in Berryville?"

"No ma'am, I lived there in seventh and eighth grades. She was a couple of years ahead of me and wouldn't have any idea who I am, but I remember her. I've seen her in here a few times, and she hasn't changed hardly at all."

"Yes, she's a beautiful girl," agreed Tennie. I waited to see how she would introduce the subject of Everett Crockett.

"Her husband must have taken up fishing. He didn't strike me as a fisherman," said Tennie. "I guess you just never know."

Lou looked uncomfortable. "I'm not sure she was with her husband. The man was quite a bit older."

"Her father, then?"

She fidgeted. I felt sorry for her. Tennie was tenacious.

"I shouldn't say this, but I don't think it was her father. He didn't act like it."

"Oh, I'll bet it was her uncle. Hoyt knows him. He has a place around here," said Tennie. "Do you by any chance know the man's name?"

I could tell poor Lou wanted to extricate herself from this conversation, and she was saved by the arrival of our meals, brought to us by the older woman who manned the check-out register.

Tennie immediately started in on her. "Hi, I'm trying to remember the name of one of my husband's friends who comes in here with his niece, a pretty young blonde. She's a little taller than he is and has long blonde hair. Her name is Stacey, but I can't remember his."

The woman raised her brows with skepticism. "I know who you're talking about, and if she's his niece, I'm his nephew. That's Everett Crockett. He has a fishing camp on the peninsula across the lake from us, on the Texas side."

"I must be mistaken," said Tennie. "Or more likely, my husband gave me the wrong information. You know how men are!"

They left the table, and we tucked into a delicious meal. "What's your plan now that our suspicions are confirmed?" I asked, before biting into a now touchable hushpuppy.

"See that marina? We're gonna take a little boat ride."

I nearly choked. "Oh, no you don't. You aren't getting me into one of those little fishing boats with you." She just dipped a piece of her catfish in tartar sauce and smiled.

I PULLED THE straps of my life jacket as tight as they would go and still allow me to breathe. The boat rocked gently back and forth at the dock, and for the second time that day I questioned my sanity. Tennie sat in the back of the boat with her hand on the steering thingie, and we took off with a roar as she totally disregarded the "NO WAKE" channel markers. I held onto the side of my seat with the grip of a redbone hound chewing a soup bone, as I thanked God there were no other boats near us.

We skimmed across the water, and I felt us go airborne more than once when we hit the wake of other craft. Tennie's laugh trailed behind us like the cackle of a cheerful witch, and I willed myself to relax and enjoy my last few minutes of life before she drowned me.

"I never expected those boring Saturdays I spent steering Hoyt's boat while he fished would pay off," she said, as she slowed almost to a stop and approached land.

Before us was a densely wooded shore, and I recalled the show I'd watched on the nature channel the last time I'd ironed my linen shirt. Maybe my death wouldn't come by drowning, but by alligator. "I don't see any sign of habitation, and there's no way I'm wading through that swampy mess to look closer."

"The guy at the marina says it's here but hard to find. We'll just scoot along close to the shore and look. There's supposed to be a big pottery turtle on the walkway." She steered the boat around a small promontory and pulled smoothly up to a low dock adorned with a bright red flowered turtle. Throwing a rope around a post, she turned and motioned me out onto land clearly labeled private.

"I'll repeat, I don't like this at all. We're trespassing on someone's property, and I don't know what you expect to find." This was said while I was hauling myself out of the boat and onto the dock, so I don't think my complaints were particularly effective. Not that it mattered. My fate was sealed the moment I agreed to leave my house with my questionable companion.

How could anyone get away with calling a place like this a camp? The large house was made of split cypress stained a mossy green. A screened porch ran the length of it and was furnished with high-end outdoor furniture. Even the rustic hardware on the doors and windows had a hand-crafted look.

We spent ten minutes walking around and peeping through windows into the immaculate dwelling, with me expecting to encounter a snake with each step. "I suppose at least we know it's nice enough for a tryst. Frankie has described the place Boots and his brothers own as nothing more than a shack. She thinks they don't improve it because it keeps the wives away, but Crockett spent some bucks on this. Bonnie must have been involved in the planning and decorating."

"She probably did every bit of it. I wonder if she had any idea that her hard work and good taste would be used to entertain her husband's girlfriend," said Tennie.

"We still don't have proof they're involved," I reminded her primly. "He might just be a father figure to her. That woman at the restaurant could be mistaken."

Tennie turned and looked at me with her hands on her hips. "She didn't strike me as a woman with a wild imagination. Do you really believe they aren't doing the horizontal cha cha cha?"

"Okay, okay," I agreed. "You're right, distasteful though it is to contemplate. But does that lead us to a murder charge?"

I followed her footsteps back to the boat dock, and on a whim, tried the door of the storage room that stood behind a large sink designed for gutting and cleaning fish. I flipped the switch on the wall and the windowless room flooded with light. It was even neater and more orderly than the house. Crockett was as rigidly careful of his fishing equipment as he was his wardrobe.

I looked at the pegboard on the wall and was amazed that so much equipment was necessary to catch and prepare a few fish. A container of hooks sat next to a box of lures. Lead weights of various sizes filled small bowls, and one basket overflowed with red and white bobbers.

On the pegboard itself were specialized scissors hanging next to strange pliers, which were close to an odd saw. The one thing I didn't see were knives. I turned around and saw they were attached to their own special display board in hollowed out spaces tailored to fit each one exactly. I saw five spaces. I saw four knives.

# Chapter Thirty-Three

"DIET OR REGULAR?" I asked, before I went into the bait shop.

"Regular. At my age, why deprive myself?"

I came outside with a Coke for her and a diet Dr Pepper for myself and slid behind the wheel of the truck. We hadn't said much; it was impossible to have a conversation in the boat.

Tennie broke the silence before we'd driven too far. "That was fun, right up until the part where you found the knives. Then it got too real. That man may really have murdered Ryan."

"What do we do now?" I asked. "I can't see myself telling Sheriff Boots Lacasse where we were and what we were doing when we found out something that may or may not be important. That other knife could be on the drain board in the kitchen, or he could have accidentally dropped it off the boat dock. And those are just the normal things that could have happened to it. If he used it to kill Ryan, he's probably disposed of it someplace it will never be found."

"Do you think he drove up here the night of the reunion and then drove back to Nacogdoches?"

"I guess. It's not too far. You could do the round trip and stab someone in two and a half hours. I've been there twice this week, and it's a pleasant drive."

"Where would he have parked the car? And wouldn't someone have noticed that big Mercedes of his with its Texas plates?"

I tried to recall that night. "There were maybe a hundred vehicles there, and lots of out-of-state tags. And there are more places to park than the main lot. Plus we don't know that's his only car. I don't imagine he drives the Mercedes to his fish camp."

"He could have pulled it off. Especially if Stacey helped him," she said.

We both fell silent.

"ONE OF MY patients brought me a smoked turkey and two loaves of homemade bread, and Boots picked the last two stragglers from the tomato plants. I know it isn't chicken enchiladas, but do you want to grab Caleb and come over for sandwiches?"

"That's the best invitation I've gotten today," I said to Frankie. "Do you need me to pick up anything on the way?"

"Run by Bubba's and grab a jar of Hellman's. I used the last of the mayo trying to duplicate Tennie's pimiento cheese. I'm still not at her level of expertise."

CALEB INSISTED I wait in the car while he went into the store, and I lowered the window to enjoy the crisp fall air. I watched as a woman took a baby out of his car seat and placed him gently into the seat of a shopping cart. I recognized Lydia Morrison and Danny. He was a beautiful child, and just like the last time I saw him, he was smiling and happy. Surely it was a comfort for Dinah's parents to have him to love.

As Mrs. Morrison buckled him in, I heard steps approaching. Stacey Dawson came around a parked panel truck and into view as the child's safety strap was secured, and he waved cheerfully at her.

They were just a few feet away and seemed not to notice me as I sat in the deepening dusk. Stacey stopped close enough for Danny to reach out and touch her, which he did with a small chubby hand, while babbling nonsense words of greeting. Lydia moved the cart and put herself between the two of them, ignoring the child's frustrated grunts as he stretched his arm toward the newcomer. Her face revealed apprehension and a determination to shield the child from whatever was coming.

Stacey's face twisted into a grimace of a smile, as if the effort hurt. "I just want to let you know how sorry I am about Dinah. It hurts so much to have lost my husband, and I can't imagine how much worse it must be to lose a child."

The other woman's face registered surprise, and the tension in her stance subsided. "Thank you, Stacey. It's been very difficult, but we'll make it through. I hope you can find your own comfort."

That won her a slightly less pained smile, and Stacey reached out to grasp Danny's little fingers. "He's so cute. You're lucky to have him." She paused, as if searching for her next words. "You know he isn't Ryan's. People are talking, but it isn't true. Just remember that."

She left abruptly, and Lydia stared as she walked away.

As USUAL, WE entered the Lacasse household through the kitchen door, and I dashed across the room to the sink. Frankie had some sort of fancy hand soap, and I hit the pump on it at least five times in my effort to wash off the slobber from Boots' hunting dogs. I had to wash all the way up to my elbows.

"They got her good," said Caleb. "She tried to shoo them toward me, but she's irresistible."

I looked down and saw little Miranda's paws on my thigh as she sought my attention. She had grown a couple of inches since I'd last seen her. I picked her up with my clean hands and tucked her head under my chin as I walked to my usual seat on the den sofa.

The TV was off for a change, and the lamps were low. Frankie delivered drinks to us and opened the windows. "It's a little cool, but an owl has moved into the back yard, and we love to listen to him at night."

A peaceful, yet mournful, "hooo" floated into the room, and I felt a shiver go up my spine. It was the perfect scene-setter for a conversation about murder. Boots, wearing sweatpants and an LSU sweatshirt, emerged from the back of the house, and the mood was broken.

We chatted for a few minutes until Caleb brought up my recent experience—the one at Bubba's, not the one at Toledo Bend. I hadn't told him about that yet.

Boots shook his head. "I hope Stacey gets some counseling. I think she's in denial about the man she was married to."

I turned to Frankie. "I don't guess there's anyone in town who can vouch for the fact that Danny looks like Ryan."

"Since the Dawson family didn't move to Louisiana until Ryan was in kindergarten, there's no one here who would know if Danny looks like he did as a baby, although there might be a resemblance to the kid I knew as a five-year-old. I'm expecting the DNA results to show they're related."

"Can you tell us why you expect that?" asked Caleb.

"I can't say anything other than to tell you I had a conversation with Ryan's parents which led me to connect some of their information with Danny. The Dawsons were angry at the time, because they were looking for immediate answers. I convinced them to wait until I could talk to the Morrisons. I was willing to broach the subject in a way that would perhaps not be as emotionally charged."

"That was kind of you," I said.

"The whole family sees me for health care. I thought I had a duty to them in what is an extremely unusual situation. We put a rush on the test with a private lab, and I expect to hear from them before the weekend."

"Are you planning to tell Stacey yourself?"

"Gosh, I don't want to. I don't really view it as my job, but we'll see what happens. I'll probably take whatever role the Morrisons want."

We went into the kitchen to fix our sandwiches. The whole-wheat bread Frankie's patient made for her was dangerously delicious. I wanted to grab the loaf and a stick of butter and make a run for it, but the thought of the eager pack of dogs waiting outside stopped me.

We sat down around the wooden table that had come from Boots' great-grandmother's house and continued our conversation. I needed to find a way to bring up the murder weapon.

"Boots," I said, "has this revelation about Ryan and Dinah done anything to make you question your arrest of Valonda?"

"It's darn strange, but I can't see that it changes the facts we currently know."

"You still haven't found the murder weapon?"

"No. We've done a thorough search of the grounds and Valonda's place. She's not being very forthcoming, but we've reconstructed her whereabouts on the days after the crime. She had plenty of opportunities to get rid of it."

I thanked Frankie for topping off my wine and took a gulp. I was gonna go for it.

"What would you say if I told you I think Stacey and Everett Crockett are having an affair?"

The answer to that was he wouldn't say anything. He would, however, laugh until he got the hiccups.

"You have the most creative imagination," he gasped. "She wouldn't choose that old fart even if she knew her husband was running around with Dinah. The man and his wife just spent the week with her at her parents. Does that sound romantic?"

"Fighting off the mosquitoes and snakes at a Toledo Bend fishing camp doesn't sound romantic either, but that's what the two of them have been doing for several months."

He gaped at me.

"Close your mouth, Boots, it makes you look dumb," Caleb said, with more than a little enjoyment.

"There are too many twists to this tale," complained Frankie. "Sweet potato pie, anyone?"

I'd skipped dessert at lunch so I held up my hand. "*And* I know more. No, don't look at me like that, it isn't from snooping. I happened to be in the right place at the right time." I related the conversation between the Crockett kids that Tennie and I overheard Tuesday. "We came to the conclusion that it was unlikely Bonnie was messing around because she seemed to spend so much time catering to her husband, and we also figured no one would be willing to have an affair with him, what with Everett being pretty unattractive and extremely unpleasant."

Boots raised a skeptical eyebrow at me. "Is that all? Are you finished?"

"No."

He turned his gaze heavenward. "Do go on, Miss Wyatt."

"I had to make another trip to Nacogdoches yesterday to pick up some more jewelry. More incredible, one-of-a-kind pieces, things I never thought would be in my possession. One is Cartier and the other one is *Boucheron.* Can you imagine? *Boucheron.* Fifteen carats of emeralds. I still can't believe it."

All three members of my audience stared at me. "Okay, okay, I get that you aren't as excited about it as I am, but wow. Anyway, I ate at the same restaurant, and Bonnie was there enjoying happy hour with a friend. I mean, they were really *enjoying* happy hour. They invited themselves to join me, and Bonnie said she's divorcing Everett because she discovered he's been buying expensive jewelry for someone who isn't her."

"Does she think it's Stacey?" asked Frankie.

"I honestly don't believe the thought has occurred to her. She's afraid Stacey knows about it and has been too sympathetic and distressed to tell her."

I paused to let that sink in and ate my pie while they discussed the importance of the news. When I'd finished, I pushed my chair from the table and lifted Miranda back onto my lap, then tapped my glass with my knife for attention. "I'm finished with dinner, but not with my story. Who wants to know where I went today?"

# Chapter Thirty-Four

"I CAN'T BELIEVE you and Tennie went to Crockett's fishing camp," said Caleb, for at least the tenth time, although he did vary the phrasing slightly with each new comment.

I guess he was trying to find the emphasis that would make me sob with contrition, but if so, he was out of luck. Given the sheriff's reaction to my news, it was a darn good thing we'd snooped.

"That trip across the lake opened Boots' imagination to the thought that maybe he couldn't find the knife Valonda used because she isn't the killer. Therefore I'd say it was worthwhile." I left out any mention of the death-defying trip across the lake in a bass boat with Captain Tennie. I'd save that for my nightmares.

He stared through the windshield at the dark road ahead of us. "I understand that it might prove helpful, but you put yourself in danger for no other reason than curiosity. I'm pretty sure you're smarter than that."

That stung. "You know the Nelson family asked me to look for information," I said. "You're implying I'm just dumb and nosy."

"I didn't mean it like that," he backpedaled. "You can be curious without being nosy. I wish, though, that you wouldn't take risks on someone else's behalf. There's a long history in this area, dating back to the Spanish and French settlers, of the right to defend your property with a gun. It's ingrained in the local DNA."

"You're saying you think Everett Crockett would have shot the two of us and gotten away with it if he'd been at the camp?" I was dubious.

"He'd have been too shocked to see the two of you to pull the trigger. You admitted you lucked into his place, though. What if you'd pulled the boat up to the wrong dock?"

Our directions from the marina owner had been rather vague, I remembered, but my concern regarding that had been eclipsed by my worries of drowning and/or being eaten. "The red turtle was there. Also, I was more worried about alligators, but I suppose you have a point. I will be more careful in the future, but at least Boots is going to look into Crockett's whereabouts the night of the murder."

"I'm not going to ask the significance of a red turtle, but I'd be a lot more relieved by your promise if you hadn't included the word 'future.' You have a safe full of valuable jewelry to sell. You don't have time to skulk around with a seventy-year-old woman."

There was a new sign in front of the church, and Caleb was smart enough not to comment on it.

ARTIFICIAL INTELLIGENCE IS NO MATCH
FOR NATURAL STUPIDITY

*

I WAS STILL a little miffed by Caleb's unasked-for opinion about my recent activities when I awoke the next morning. My annoyance led me to choose a Pilates workout rather than a more Zen-like yoga session, and I finished feeling like I'd gotten rid of some hostility. I don't handle criticism very well, and that's a fact I don't like to share.

I polished off a couple of fried eggs and a piece of toast, then retired to the study with my second cup of coffee. As a certain busybody told me the night before, I had jewelry to sell. I pulled several reference books from the shelves and began documenting what I'd gotten from Janice.

I'm extremely meticulous when I establish the value of a piece of high-end jewelry, and luckily for me, most of the items were hallmarked. I'd just finished writing up the chrysoberyl brooch, having estimated the carat weight of the diamonds, and moved on to photographing it.

The doorbell rang, and I paused. I wasn't expecting anyone. I looked around the room and decided to lock the study door behind me before answering.

Valonda stood waiting on the porch, and I was glad I'd secured the other door. Her lack of honesty about the salamander left me distrustful, even if I was reasonably convinced she wasn't a murderer.

"Sorry to drop in like this, but I haven't heard from you since you came by the house. Any luck?"

"I haven't contacted you, because I can't depend on you for the truth," I said, with brutal bluntness.

"And what's that supposed to mean?"

"That means I know you lied about how you got the pin, and also you lied about not leaving the party with Ryan." For a moment I thought she was going to spin me another one, but instead her expression turned petulant.

"I don't really know what difference it makes. You know I didn't kill him."

Leaning against the door frame, I crossed my arms over my chest. I still hadn't invited her in. "At this point, Valonda, I'm not so sure."

She pushed her way past me and sat down. The cat and dog both left the room. Lafitte shuffled to the far end of his perch.

"You want the truth? After Stacey left, Ryan and I went out behind the gym together and made out. See? I'm just as bad as my reputation."

"How did you acquire the jewelry?"

"It was on the lapel of his sports coat."

"That's an odd place for his wife's jewelry." I didn't let on that I knew it already. Her legs were crossed at the knee, with the topmost one swinging rapidly while I questioned her. I was still standing by the door, so I crossed the room and sat directly across from her.

"Ryan told me they'd had a big fight. He laughed and said she probably wanted to stab him with it instead of just sticking the pin through his jacket. That's why I think she may have killed him," she said. "So that's the true story."

"Not quite. How did the pin get from his lapel to your bedroom?"

The swinging foot picked up speed, and she looked uncomfortable. "He was never in my bedroom; that's the truth. He got pretty friendly, I guess you could say, and gave it to me. I guess he thought I'd let him go ahead with what we, what we had started, I guess."

"You're guessing a lot. Did you have intercourse?" I couldn't believe I was asking that question. How embarrassing for both of us.

"No!" she snapped. "We didn't. We probably would have, but he started talking about Dinah Morrison. He said she was supposed to meet him somewhere, and he had to cancel. He wanted me to talk to her because she wouldn't return his phone calls. I got mad and went back to the gym."

"Oh, good grief, Valonda. You knew Dinah was missing then. They found her body the week after the dance. I want you to call the sheriff's office and tell them the truth. Your information may be helpful."

"They'll make me give the pin back."

She glowered at me, and I knew it was unlikely she would follow my instructions, so I added, a bit nastily, "In case it hasn't occurred to you, they don't let prison inmates wear jewelry."

"I didn't *do* it. How many times do I have to tell you?" she practically hissed.

"I'm not the one you have to convince," I answered. "But as many things as you've lied to the sheriff about, I'm not sure he'll believe you now if you actually tell him the truth."

I FELT A marvelous sense of relief when my unexpected guest drove away. As far as I was concerned, I'd made good on the promises I'd given the reverend and his sons. Now it was up to their errant family member to cooperate with the authorities. True, all I'd discovered was Valonda's lies, but it was bound to improve her odds if she stopped her damaging fictions. The ancillary information I'd come across in the process didn't apply to her, but did give a new direction for Boots to investigate.

Before I could return to my work, Clotille came around the corner of the house with a pink armful of amaryllis lycoris, or, as I'd delighted to call them as a child, naked ladies, since the blooms shoot up without foliage in the fall. She followed me inside and we arranged them in a tall, cut-crystal vase.

"They smell like bubblegum, but in a good way," I said, taking a big sniff and emerging from the process with a golden coating of pollen on my nose. "Where did you find them?"

"There's a big bed of them behind the log cabin. I tend to forget they're there since they're out of the normal sightline. I saw Valonda leaving; did you have helpful news for her?"

I filled her in on all the sleuthing I'd done since I last saw her. I was afraid to tell her about my boat trip with Tennie, but considering the chewing out I'd just given Valonda about lies, I had to confess. She wasn't happy.

"Do you know, Anna Leighton Wyatt, that I promised your Aunt Josie on her deathbed I would look after you?"

"No, ma'am."

"Well, I did, and you are making it awfully hard for me. I have warned you about that woman, and it hasn't made a lick of difference. I just give up, I swear, I give up. I'm gonna pray on it. I think I'll talk to the minister about it tomorrow."

Guilt settled on me like somebody tilted a dump truck full of pea gravel over my head. Clotille was nearing eighty and shouldn't have to contend with worry over my well-being.

"I'm sorry. I truly am. But, Clotille? Tennie was one of my aunt's best friends. Are you sure Aunt Josie wouldn't be happy that she's becoming one of mine?" I said, timidly.

The older woman's expression softened, and she gave my fanny a swat hard enough to make me jump. "You're probably right, you rotten child. Go on and do what you're going to do anyway. But I'm still going to pray."

And for that, I was thankful.

# Chapter Thirty-Five

THE LALIQUE CHOKER lay on a black velvet ground. I adjusted the lighting, then began snapping pictures. When I finished, I moved it to royal blue velvet and started over. I wanted to compare the two and see which set it off better. I had a feeling the blue would complement the green of the enameled leaves. Only a hundred and three more pieces to go.

I planned to list the most valuable of these items on one of the high-end jewelry sites after I offered some of the more unique things to private collectors. An unexpected video call came in on my laptop. When I accepted, Caleb popped up on the screen. Immediately one of my hands went to my hair while the index finger on my other one tried to surreptitiously remove the mascara circles that always appear under my eyes at this time of day. I'm not a fan of the unplanned face call in general, and even less from someone I was dating.

Since we were looking at each other there was no way to hide my wariness, which came through in my voice, anyway. "What's up? Is something wrong?"

"What time should I pick you up?" he asked.

"Do we have a date?" I didn't remember him asking me out and wasn't sure I liked the expectation I'd be available.

He looked startled. "Don't we? Did I forget to ask? I probably forgot to ask. Do you have plans with someone else?"

That was better. He didn't look complacent any more. "No, we don't have a date because you didn't ask me out. Luckily for you, I'm free, and I'll be starving by the time we go somewhere. Come on over, but don't plan on any place I can't wear jeans. And don't think you can pull this one again. This girl requires invitations, not assumptions."

AN HOUR LATER we arrived at one of my favorite pizza joints. There was an LSU game on four TVs with a fifth showing the Arkansas Razorbacks, and the place was full of fans, including what looked like an entire third grade soccer team. We squeezed into the last two seats at the bar and ordered drinks; beer for Caleb and a frou-frou cocktail for me.

I reached up to my bun and checked that the fresh rose pinned next to it was still securely fastened. "I want you to be honest. Did you raid your mom's rose bushes on your own, or did she suggest it?"

"I get complete credit. I was afraid you wouldn't let me in the door. Between taking a date with you for granted and instructing you how to conduct yourself last night, you had a right to keep it locked. Or if you did open it, you might tell me to leave and never bother you again."

"I was mad at you last night, but not mad enough to kick you to the curb."

"But mad enough to kick me?"

"Your complaints were legitimate. We shouldn't have gone to the fishing camp. I've never thought of myself as being easily led, so I guess I wanted to go as much as Tennie did. I'm not normally a risk-taker."

"You think not? You run your own business; you took on the care and feeding of a one-hundred-and-thirty-year-old house by yourself, and you are completely unfazed by sharing your property with a ghost."

"Repentance isn't exactly spooky," I pointed out.

"Speak for yourself. I'm still nervous whenever he's around. Even if I just think about him being around."

"There's something sweet about a guy who admits he's afraid of a ghost," I grinned.

He rested his hand on my knee and leaned forward. "What would you think about a guy who helps you fight crime?"

"Why, Mr. Bright! You're making my heart go pitty-pat," I drawled. "For real. Do you know something I don't?"

We had ordered food at the bar, and we stopped our silliness when the pizza arrived. I took a piece of my pear and gorgonzola while he maneuvered the stringy mozzarella that hung from his slice of pepperoni and mushroom.

"I called Boots today. We didn't talk about Dinah's death last night, and I started wondering if there was any news. I had to work it into the conversation, but he finally told me that her car was discovered a couple of days ago at the bottom of a pond. Some teenagers admitted finding it by the side of the road, complete with keys. They took it joyriding, then drove it into the water."

"Were they able to get any clues from it?"

"The biggest clue is that the kids picked it up within walking distance of the bartender's house, the guy who was the last person to see her alive. He's now the major suspect. They're working on breaking his alibi."

"That's wild. I don't know what to think now. I was almost positive her death would tie into Ryan's somehow, but this seems random. What are the odds of two people who are having an affair dying within a couple of weeks?"

"He also said Frankie got a phone call this morning. The DNA is back. Danny is Ryan's child."

My stomach did an inadvertent flip, which was unfortunate considering it was full of pizza. "What a total mess. Stacey is going to need more than grief counseling after this comes to light. I wish you could have seen her yesterday in the grocery store parking lot. She was very gentle with the baby, but the look on her face was eerie. She was in total denial of the possibility that Danny is Ryan's. I don't know how she's going to cope with the truth."

"Maybe she'll go back to Nacogdoches. They've lived there several years now; it should feel like home to her. She needs to get out of her childhood bedroom and begin to move on with her life," said Caleb.

"That may take less time than usual if she and Everett are having an affair. Poor Bonnie."

It was a cold, clear night, and we settled on the front porch when we went back to Goat Hill. I put a blanket behind us to keep the air from coming through the slats on the back of the swing and then tucked one over our laps. Caleb took his cell phone out of his pocket, set it on flashlight mode, and shined it at my wrist.

"What are you doing?" I giggled, as he moved my arm up to eye level.

"I've been looking at this weird bracelet all evening. Are you wearing bugs?"

"You caught me. I confess I'm wearing something from the Nacogdoches estate. I'll only wear things I can afford to replace, which narrows it down quite a bit. This is pietra dura, from Italy in the nineteenth century. It's similar to mosaics, where they use tiny pieces of stone to create a picture. These are slightly bigger slices of things like coral, malachite, lapis lazuli and different colors of onyx, and yes, you're looking at bugs, including a few flies. No Louisiana mosquitoes, though."

He shook his head and let me reclaim my arm. "The gold part of it is pretty, and the colors are bright, but that's probably one of those pieces that requires a special buyer. I'm guessing you couldn't pay Stacey enough to wear it."

"Nope, it doesn't fit her aesthetic. I'm not even sure it fits mine, but it's fun. Did I tell you that Everett won't let Bonnie wear any jewelry that he didn't buy for her? Including what she inherited from her mother."

"Why has she put up with that for so many years? She's nice, seems smart, and is a lot more attractive than he is. They have two kids together and grandkids. What's wrong with a man who can't appreciate what he has? Selfish old fart."

"And Stacey? What do you think about her behavior?" I asked, pleased that he nailed Everett Crockett's bad decisions so neatly.

He frowned. "I don't approve of what she appears to be doing. I know Ryan was a crappy husband, but she should have gotten a divorce instead of having an affair.

And how she can rationalize doing to Bonnie what Ryan has done to her is beyond my imagination. Sooner or later it's all going to come out, even if she and Everett had nothing to do with Ryan's murder. I hope she's ready for the fallout. It will sure put a damper on the grieving widow sympathy."

I shifted and pulled the blanket higher, using the opportunity to snuggle just a little bit closer. "Valonda came by today to see if I had any news. You know I had been feeling kinder toward her; that's one of the reasons I snooped around."

"You sound like you've changed your mind and gone back to your original opinion."

"That girl is a piece of work. I think, wouldn't swear to it, that she finally told me the truth about that evening at the party. She did go outside with Ryan, and he gave her that pin to soften up her resistance. She admitted to me that it would have worked if he hadn't mentioned Dinah to her."

"You mean he talked to her about Dinah? Did he tell her anything about Danny?"

"No, just that he'd been supposed to meet her, and he couldn't make it. She refused to talk to him afterward." I stopped, aware that I was missing something important. "No, wait, he couldn't reach her. He called and left messages and she wouldn't respond. He assumed she was mad at him."

Caleb nodded, picking up on my thoughts. "He thought she was too angry to talk, but she must have already been dead. She went to south Louisiana to meet him the day she was murdered, and he never even knew she was missing."

# Chapter Thirty-Six

*Dare we try walking again?* texted Frankie.

*Let's throw caution to the wind. Meet you at two*

I SHOULD HAVE spent my time working on jewelry, but I couldn't concentrate. The events of the last couple of weeks kept churning in my mind, and I found myself too distracted to appraise all the pieces that awaited my attention. I decided to clean out closets instead.

I went into the bedroom and opened my closet door. I closed it and went back downstairs. I wanted a distraction, not an impossible task. I'd start with the kitchen. Opening the pantry, I began with the canned goods and was soon deep into decoding the expiration dates on Aunt Josie's spices.

My phone rang, and I exited the small closet, dropping a can of ground pepper in the process. A cloud of fine black dust drifted into the air around me, and I answered the call in the middle of a sneezing fit.

"What's going on over there?" asked Caleb.

"Housekeeping tasks," I said, through my sniffs and snuffles.

"I didn't think the place was that dusty. I'm heading out to play tennis with Parker. Will you spend the afternoon reading the paper without me?"

"You're wasting your envy on me. Frankie and I are walking the track at two."

"We're playing tennis on the school courts. Maybe I'll see you there. You'll recognize me. I'll be the one who looks like he's never held a tennis racket before. I'm not sure I remember which end to pick up."

"Don't forget to be a gracious loser, and don't stumble over any crime scenes. That's a job for me and Frankie."

FRANKIE AND I arrived at the track at the same time, and were faced with a stream of cars exiting the parking lot by the field house. An elementary school football practice had just ended, and every parent was leaving through the same drive. We drove around the corner and parked our cars in the lot at Doc Reynolds' dental practice, then cut across the grass to reach the athletic complex. I could see two figures on the tennis court in the distance and recognized Caleb's long, lean frame. He seemed to be holding his own, so his long-unused skills had surfaced when he needed them.

Before we began our walk, I took Frankie's hand in mine. "Let's promise each other that we won't come across something terrible today."

She shook my hand in agreement. "Absolutely no dead bodies allowed."

We began our first lap and didn't stop until we hit three miles. By unspoken agreement we'd both brought water bottles. Neither of us wanted to drop by the field house water fountain. The campus grounds were empty except for Caleb and Parker when we finished, and we decided to relax and visit.

Berryville High is an old facility. My great-aunt Josie went to school there, and her mother before her. It's pretty, in that red-brick classic schoolhouse style, and all the new additions have been to the other side of the building. They've managed to keep a large area free from "improvements." In addition to spreading oaks, there are stands of longleaf pine trees that top out well above a hundred feet, some of which have veritable groves of old azaleas growing tall beneath them. The trees and shrubs are both native to the area, and have a sort of symbiotic relationship. We chose a spot by one of the thickest clumps of shrubs and sat down on the lush St. Augustine grass.

"What do you think about everything that's happened, Frankie? Does Boots still believe Valonda killed Ryan?"

She shook her head. "He hasn't said anything to me, but I overheard him talking to Seth Hammett. They were coming up with a plan of action for tomorrow. I think Seth is going to Texas to question Everett Crockett about his whereabouts on the night of the crime."

"Boots told Caleb that the DNA on Danny came in yesterday, and he's definitely Ryan's child."

"Yes, there's no doubt at all. I went to the Morrison's house yesterday afternoon to tell them, and then I called Ryan's parents from there. It was awkward, but his parents were pitifully happy. When I left, the four grandparents were on speakerphone crying together," she said. "What the hell were Ryan and Dinah thinking about when they decided to keep a secret like that? If they were here, I'd kick each of them in the rear end. They left an unspeakable mess behind for their parents."

"Will you have to tell Stacey?"

"Nope. I changed my mind about being involved and flat refused. I told Boots he'd have to come up with another plan that didn't involve me. It's such a weird situation that I'm not even sure about her right to know. She has no biological relationship to the baby, and the father, even though he was her husband, is dead."

"I wonder if he had a will. Surely he did, he was an attorney; he would know how important it is to prepare for the unexpected. Maybe he left some money in trust for Danny," I said. "I bet they haven't read the will yet since she hasn't been back home since his death. I'd like to be a fly on the wall for that one."

We said nothing for several minutes afterward, enjoying the cool breeze and companionable silence. The quiet was broken by the sound of voices on the other side of the azaleas. I recognized Stacey as she greeted someone.

"What do you need to talk to me about that couldn't be done in a phone call? I'm still not ready to come back to Nacogdoches."

We heard the lower rumble of a man's voice, which became clearer as he neared the trees. "Let's just sit and talk awhile." It was Everett Crockett.

Frankie and I stared at each other as we heard the creak of a wooden bench. Should we get up? There was no way to return to our vehicles without walking in front of the couple. I can't vouch for what was going through my friend's mind, but I'll admit I really wanted to stay and eavesdrop, nervous though I was. The bushes between us and the other two were eight feet tall and thick as an English garden boxwood hedge. It was highly unlikely that we'd be found out if we kept quiet.

Frankie shrugged her shoulders, and I hit the silent button on my phone. She followed suit. At this point there was no pretending—we were about to listen in on a private conversation.

"Why don't you come back, Stacey? Nacogdoches is your home now. If you don't want to stay at the house you and Ryan shared, stay with us."

"That sounds like an excellent plan, Everett. You're always so thoughtful." Her genial words had a tinge of good-natured sarcasm.

"Then don't stay with us; I'm sure Bonnie would be willing to help you settle back into your home. She has a real knack for helping the bereaved. There are things that need to be taken care of in Nacogdoches, like reading Ryan's will. Our business contract put things in place to handle the death of one of the partners, but you need to be there for his will to be probated."

"What's the hurry? Every bill I pay at the house is set up for direct withdrawal, and I logged onto the banking site yesterday. There's plenty of cash in our—I mean, my account."

"Don't you miss your friends?" he asked. "They would be a source of comfort to you now. Bonnie and I have both had phone calls from people who'd like to see you. I understand you're going to be president of the league this year."

"I don't care about any of that. I miss my husband. He's the *only* person I'd like to see," she said fiercely.

Frankie and I looked at each other. Perhaps she was also thinking that response sounded a little pointed. I guess Everett did too. He turned on the persuasion.

"I miss you, Stacey. I miss our nights at the lake and our trips to New Orleans. I hope that with time, you'll remember all that and miss me, too. As I've told you, Bonnie and I don't have the same sort of relationship that you and I have. We never did, even when we were first married, back before she let herself go. She was cute and fun to be with when we were in college, but I made a mistake when I proposed. I guess you'd say I settled. I settled for good enough, when I should have held out for best. You're the best, and I want to spend the rest of my life proving it to you."

I rolled my eyes at Frankie, and she made a silent barfing motion. I couldn't stop myself from looking at Caleb in the distance, still doggedly whacking a tennis ball back and forth across a net. Somehow, I knew he wasn't the type of man to make a commitment to a woman and trade her in for a younger model. I heard Stacey clear her throat.

"Everett, I wasn't even born when you and Bonnie got married. Are you saying you should have waited for me? That's sort of sick, like you saw a little girl and wanted to marry her. Would you give up your great kids? Do you truly regret the life you and your wife have together?"

Maybe I'd been too harsh on Stacey. Although I didn't approve of her affair, she was making a lot of sense.

"You have the wrong idea about you and me," Stacey continued. "I told you this before; you were basically my revenge on Ryan. Even though he didn't know, it made me feel like I was getting even for the women who threw themselves at him. You were so sweet when you bought jewelry for me. I loved the fact that we went shopping together; Ryan just told me to charge what I wanted. You did make me feel special, but I never planned on anything more. I still loved Ryan. I spent my whole life loving him.

I would have done anything to keep him happy. No one will ever measure up to him and the love I know he had for me. I was the one he always came back to; I was the one he wanted to grow old with."

There was a long stretch of silence before the older man spoke. "Would it change your opinion to find out that his estate will be shared? You aren't the sole beneficiary."

"It's fine with me if he left something to his family. He'd been concerned about his dad's health; it would be normal to leave them some money."

"He didn't leave anything to his parents."

"The LSU booster club? He was a big supporter," she said. Then her tone changed. "And how do you know, anyway?"

"I drew up the will for him. Half of his estate goes to his son."

I heard a horrible gasping intake of breath, followed by the sounds of fists pummeling a chest. Frankie and I met each other's eyes with identical looks of dismay.

"It's not true; it's not; it's not; it's not! That bitch did not trap him with a pregnancy. I don't believe it." She broke into heaving sobs, but I didn't feel a bit of pity for her at that point.

Everett seemed to. His voice gentled. "I'm sorry, honey. I know it's hard on you, but Danny really is his. He's been sending child support since the birth, and he also paid for all of Dinah's hospital expenses."

"How long have you known?" she sniffled.

"Since the baby was born, so about eight months."

"Right about the time you and I started seeing each other?"

"Yes. That's when I knew for sure that he didn't

appreciate what he had with you, and I felt free to make my feelings known. He didn't deserve a woman as wonderful as you are."

Stacey's voice grew strained. "It's nice that you think I'm wonderful, but you've got to know that I don't feel the same way about you. Our time together was a pleasant distraction, but that's all it was. And I love Bonnie; she's a saint. You, to be honest, you're kind of a pain in the ass. I can't imagine why she's put up with you all these years. You're rude to her in public and treat her like she's nothing more than an annoying convenience. You take all the things she does for you for granted. I'd be a fool to take her place, because it wouldn't take you long to start treating me the same way. No, I'll wait here till Valonda is tried and convicted, then I'll go back and shut things down. I can forget about the baby, because I know I was more important to my husband than anyone else. Maybe I'll move to Dallas."

I heard footsteps, then a yelp from Stacey.

"What are you doing? That hurts! Let go of my arm, right now."

"I didn't drive all the way up here and kill that SOB just to have you walk away from me," snapped Everett. "We are bound together now and forever. Get used to it. I'll divorce Bonnie, and we'll get married. You don't really have a say in it anymore."

By this point Frankie and I were holding hands and our looks of dismay had changed to ones of horror.

"Marry you? What are you talking about? Valonda killed Ryan! She has my alligator pin."

The salamander versus alligator issue was obviously a lost cause.

"Why are you so obsessed with Valonda Nelson? If you honestly thought she and your husband were screwing each other, why didn't you kill her?"

"Kill her? Are you insane? Where did that idea come from? I'm no murderer, but you just admitted that you are. You stabbed my husband. I'm going directly to the sheriff's office and tell him you're guilty. They'll give you the death penalty, for sure."

That's when we heard a cold, terrifying laugh from Everett.

"Ryan told me more than once that you aren't playing with a full deck, but I didn't believe him. I should have. You murdered Dinah Morrison, Mrs. Dawson. And I watched you do it."

# Chapter Thirty-Seven

Frankie's fingernails dug into my arm so deeply that I figured I'd need stitches later, but I wasn't worried about blood loss at the moment. I held my breath as I waited for Stacey's reply to Everett's horrifying accusation. There was an interminable moment of silence before she responded, and when she did, her voice was tremulous.

"Why are you making up such a crazy story? I did no such thing. I was on my way home from New Orleans when she died."

Another creepy chuckle. "Cut the acting. You aren't very good at it. Don't you think I wondered why you had me call and ask Ryan at the last minute to stay in Nacogdoches and work that weekend? I followed you when we left New Orleans. I admit I don't know how you knew where Dinah would be, but I saw you pull the trigger and drive away like you'd never be tied to the crime.

"Hell, Stacey, you left the woman's body by the side of the road. I'm the one who dumped it in the swamp. Did it ever occur to you to wonder why it was found miles from where you killed her, or did you even give it another thought? I saved your fanny, and now you tell me we're finished. I don't think so."

Once again I heard footsteps, followed by stern instructions from Everett.

"Stop right there. This discussion is not over. I'll tell you when you can leave." There was the sound of scuffling, then a sudden silence, broken by a new voice.

"Are you giving your girlfriend orders, Everett?" It was Bonnie Crockett, and she wasn't happy. "Give her all the orders you want, but don't try to tell me what to do anymore. Those days are gone. As a matter of fact, I'm calling the shots for the afternoon. Stacey, get back on that bench and sit down next to my husband of forty years. Why don't the two of you hold hands?"

Everett tried to speak, and Bonnie's reaction was swift. "Shut up, Everett. As you've said to me so many times, no one is interested in what you have to say." She then added a pithy description of his character and physical status.

"Bonnie, thank goodness you're here," said Stacey. "Everett just told me he killed Ryan."

"I thought as much," the older woman answered. "Was that before or after you began sleeping with him?"

By this point, Frankie and I had thrown our arms around each other and tried to bury our heads. Our efforts didn't last long.

"Annalee, you and your friend can come out of the bushes now," called Bonnie.

We rose slowly and edged our way into the open while holding hands tightly. I would have laughed at the shocked expressions Stacey and Everett wore if I hadn't been so terrified. Bonnie stood casually in the clearing with a pistol pointed at the two on the bench. I once had an unfortunate experience with a handgun and had hoped never to encounter another one.

"Have you two been back there listening to our conversation? That is *not* polite." Of all the things she could be worried about, Stacey chose to be indignant at our bad manners.

"They've been there the whole time," said Bonnie. "I saw them sitting there before you two ever walked up. Since I brought my binoculars, I could also see the expressions flitting across their faces while you two talked." She waved the gun in our direction as she spoke, and I thought I would wet my pants.

"Oops, sorry. I don't have any reason to aim at the two of you," she said, including a pointed expletive. I didn't feel any safer.

She pointed at the couple sitting on the bench. "Stacey, I probably won't shoot you either, but don't get too close to Mr. Sexy-pants. That's the direction the bullet will go."

Everett Crockett pushed himself to his feet and stepped toward his wife. "Now see here, Bonnie. I've had about enough of—"

She pointed the gun directly at his head with an ease that suggested she wouldn't miss her target. He sat down.

"Allow me to explain what this gun means. This gun, this big 44 Magnum semi-automatic, held in my little pudgy hand, means that I talk and you listen. Unless I ask you a question. In that case, you answer. So, what have you had enough of, Everett?"

I watched his small ears redden. "I've had enough of our marriage. We've grown apart. We have nothing in common anymore."

"Hmm. Let's think about what we had in common for the first forty or so years of our marriage. I worked while you went to law school; no, that's two different things. I entertained your colleagues and clients with parties and dinners while you built your practice; no, that's two different things. I raised our children so that you could show up at awards ceremonies and take credit for their accomplishments, but I didn't do that for you. I did that for them.

"I made sure you were fed, that your clothes were clean, that your house was a warm and welcoming home, and treated you like you were the most important thing in my life. The thing we had in common was you. You think you're the most brilliant, important lawyer ever, and so did I."

Stacey chimed in. "She's right. You're horrible to her, and she's the best wife I know."

Bonnie looked exasperated. "Yet you went to bed with him. I am not happy with you."

The younger woman looked toward the leaf-strewn ground. "I know. I'm sorry. You were so nice to me, and I betrayed you. If it's any help, I didn't enjoy it."

"What do you mean, you didn't enjoy it?" yelped Everett.

"You're pathetic," said Stacey. "You can't even recognize a fake orgasm. Maybe you've never seen a woman have a real one."

I snickered. I couldn't help it; he looked so darned offended.

Bonnie continued: "There's only one more question I want to ask. Why did you kill Ryan? I don't think either of us suspected the affair. Did he really have to die?"

"I could no longer stand by and watch him mistreat his wife," said Everett. "She deserved better."

Bonnie smiled. “Too bad I didn’t have someone do me the same favor years ago.” She nodded at us. “Can I assume you heard enough to put Everett away for the rest of his life?”

Frankie and I exchanged nervous glances, and she spoke first. “Yes, Mrs. Crockett. My husband is the sheriff, and I’m pretty sure what we heard will stand up in court. But you should let the law take over this situation. Don’t shoot them.”

“Oh, honey, I’m not going to shoot anybody. I’m executing a citizen’s arrest. Do me a favor and call your husband. Tell him to bring a set of handcuffs.”

I realized then that she’d missed the conversation between the two lovebirds that we’d overheard. She didn’t know about Dinah. I corrected her request.

“Frankie? Tell him to bring two sets.”

Two hours later we gathered at Katie’s Kitchen. We weren’t alone; Caleb and Boots were there, along with Tennie and Hoyt. Caleb’s account of his thoughts as he walked toward the scene from the tennis court had left us in laughter.

“The last thing Annalee said to me on the phone was an instruction to stay away from crime scenes; they were reserved for her and Frankie. When I saw Bonnie Crockett holding a gun on Everett and Stacey, I decided I’d pay more attention to her guidance from now on. She’s serious.”

I looked heavenward toward the pressed tin ceiling. “At last, someone believes in me.”

“I’m so glad you called us when it was all over,” said Tennie, as she batted Hoyt’s fork away from her mashed potatoes. "Tell me again what Bonnie said while you were waiting for Boots to arrive."

"Let's just say that like most Southern women, she knows all the words a lady should never utter, and she pulled 'em forth and let 'em loose," said Frankie. "The best part of witnessing her chew her husband up and spit him out was that she did it in front of an audience. He couldn't open his mouth and respond without possibly incriminating himself, so he had to stand there and take it. The gun she had pointed at him got his attention, too. She did save a few choice words for Stacey."

"I liked the comparison of him and a pile of dog poo, followed by a ladylike 'Bless your heart'," I said.

"And the murder weapon?" Tennie asked over the laughter. "Was it really the missing fish knife?"

"We think so," said Boots. "Mrs. Crockett found a knife in her husband's closet that fits the description. She put it in a plastic zip bag and brought it along with her, but of course he had already cleaned it. Forensics probably can't get any DNA from it, but they can tell if the size and shape fits the wound that killed Ryan."

"Why on earth didn't he dispose of it?" I asked. "There's miles of woods between Berryville and his house, not to mention the Sabine River. It would have been so easy. Why would he risk taking it home?"

The usually silent Hoyt chimed in. "I'll bet I know. Tennie told me how perfectly organized his fishing closet was. He was afraid he'd never find another knife to fit that space on the wall."

There was a moment of silence followed by laughs of recognition from everyone.

"We're all laughing," said Boots, "but according to his wife, that is the most likely reason. Thank goodness for his touch of obsessive-compulsive disorder."

I was still troubled by my memory of Stacey in the grocery store parking lot. "How could Stacey have walked right up to Mrs. Morrison and sympathized with her on the loss of her daughter? I mean, she killed Dinah herself. Was it some sort of sick joke on her part?"

Boots looked to his wife. "Does the doctor have an opinion?"

Frankie put her chicken-fried steak on hold as she considered the question. "I'm not her physician, but she seems to have a serious disconnect with the facts where her husband is concerned. She may be the only person left on the planet who believes Ryan was helpless to resist the women who, in her self-protective mind, threw themselves at him. That said, her conversation with Dinah's mom was extra creepy given what we found out today. Something in her head is not clicking in a normal fashion."

"So, as Everett described her this afternoon, she isn't playing with a full deck?" I asked.

"A few crumbs short of a biscuit?" That one was from Tennie.

"A bubble off plumb?" chimed in Caleb.

Frankie gave us a reproving look.

"Come on, it was a stressful afternoon," I argued. "Allow us to be a little unkind."

"We will be looking at all of the facts in the case," said Boots, with the sincerity you'd like your local law enforcement official to employ.

"So, is Valonda completely cleared of suspicion?" asked Caleb.

"And what about that demantoid brooch?" I demanded. "Surely she won't be allowed to keep it."

Boots looked at his watch, then back at all of us. "You people do realize it's only been a couple of hours since Stacey and Everett were taken into custody? Even if it was appropriate to share everything with you, that particular dilemma isn't high on my list of priorities. As soon as I finish eating, I'm going back to the jail to see that all the paperwork is perfect. The pin will stay in the evidence safe at the station for the foreseeable future."

"It didn't take you long to turn on Valonda," said Frankie, accusingly. "You've flipped from feeling sorry for her to wanting to take her jewelry away."

I felt a twinge of guilt. "You're right. I'll try to develop a neutral stance; it's no skin off my back if she gets to keep the salamander. Stacey didn't have any appreciation for it, and I do think the final truth is that Ryan gave it to her."

CALEB GAVE ME a hug and a lingering kiss in the parking lot before I got in my car. Our embrace was broken when Tennie yelled, "Hey, no public displays of affection on Main Street!" Reminded of Valonda's behavior a couple of weeks before, I jerked my hand off Caleb's lean rear end and laughed.

"I could get away with that in Houston," I said. "No one who knew me would see it."

"Let's get in the car and head south," he said in my ear. "We can hit the Houston city limits before bedtime."

"The only place I'm going now is Goat Hill Farm," I smiled, "but you're welcome to follow me home."

As Caleb drove behind me, he tooted his horn and pointed at the First Church of the Devil's Destruction. I saw Reverend Nelson changing the sign once again, accompanied by a conservatively-dressed Valonda.

IF YOU AVOID THE BAIT, YOU WON'T END UP ON THE HOOK

I must admit, the reverend has a remarkable ability to tell us what we need to hear.

Mabry Hall created Annalee Wyatt, *18 Karat Cold Mysteries*' bling-bedecked sleuth, out of her love of antique jewelry. She gets a vicarious pleasure when Annalee buys, sells and sometimes wears the beautiful pieces of jewelry she would love to have for herself. She's quite happy to leave the murders to her fictional creation and lives a quiet life in Louisiana, not far from the imaginary town of Berryville and Annalee's Goat Hill Farm. You can follow Mabry on Pinterest at http://www.pinterest.com/mabryhall/ and see pictures of some of the beautiful antique jewelry that inspires her, including jewelry specific to *A Regrettable Reunion.*

Join her on Facebook at Facebook.com/18KaratCold
Email her at mabrydhall@gmail.com

45220211R00178

Made in the USA
San Bernardino, CA
26 July 2019